THE REMNANT FLEET

Geonn Cannon

Supposed Crimes LLC • Matthews, North Carolina

THE REMNANT FLEET

Riley Parra: Season 1
Riley Parra: Season 2
Riley Parra: Season 3
Riley Parra, Season 4
Riley Parra, Season 5
Underdogs (Underdogs #1)
Beware of Wolf: An Underdogs Novel (Underdogs #2)
Wolf at the Door: An Underdogs Novel (Underdogs Historical)
Dogs of War: An Underdogs Novel (Underdogs #3)
Red in Tooth and Claw: An Underdogs novel (Underdogs #4)
Railroad Spine
Gunfire Echoes
On the Air
Gemini
World on Fire
The Following Sea
Tilting at Windmills (Claire Lance, Book 1)
Only Flame and Air (Claire Lance, Book 2)
Confused by Shadows (Claire Lance, Book 3)
Chasing Dragons (Claire Lance, Book 4)
What Matter Wounds (Claire Lance, Book 5)
The Rise and Fall of Radiation Canary
Radiation Canary: Greatest Hits
Silence Out Loud
Girls Don't Hit
Cinder and the Smoke
Sojourn
The Virtuous Feats of the Indomitable Miss Trafalgar and Erudite
Lady Boone
Into the Furnace

CHAPTER ONE

EVERY SOUL aboard the Quay was far from home. The vastness of space yawned across empty stretches in all directions around the station.

The Quay was a mere fifty AU from Earth, at the very edge of their solar system, and yet that was considered far for the Humans who were elected to serve there. Even two hundred years after its first foundations were set up, most officers considered their journey to the station a one-way trip. The aliens who traveled from other systems to take up residence aboard the Quay were hundreds, sometimes thousands of light-years away from home.

Executive Officer Bauwerji Crow's home was twenty-one hundred and seven light years away from where she currently stood. She was Balanquin, dark red of skin with mustard-shaded eyes, one of six humanoid races that resided aboard the station. Currently she walked along one of the wide avenues that cut through the interior like veins and arteries connecting the vital sections. It was crowded this morning; she passed the Humans with their shades-of-tan skin and multitude of hair colors, nodded greetings to the other vermilion-skinned Balanquin, and tried to avoid the lecherous gaze of the slate Acapsian couples she passed.

They were scientists and explorers, thieves, fugitives, tourists, engineers. They were sightseers at their end of their lives who had finally saved up enough to see the universe before finally passing out of it. They were soldiers on leave. Those who were stationed on the Quay wore uniforms similar to Bauwerji's, differing only in color to denote rank. Some of them nodded a greeting to her while others were too busy with their duties to even notice her passing.

She was the second-in-command, which was a rank with enough esteem to greet their incoming guests but not so high she could refuse the duty. She disliked it immensely, but playing host to wide-eyed neophytes was far from the most odious task she'd ever been assigned. She could suffer through a few hours of meaningless conversation.

The docks were located along the lower edge of the station, a saucer upon which the teacup of the station was situated. She walked along the outer rim and watched through the windows as the ship she was going to meet positioned itself along the proper slip. High above in the pilothouse, techs were in communication with the captain of the small shuttle, guiding it where it needed to be so that it didn't collide with one of the other ships weaving around in the space beneath the station.

Bauwerji picked up her pace, jogging the rest of the distance so she would be there when the passengers disembarked. In a rare show of diplomacy and cooperation, the Aphelion Project had agreed to fund a civilian reporter's stay aboard the station. A volunteer was found who agreed to spend the rest of her life on the edge of her home solar system. That sacrifice was enough for Admiral Indira Reshef to send a high-ranking member of her command crew to act as a welcoming party.

The shuttle docked and went through its typical clearance procedures. The ship had undergone a quarantine period on Earth, and their two-month journey gave the onboard physician more than enough time to catch any diseases that the passengers might be carrying. Regardless there was still a fifteen-minute wait as the ship was cleared by the Quay's own diagnostic scanner. It was Paisian-built and therefore infinitely more reliable than anything Earth could have run.

Finally the new arrivals were cleared. Bauwerji straightened the dark blue tunic of her uniform as she took position in front of the gangway as the first group appeared. Bauwerji was a few inches shorter than the average Human, but she was solid enough that none of them considered her petite. She was well-muscled and fast due to the station having lower gravity than Pelorum. Her hair, a shade darker than her skin, was shaved above her right ear save for the four braids that represented the women in her family who served before her in their country's military.

She was acting as diplomatic escort. Her duty was to meet a journalist from Earth and guide her to the habitation ring. It was the sort of dull busywork that she'd been promised when she first signed up to serve for her people's military. Instead she had seen two active war zones and been instrumental in starting a cold war that her people were increasingly unlikely to win. She told herself she should cherish the boring days afforded to her by enlisting with the humans.

Bauwerji recognized the reporter from the data packet she'd gotten that morning. She crossed her arms behind her back, hands clasped on the opposite forearm, and put memories of Pelorum out of her mind and lifted her chin to acknowledge contact had been made. The reporter smiled and lifted her hand in greeting. She was an Earth race called Indasian-Human, tall and elegant, with a disarming smile and a harried look about her.

"Bowery Crow?"

"Bah-whir-j-yee," she corrected, though no one except other Balanquin seemed capable of pronouncing it correctly. "Lalan Paget?"

"Correct." She extended her hand.

Bauwerji ignored the gesture and turned to lead Paget away from the docks. "I hope your journey wasn't too arduous."

Lalan shook her head and hoisted the strap of her bag higher on her shoulder. "Just long and tedious. But the payoff is worth it." She gestured toward the windows. "Do you mind if we take a moment...?"

"Not at all."

The row of observation windows had been installed to cater to the new arrivals. Bauwerji stood a few paces behind Lalan so the other woman wouldn't feel rushed. On the other side of the partition, at a relatively scant distance of four hundred thousand miles, the Kuiper Belt began. The Quay was stationary in relation to the belt, so it looked as if they were parked on the side of an extremely busy thoroughfare. Billions of small icy projectiles skidded past them every day, with the occasional large planetoid making an appearance.

"Will we see Pluto?"

Bauwerji was stymied by the fact that every Human visiting the station asked the same question. The nostalgia for a single dwarf planet was a testament to Human obsession, and she considered it both a plus and a minus to their character. "No. Pluto's orbit is nearly two-hundred and fifty years. There was a pass-by one hundred and seventy-five years ago, when the Quay was still under construction."

"I've seen pictures of the celebration. I was just... hoping, I guess. It is beautiful though, isn't it?"

"It is." She crossed her arms behind her again and waited. Lalan had just said goodbye to her home planet. She deserved to take a few minutes to look around her new neighborhood.

Finally, Lalan turned away from the vista. "They said my bags would be taken care of?"

"Yes, they'll be transferred to your quarters." Bauwerji gestured for Lalan to follow her. "We've arranged for a standard orientation package for you and the other new arrivals. A where's where and what's what of the Quay."

An Acapsian couple walked past them and Lalan slowed to stare at them. Acapsians had small chins and long, slender noses. Their eyes were elongated but wide. The female smiled at Bauwerji and Lalan as she passed, lifting her skirt to one side so it wouldn't brush against them. Lalan turned to watch them go and Bauwerji resisted the urge to sigh.

"There is also sensitivity training, should you wish to attend."

"I didn't... I-I was... I've never seen an alien before."

Bauwerji looked at her and raised an eyebrow.

"Well, I mean, I've seen you. They showed me your picture on the shuttle so I'd know who I was meeting. But that..."

"That," Bauwerji said, "is something you will have to get used to. There are six different races residing on the Quay, along with however many are visiting at any one time. You will be subjected to completely alien cultures every time you leave the comfort of your quarters. There is a food pavilion which caters to other races, and you might find their cuisine distasteful. The sensitivity training isn't required, and it's not intended to imply you might be willfully prejudiced or discriminatory. But despite their best intentions, Humans are overall a fairly xenophobic species."

Lalan said, "I suppose that's true. We've spent centuries fighting wars amongst ourselves based on skin color. I'd like to attend the training."

"I'll have the schedule uploaded to your Cloud."

Their walk took them along a promenade that overlooked a

concourse full of shops and teeming with people. Lalan moved closer to the railing and peered down at the ebb and flow of bodies. Bauwerji impatiently crossed her arms behind her back and waited again. She had no further duties until her shift began in three hours, but the stop-and-go of escorting Lalan to her quarters was beginning to chafe.

"This is partially what I was referring to," Bauwerji said. "Human, Balanquin, Irikoan, Ladronis. Some establishments cater to all races, some are only visited by their own people." She pointed to one dark shop. "Irikoan clothier. They're nocturnal, and there are only about a handful of them on the station. No one would wear Irikoan clothing unless they were Irikoan themselves, so the shop closes when they're all asleep. And that..." She pointed to a blank, unmarked door. "What do you think that is?"

"Could be anything," Lalan said.

"Acapsian fine-dining. They consider eating to be a sensual, private affair. They go in, buy their food, and take it home to partake out of the public eye. Whereas sex can be a communal event."

"Acapsians... like..." Lalan gestured back the way they'd come.

Bauwerji nodded. "If you had asked them to dinner, they might have been offended. If you had asked to join them for a threesome, they might have welcomed the offer to get to know you better."

Lalan blushed. "I see."

"As I said, the sensitivity training is more about convenience than correcting behavior. We want to make sure everyone knows the... guidelines..." She trailed off as something caught her eye down on the concourse. She cursed under her breath and moved quickly toward the stairs. "Stay here."

She used the stairs as a platform for her controlled plummet, one hand on the railing and her feet only touching down when absolutely necessary. Her eyes were locked onto the Sautoriaun woman shuffling toward one of the lifts that could take her to the residential hub. It was hard to tell ages on the bastard Sau, but the way she moved indicated she was at least a century old. She glanced up and saw Bauwerji barreling toward her. She gave up any pretense of remaining casual and decided to make a run for it. Bauwerji bared her teeth and gave chase.

A Paisian was nearly trampled by the Sau, and Bauwerji uttered a quick, "Pardon me," as she ran by the startled scientist. The Sau was at the lifts and slapped her hand against the call screen a few times before deciding it was futile. She saw Bauwerji closing in and ran down the corridor. Bauwerji freed her earpiece from the collar of her tunic and plugged it in.

"XO Bauwerji Crow in pursuit of contraband on concourse level two, currently traveling starboard along the red path. Suspect is Sautoriaun. Roadblock required at intersection T-104."

The corridor ahead of the Sau flashed as security measures were enacted. Bauwerji found reserves of speed she hadn't yet tapped to close in on her prey. A Human passed through the intersection without incident, but the moment the Sau woman crossed the seam, she froze. Her limbs tightened and pulled tight against her body, and her face was twisted in a rictus of pain. Bauwerji slammed into the thief from behind and tackled her to the ground. The security measures were set to respond only to Sau genetic code, meaning Bauwerji was unaffected as she restrained her prisoner.

Lalan trotted up behind her, out of breath from running, and stared wide-eyed at the prisoner. "That was amazing! What... what was that? How did you know she was breaking the law?"

"Because she's Sautoriaun, and she was coming out of a Ladronis market." Lalan stared at her blankly, and Bauwerji sighed. She got to her feet and hauled the immobilized Sau up with her. "Ladronis don't like the Sautoriauns. They're considered unclean. So any Ladronis in that market would have averted their gaze or turned their backs. The distaste goes both ways. So the only conceivable reason a Sau would have for being in an exclusively Ladronis place of business is to move about unseen." She looked at her prisoner. "What were you hiding? Theft of goods or money?"

"I'll be sorting that out."

Bauwerji tensed. She and Lalan both turned to see a Karezz woman coming toward them. Her uniform was identical to Bauwerji's in everything but color, red rather than blue. Her skin was orange-brown, her nose beaked, and her plate of a forehead was crowned by a fringe of black hair. She looked like a flat-faced bird of prey, some creature alighting on a high branch to watch its prey from a safe distance before swooping in for the kill. The dark eyes of the constable swung toward Lalan.

"I'm not sure I know you."

"Lalan Paget." Bauwerji shoved the Sau at the newcomer. "Journalist from Earth. Lalan, this is Constable Mara Heely."

Lalan smiled genuinely. "It's a pleasure to meet you."

Mara ignored the pleasantries and focused on Bauwerji.

"Excellent capture, XO Crow."

Bauwerji said, "Just doing *your* job, Mara."

Mara smiled and winked as she gripped the Sau's upper arm. "Don't worry about what she was up to. I'll spend the rest of the afternoon sorting that out." She finally looked at Lalan again. "Welcome to the Quay."

The security officer marched the prisoner away. Bauwerji watched them go, barely able to keep the disgust and anger off her face. She noticed Lalan watching her and brought one hand up to reactivate her earpiece. It had the added benefit of hiding her expression from the curious Human. "Disable security measures in T-104. Suspect has been apprehended and is in the custody of Constable Heely." She tucked the earpiece back under her collar. "Sorry about that, Miss Paget. Shall we continue?"

Bauwerji started walking without waiting for a response. Lalan was forced to catch up with her.

"That woman was Karezza, right?"

"She's Karezz. Singular. Karezza is plural, for the race."

"Right. And... well, with you being Balanquin... I don't want to pry or seem invasive, but for the two of you to be working together..."

Bauwerji said, "We don't work together. She is in control of the station's security. I am an officer. We both report to Admiral Reshef about our respective jurisdictions. We can be professional."

"Considering what they did to your people..."

"Constable Heely had no part in that." Bauwerji stopped and faced Lalan. "I don't wish to talk about what happened on Pelorum, nor do I wish to turn this tour into a history of the Karezza occupation. If you want to know about that, you can certainly find more than enough in the database. Now I apologize for this interruption to our schedule. Shall we continue?"

Lalan nodded sheepishly. "Yes. Of course."

Bauwerji turned and walked back to the stairs, ignoring the crowd which had gathered in response to her pursuit as she tried to get back into the mindset of a tour guide. The truth was that she hated having a Karezz in such a vaunted position. Heely was the Law, and she could arrest anyone she wanted and figure out the charges later. Bauwerji was extraordinarily uncomfortable with that dynamic given what she had suffered and what she knew about Karezza who had been given any sort of power. She had worked alongside Heely long enough to know she didn't need to worry, but that didn't mean she would let her guard down around the flat-faced fiend.

She thought about everything she'd said to Lalan about sensitivity training and how she had declared Humans as xenophobic sectarians. But the truth was, if every Karezza could be gathered in an airlock, she would gladly hit the button to send them into space.

CHAPTER TWO

THE MAIN floor of the pilothouse was taken up by two sunken areas separated by a central walkway. Operations, communications, sensor officers, navigators, and dispatchers occupied the lower level, their heads and hunches shoulders rising up like the shoal-burrowers Bauwerji spent her childhood hunting. Their voices filled the shell of the pilothouse's amphitheater, a comforting hum that only drew Bauwerji's attention when it stopped or changed tone.

After depositing the journalist to her quarters to get situated, Bauwerji returned to her post. She kept an office on the pilothouse deck, but she was rarely at her desk. She preferred to be present among the crew just in case a situation arose that required her attention. Monitors throughout the room showed real-time displays of the space just outside the station and revealed just what their dispatchers were forced to deal with. She moved closer to one monitor as a piece of debris tumbled across the screen. It was large enough to identify the craft as Karezza design, but nothing more.

Nine years earlier, a massive fleet from every spaceworthy species had gathered to fend off powerful and unknown invaders. Their foe's initial message demanding surrender identified the aggressors as Cetidroi. The commander of the Acapsian vessel they contacted refused, and his ship was destroyed as a result. After that there were no further attempts at communication. The Cetidroi army came from the unknown space beyond even the Paisian's ability to explore and began attacking any ship or outpost they came across. Responding to the attacks was suicide, victory apparently impossible, but forcing the Cetidroi into conflict worked as a distraction. It slowed them down and gave every race a chance to come up with a solution.

The combined fleets used the Quay as a rallying point. It was far enough away from the Cetidroi targets to serve as safe harbor. They used the docks to effect repairs, and the concourse became filled with soldiers and generals trying to come up with a new angle of attack. Ships limped to the Quay for help and occasionally were forced to remain behind to be used as spare parts for others. Before long, the empty space ahead of the Quay was littered with the remains of what had once been a mighty and impressive fleet.

With the Kuiper belt behind them and the ship's graveyard ahead, the dispatchers and navigators were tasked with safely guiding visitors to the docks. There were tenders and towships that monitored the graveyard to make sure there was enough room for the larger ships to get through, but trying to maneuver through the minefield was a daunting task for both pilot and navigators. Bauwerji had done it herself without the benefit of a spotter and it wasn't an ordeal she anticipated doing again.

She turned when she heard the lift activate behind her, and Admiral Indira Reshef arrived on-deck. She was Indian-Human, middle-aged by Earth standards. She assumed command of the station twenty years earlier, its youngest and currently longest-serving leader. The Quay had been built by Humans and it was officially still their property, but every other race aboard had been allowed to approve of Admiral Reshef before she became their leader. She'd proven herself time and again to be a just and considerate officer, and Bauwerji believed she truly had every race's best interest at heart.

Indira smiled as Bauwerji approached with the overnight reports. "It seems everything is going well down here," the Admiral said. "Did the journalist from Earth arrive safely?"

"She's tucked away in her room, ma'am." Bauwerji handed over the tablet with the nightly arrivals displayed on-screen. "The only major arrival was the Karezza vessel *Mae fy hofrenfad yn llawn llyswennod*. They docked just after midnight."

Indira skimmed the page. "Speaking of the Karezza, I understand you had a run-in with Mara Heely this morning."

"I subdued a Sau thief," Bauwerji said. "Constable Heely took custody of the prisoner. If there was anything else to report, I would."

"I know. And if there was anything you wanted to tell me unofficially, without the report, you know where I can be found."

"Yes, ma'am."

Indira handed the tablet back to her. "Very good. How long have you been on-duty?"

Bauwerji checked the chronometer above the nearest monitor. "Eight hours."

"I'll take over here. Go get yourself something to eat, have a rest."

Bauwerji thought about arguing; the Balanquin day was thirty-seven hours, and a typical work shift ran anywhere from eleven to thirteen hours. But the Humans set the schedule aboard the Quay and they insisted on a twenty-four hour cycle. She would accept the break as prescribed but she would report back in four hours for a second shift.

"Will do, ma'am."

"The journalist. Paget, right?"

"That's right."

"What did you think of her?"

Bauwerji shrugged. "I didn't have much chance to form an impression. She seemed taken with the station and overwhelmed by the diversity of our population." Indira raised an eyebrow. "Not in a problematic way. You know how Humans are."

Indira smiled. "That almost sounded like prejudice, XO Crow."

"I'll assign myself to a sensitivity class immediately, ma'am."

"See that you do." She winked.

Bauwerji signed out of her console and tried to think of where she could spend the next four hours. She could nap, but then she wouldn't be able to sleep for a full night. Most officers used the Sensuite, but she didn't like having her eyes and ears closed to the real world around her. Her time would be better spent on-duty. When the lift arrived she sent it to the pavilion. She could at least have a little *suchale'nt* as a mid-duty snack.

When she did reach the pavilion, she wished she had gone absolutely anywhere else. Selina Rogers, Acapsian diplomat, was seated by herself at a table in the common area. She was centrally located and casually scanning the crowd with slow movements of her large blue eyes. Acapsian and Human features were mostly interchangeable, save for the exaggerated features and slate-gray skin of the Acapsian. Selina's hair was blonde and cut short in a male's style, and she wore a blue suit that showed off her curves. Her eye landed on Bauwerji and her grin widened to reveal small white teeth.

Bauwerji fought the urge to look away as she marched over. It would be rude to simply ignore the diplomat, but she could think of a thousand other places on the station she would have rather been. Hell, hanging outside in an at-suit would have been preferable to pulling out the chair across from the smirking Selina Rogers and taking a seat at her table.

"You are perverted," Bauwerji said.

"They don't seem to mind," Selina said, eyeing the crowd.

Bauwerji said, "They have to eat. Maybe they would prefer to do so without some letch staring at them the whole time getting her rocks off."

"Anyone who wishes to spend the evening in my quarters is more than welcome to do so." She held Bauwerji's gaze, daring her to look away.

Bauwerji crossed her arms and refused to play Selina's games. She broke the staring contest without fanfare so she could scan the area behind the other woman's head. When Selina first arrived on the Quay, she had invited Bauwerji to dinner. Bauwerji accepted and, though she found it odd that Selina wasn't eating, actually enjoyed their conversation. She went back five times before Indira revealed the truth: Acapsian culture considered dining in public to be taboo, while sex was a communal activity. Bauwerji had basically been masturbating in front of the diplomat for five evenings.

She couldn't even be angry at Selina for the deception. She'd assumed Bauwerji knew about their customs, and she actually should have been aware. It was her own fault for not investigating. But that didn't mean she had to suffer through the Acapsian woman's smug voyeurism.

"I think you should go back to your quarters, Miss Rogers."

"Why?"

"Because not everyone in the pavilion is aware of your proclivities. It's not fair to them."

Selina said, "They're just eating. They don't find it prurient or objectionable." Her eyes had drifted to the left, and Bauwerji followed her line of sight to an Occamian licking sauce from its fingers. "If I become overly stimulated, I will resign to my quarters before I take care of myself. Because every other race on this station finds sex to be private, I restrain myself for their benefit. What would happen if I requested everyone eat in private to accommodate my needs? It would be madness. No one would want me aboard the station. So I'm just making the best of a bad situation."

Bauwerji lifted her left hand and twisted the wrist downward, a Balanquin gesture that indicated turning down the flow of water.

"Dismiss me all you want," Selina laughed. "My way works out for everyone. No one has to change their dining habits, and I don't have to pay for Sensuite pornography."

Bauwerji pushed her chair away from the table. "I'm asking you politely to... at least be less obvious about it."

"You're forgetting something, XO Crow. Many people know about Acapsian culture. Some of them only come here to eat if they see I'm here... people-watching."

"Perhaps you could all have a dinner party."

Selina shivered. "Ooh, talk dirty to me more often, Bowery."

Bauwerji shook her head and walked away. The Acapsian were odd, to be sure. They were the most technologically-advanced race on the Quay, other than the Paisian, but they were infatuated with Humans to the point of obsession. Acapsian names were difficult to pronounce, so any Acapsian who had to deal with other races chose a Human name. They affected Human idioms, gestures, and fashion. They had perfected cloning, and some claimed they were even programming more Human features into each successive generation. The Acapsian claimed it was just natural progression and refinement of the process, so it was difficult to prove the allegations.

The encounter with Selina had put Bauwerji off her appetite, so she wandered up to the concourse. At the top of the stairs, she was nearly run down by one of the small three-wheeled carriages that people used to travel from one point of the station to the other without using a lift. They were slower but she had to admit they were a lot more fun. There was a track on one of the mid-levels where people could race. It was the kind of mindless entertainment she could have used right then, but she didn't want to take the time to gear up just to drive around an oval.

She turned away from the carriage and nearly tripped over her feet when she saw the group coming up from the dock level. Karezza. Eight of them, all dressed in diplomatic attire but still undeniably Karezza. They were caught up in conversation so there was time for her to avoid them, to go back downstairs and duck out of sight, but her legs refused to obey her. She moved her hand to her belt for a knife she no longer carried there, breathing heavily and smelling the thick copper of her raised blood pressure. Her eyes were wide and her body was poised for a brawl when the first Karezz spotted her.

He wore a purple robe with a red mantle, his gnarled hands extending out beyond the sleeves as he held one up to pause his friend's conversation. His friend looked to see what had caught Purple's attention, and then all eight men were looking at her. They were young, perhaps three cycles or even late-two. Students of law and government, but they were still Karezza. Scholars. Karezza scholars. She pressed her lips hard together to prevent them from pulling back to expose her teeth to them.

The Karezz slowed and parted around her like a river around a stone. They said nothing, but each man swiveled his head to keep their eyes on her until they were past. The final one smirked and nodded his head in greeting.

"*Baqua'hin'qo.*"

Bauwerji dug her fingernails into the meaty part of her palm to stop herself from lashing out at the insult. She didn't look back when she heard the men laughing. It wasn't a quinlitz phrase, and it wasn't even really from chelseet, the Karezza language. It was a bastardization of the two made popular when the Karezza occupied her world and turned the native Balanquin population into second-tier citizens. Crudely translated, and there was no other way to do it, the word meant "meat toy."

When she was sure they were gone, she finally turned to look after them. Indira was well aware of what the Balanquin had suffered at the hands of the Karezza, and she knew Bauwerji's history before coming to the Quay. If these delegates needed any escort or handling from a member of the senior crew, she would make sure someone else was assigned. She shook off the encounter and looked around for the nearest lift that could take her back home.

After encounters with Selina Rogers and now a horde of roaming Karezza, logging on to Sensuite and cutting off the outside world suddenly didn't seem like such a bad prospect. There were customizable battle programs, safe virtual worlds where she could kill as many Karezza scum soldiers as she wanted without worrying about being reprimanded by Indira.

CHAPTER THREE

THE ROGUE planet Xibalba was ejected from its solar system several millennia before the first settlers landed on its icy inhospitable surface. There was an atmosphere and enough large flat plains for an enterprising group to create a rudimentary camp. Outside the jurisdiction of any species' law, the governor of Xibalba could grant immunity to anyone who found the planet and managed a safe landing. Soon the little camp grew into a colony, then a sprawling megacity with an ever-changing population. The only law recognized on the cold stone was whatever the governor or his family decreed, making it an ideal site for all manner of disreputable travelers.

Currently it was orbited by dozens of small ships. There were representatives from every spacefaring race, patchwork go-fasts and hail-makers that carried contraband from one port to another. The hail-makers would skim across at low altitudes to drop their packages in remote areas of a target planet. Go-fasts were eviscerated ships that were designed to break atmosphere faster than anyone pursuing them. The hulking vessels orbiting the perimeter of Xibalba's orbit were designed to ensure that every law-keeping organization in the vicinity respected the rogue planet's accords.

Cicerone Drayton considered Xibalba her second home. To be more honest, she considered it her first home. Earth was just the rock where she happened to be born, a place she'd escaped as soon as she was old enough to sign up for a trip to the Quay. She lived there from the age of twelve, sleeping in dead-ends and repair tubes. The station was large enough that she didn't have to worry about work, but soon work found her. She was a very good thief, a pickpocket and confidence artist who could convince anyone to give her anything. When she couldn't filch enough money to buy food, she convinced clerks and butchers to provide a free meal.

After a few years of saving and trading up, she was able to buy her own ship, free and clear. Her original goal had been to escape, get away from Earth and other Humans to see what the universe had to offer. The other races capable of interstellar travel refused to share the technology, although they had been willing to "cooperate" when it came to building the Quay. It was easy to understand why. The Paisian, the Karezza, the Acapsian, they all found the station useful. Giving Humans the ability to leave their solar system and visit others would be granting them far too much freedom.

Cicero wasn't a self-hating Human. She was proud of who she was, and she wouldn't trade her Humanity to be any other race. And there was a certain distinction to being the only Human to travel so far. She was the only Human many aliens had ever met, and they treated her like the rare breed she was. Then there were the kinks. Acapsian who had never seen a Human naked before. Karezza who were intrigued at the possibility of bedding a new species. Cicero encouraged their proclivities.

She was the renegade Human, cast out from her home system to float adrift through the universe. That was why Xibalba felt like home to her. That, and the fact its population accounted for ninety percent of new business. Currently she didn't have any contracts to fulfill, no merchandise to recover, and nothing on the schedule, so she aimed her ship toward Xibalba to see what jobs could be had.

The *Sastruga* was a gorgeous little ship. It was powerful and fast and with enough nooks and crannies to hide an entire Delianes cruiser if she happened to get one and had the time to break it up into smaller pieces. The engine was a mishmash of Acapsian and Paisian tech, the weapons and structure were Karezza, and the thrusters were Sautoriaun. The only part of the ship that was Earth-designed were the creature comforts; beds, chairs, couches, et cetera. If there was one thing Humans did right, it was comfort.

She sat on the bridge with her boots up on the console. Xibalba loomed on the theater-sized viewer a few feet in front of the bridge. The little rogue planet was beautiful. It was near enough to the neighboring system that the sun caught ice crystals in the atmosphere. The harsh and unwelcoming nomad was suddenly ringed by a halo, and spires of light shot out into the darkness.

Cicero had a bag of helib roze, a Balanquin delicacy, and she popped another one into her mouth as her instruments began beeping an alert. She dropped her feet to the floor and waited for the roze to dissolve on her tongue before she activated the intercom. She opened the link to engineering.

"We're closing in, Aryana. You ready?"

Aryana Barrien, her Balanquin engineer, responded within seconds. "I'm always ready. Just tell me where you want us to set down."

"West side of the Taplinid district."

"Want me to rest it on a specific stone?"

Cicero grinned. "Not necessary. Fly loose, improvise."

"Aye."

She released the key and scooted her seat closer to the console. The Taplinid district was as good a place as any to begin looking for work. She had some contacts there who would at least have some leads for her. She was trying to think of which one to contact first when her communications screen flashed with an incoming message. She reached over and accepted the call.

"Captain Drayton of the *Sastruga*."

"Captain," a gruff Karezz man said. "Which fleet is that rank from?"

"Whichever one has the best perks, Zuk. You have work for me?"

He reclined in his seat. "That depends. How is your chelseet?"

"It clanks," she admitted. "I don't have much cause to talk to your kind conversationally. It's always 'hand it over or I'll cut your throat' kind of talk."

Zuk grunted. "There's a guy here looking to move a product. He's skittish and hard to understand even if you're fluent. But I think he can cough out some yun-voo."

The idea of speaking in yun-voo irritated her. Universal Vocalization was a language devised hundreds of years before Humans escaped their solar system. Devised by the Paisian, it put everyone on equal footing without giving dominance to any one species. Cicero found it difficult, but she could speak it well enough in a pinch.

"Okay. I'll meet him when we're grounded."

"Perfect news. He'll be waiting for you at Benjo. He's J'to-Karezza, probably the only one in the joint, but he'll be wearing a purple jerkin just so you can be sure. I'll let him know you're coming."

Cicero knew that J'to-Karezza were from the smaller subcontinent of their planet. He would have slightly different coloring than most of the Karezza she'd dealt with in the past. She watched the instrument panel as they came in for a landing, cutting through the atmosphere at a good clip. Aryana kept the engines burning at the right angle and thrust, but when they hit sky she would have to take over the steering. "Anything else I need to know? How has the world fared since I've been gone?"

"Riots on the outskirts, but what else is new. Quyan got exiled to the wastelands."

That was surprising, but she didn't let her reaction show. "I guess his bankroll finally ran dry. Protection only works if everyone gets paid. We're going to make landfall in about three minutes. Give me an hour to make my way to Benjo."

"An hour?" He looked away from the lens. "I have you coming in hard near the Taplinid district. What's going to take you an hour?"

Casing the location, checking for spies and snipers, gauging the safety of the bar, and watching the man she was supposed to meet to see if he was acting suspicious. Out loud she said, "You know how girls like to shop. Might be some fancy new gear to pick up."

"Try not to keep him waiting too long."

She disconnected the call and strapped in. The *Sastruga* was assaulted on all sides by the air rushing over its body. Cicero heard something rattling in the lower back quadrant.

"Hey, 'Yana. You hear that?"

"Rattling booster," Aryana responded. Her voice sounded small and faraway through the speaker. "It's going to hold until we sit down, but I'm going to be spending this visit tightening some couplers."

"Sorry you'll have to miss out on all the fun."

"Prefer to not fall out of the sky next time we try landing."

Cicero smiled. "Priorities, 'Yana. Hold on tight." She tapped a button to send out her message to the rest of the crew. "We're coming in for a landing in the beautiful Taplinid District. If you wish to disembark with your captain, be reminded that this little rock tops out at a gorgeous minus 43 Celsius. Hope you all have your cozy sweaters out of storage."

Below, the barren and rocky wastelands stretched out like a sea of blue stone, flanked on either horizon by jagged and angry-looking mountains. Other places, like the Quay, had docking clamps that did the majority of the work when it came to a landing. Out here Cicero had only herself. She eyeballed the quickly-approaching airstrip and guided her precious vessel down with the touch of a feather.

She undid her straps. The springs of her chair groaned as she got up, stretched out the kinks from their long voyage, and went down through the arteries of the ship to the common area. Her crew, her family, the people who counted on her to keep them safe and put food on the table, looked up as she came in. She opened the weapons cabinet and began arming herself as she explained Zuk's call.

"Shouldn't be too much trouble," she said. "Hear the guy out, see if we're interested in whatever he's selling, and then come back. It's an hour until the meeting so if I'm not back in two..."

"We'll come looking for you," Irias said. He was Ladronis, supposedly a pacifist, but she knew he would lead the charge if anything happened to her. She also knew that he had a rage within him; it was the reason he'd left his people behind and taken up with criminals.

She nodded to him and scanned the others. She was a Human, the lowest of the low when it came to species hierarchy. But aboard the *Sastruga*, she commanded the respect of Irikoan, Balanquin, Ladronis, and Acapsian alike. She had earned their trust. She nodded to them and moved her hand in a circle above her head (clearing away the clouds so the sun could shine down upon her, an old Balanquin gesture akin to Humans crossing their fingers. She found the Balanquin way made much more sense).

When Cicero reached the side hatch, she saw Aryana approaching from the engine compartment. Her sleeveless shirt was ringed with sweat around the low-cut collar. Being Balanquin helped her withstand the extreme heat of the engine compartment, but even she found it borderline unbearable. She pushed a hand through her carnelian-colored hair and made it stand up in spikes. She smiled as she approached and gave Cicero a thumbs-up.

"Am I doing it right?" She wiggled her thumb. "Good luck?"

"You are," Cicero said. "You want to come with me?"

Aryana looked at the hatch and gave an exaggerated shudder.

"Not without at least five layers on me. I'll pass. Besides, I need to get to work on that booster. Just in case we have to pitch out in a rush."

"When has that ever happened?"

"Been a whole week, I believe."

Cicero laughed and waited until Aryana was out of the section before she opened the door. It was several rungs below freezing outside by Human standards. A Balanquin wouldn't last five minutes in that kind of weather. She once again reflected on how lucky she was to have a crew so loyal that one of them didn't mind remaining ship-bound on a world that was inhospitable to her. She would have to find a way to make it up to Aryana soon.

For the time being, she had a meeting to scope out and a job offer to hear.

Xibalba didn't have seasons or cycles, but a certain rhythm had emerged among its people. There were periods of great wealth and periods of wanting. When there was too much merchandise, ships would be turned away by the Regulators. When the coffers were bare, the doors were flung open wide. Judging from the marketplace Cicero found when she came off the ship, the city was on the cusp of a time of plenty. The shops were full to overflowing with customers, so the street was crowded with secondary and tertiary storefronts.

Cicero weaved through the crowd of people buying and selling, wary of pickpockets and always on alert for Regulators undercover. Xibalba may have been outside the law, but that didn't stop incognito constables from staking it out. They waited for their target to show up and then just followed them somewhere with stricter laws. Cicero had never spent more than a few hours behind bars and she had no intention of breaking that record just because some officer was more patient than she was cautious.

The Taplinid district wasn't the worst Xibalba had to offer. There were plenty of reputable businesses on every street. Gambling could be found, but it was all strictly monitored. A debt wouldn't lead to broken bones on these streets, but they might lead to a permanent banishment. Companionship could be bought or sold. She passed a few men and women offering their wares and felt a twinge of disappointment that she was there on business. Some of her most fulfilling relationships had been purchased on an hourly basis, but she couldn't spare the time.

Benjo was at the far end of a dogleg street. Easy to hide in, easier to become a trap. Cicero used an exterior staircase to access the roof so she could spend twenty minutes watching the street. Confident it was clear, she went down through the building and checked every open room. Nothing jumped out at her as overly suspicious so she spent another half hour circling the bar just to be sure no one was giving it undue attention.

Fifteen minutes before their arranged meeting, a Karezz male in a purple jerkin shuffled down the alley and entered the bar. He ordered a bottle of Vino Tallinn and went to sit at a table in the corner as he waited for the 'tender to bring it out from the cellar. Cicero entered the bar and took the bottle when it was ready. She pointed at the man in purple, winked at the 'tender, and put the bottle down in front of the man she hoped would be her new friend.

He jumped at the sound of glass hitting wood and stared up at her. First he looked frightened, but then his features softened into curiosity.

"Your face has damage."

"Nope. Born this way. Back on Earth."

He tilted his head almost completely onto its side, a Karezza gesture of confusion that made her think of owls. "Earth? Born there? You born Earth you Human. Out here? So far?"

"Our people have a long history of exploration." She pulled out the seat across from him and lowered herself into it. "Zuk tells me you have a job. Legitimate or under the table?"

"Under...?"

She sighed. It would be so much easier if they could speak the same language. She scanned her memory to see how much chelseet she could remember and tried again.

"Is this job tri'k'zee or asce'key'ou?"

"Job is necessary," he said, struggling around the word. He reached down into his bag with both hands to withdraw a large box. "Man have died for this. Woman have died for this. Children too. Many. I killed the last four who hold it and take it from them."

"You killed?"

He met her gaze and she had to admit she felt a chill. "It was only option available to me." He withdrew a metal container, pushed the bag aside, and put the box down on the table. "This stone is spacefall. It travel very far. Very, very far." He rested his hand reverently on top of the box. "Million of years, you understand? Before you, me, here, this, anyone. This stone." He jabbed the box with his finger. "It come from origin."

"Origin of what?" She was looking at the box, wishing he'd just open it already.

The man swept his hand around them. "This. Everything. Balanquin, Karezza, Ladronis, all. Every. Origin of us."

Cicero leaned closer. "You're talking about a cenancestor." He stared blankly at her, so she clarified. "Something that can prove every species came from one source."

He nodded quickly and jabbed the box with his finger. "Yes! Last common connection. Everything goes back to this. This stone."

"How?"

"Stone contains pieces. Ah, uh, the... th-the..." He gestured in frustration. "The, the, the..."

"Genetics?"

"I don't... maybe? Look... this part of bigger. Bigger thing out there..." He gestured at the exit. "Long time ago. Then thing explode. Boom, pieces go everywhere. Piece hit here, hit there, some go far and some not so much. Some land on Karezz. Some on Pelorum or Acapsia or Earth or Pais. Life grows. Becomes Human or Karezza or Acapsian. Slightly different. Same building blocks."

"Panspermia," Cicero said quietly. Her rough and gruff exterior faded in the face of something so awe-inspiring. "Can I see the stone?"

He covered the box with both hands. "Understand why this important?"

She hesitated. "It would be a remarkable scientific discovery. Proof that every race in this sector came from the same ancestor would be monumental."

The man snorted and shook his head. "No! No one care. That is nothing, that is minor interesting thing. But this powerful. This dangerous."

"Why?"

"Stone has bits. Pieces. Things tell you what people are."

Cicero said, "Right. Genetics."

"Know what people are, know how to destroy them. Get rid of them, you have building pieces of whole new thing."

Cicero leaned back in her chair and stared at the box. "That's insane."

"That truth."

"You think someone would use this rock to target specific races?

Kill every Human and leave the Balanquin untouched?" She looked into his face, this Karezz, and knew that his people would love to eradicate every Balanquin on Pelorum to finally take the planet as their own. "You're talking about killing billions of people across half a dozen systems."

"Mm. Race who have this powerful. Evil, but who risk? Who risk not bowing to them?"

Cicero pictured what the Aphelion Project would do with such power. *You don't want to give us interstellar tech? Fine. Madam Prime Minister, kindly erase the Paisian from existence, please.* The cold war between the Karezza and the Balanquin would get real hot, real fast.

"What do you want me to do?" she asked. "I can't afford something that valuable."

"Just transport. Need to get somewhere safe, somewhere no one will find. Eventually someone will find, will kill me like I killed. They will take and do evil things. I cannot allow."

Cicero rubbed her lips together and stared at the box. If what he claimed was true, every species in the sky would have at least one faction willing to do whatever it took to get their hands on it. Then again, it might just be a rock. A bit of space junk that someone lied about to this J'to. She didn't want to be racist, but they were a particularly gullible lot. She chewed her bottom lip and decided she couldn't just walk away from the bomb sitting on the table.

"There's someone who can scan the rock, tell us if it really is what you claim."

"It is! I kill, many kill--"

She waved a hand to stop him. "Yeah, yeah, someone told you a story that you believe with all your heart. I'm not denying that you believe it. But you're an idiot."

"I'm..."

"Shut up. Just shut up. I'm going to do what you want. I'm going to give you transport to the Quay. There's a doctor on the station who can scan this and tell us if it's really as dangerous as you claim."

"Thank you," he said. "Thank you, thank you, gratitudes to you."

"Yeah," she muttered. She stood up and snatched up the bottle before she started walking away. "Come on before I change my mind."

The chief medical officer aboard the Quay was a Human named Cordwainer Littlefoot. Ze could confirm if the Karezza's story was true. And even if it turned out to be a scam, it wouldn't be a wasted trip. Going to the Quay meant an opportunity to see Bauwerji Crow again. That was always worth a little time spent in transit.

The man hurried to catch up with her. "You keep me safe?"

"You'll be on my ship, and I'll keep my ship safe. Either I get you where you're going or none of us make it."

He grimaced. "Not comforting."

"Not to you, maybe."

Cicero scanned the street again. She didn't see anything to cause alarm, so she motioned her new passenger to follow her out into the cold night.

CHAPTER FOUR

ARYANA BARRIEN was born and raised in the Birncei Desert province of Pelorum. It was often said that its people started sweating the minute they were born and didn't stop until two weeks after they died. She welcomed the heat. She thrived in temperatures that sent others gasping for fresh air. She was small enough and intelligent enough to know how to keep the *Sastruga*'s patchwork engine running, so she snagged a job that most people would have considered impossible.

She was on her back under the axial compressor cowling. She had tightened its connectors so the rattling would stop and now she was distracting herself with routine maintenance. Most engineers on ships this size remained in the engine room and used drones to handle these jobs. She finished cleaning off the elevation actuator and reached up to hook her fingers on the edge of the cowling. She pulled herself out of the crawlspace, rolled onto her stomach, and got to her feet. She wiped the sweat from her face and arms before opening the hatch and squirming out.

Aryana heard movement on the deck above as she climbed up the ladder to join the rest of the crew. Cicero's voice carried, and she mentally planned what she was going to say about the ship's status. Everything was fine and her baby would get them wherever they needed to go next. She took out a rag to wipe the rest of the sweat from her skin as she followed Cicero's voice through the cargo hold to the narrow corridor near the hatch.

"Finished tinkering with the engine bits, Captain. Everything will be smooth... sailing..."

Cicero was already moving, one arm held out to grab Aryana across the chest when she pounced at the sight of a Karezz bastard on their ship.

"What in the dark is that Kezzie bastard doing on my ship?"

"He's a client," Cicero said in quinlitz. "Calm yourself, Aryana."

"Let me go," Aryana demanded, also using her native language. "Let me go. I'll tear him apart. Or I'll tear the engine apart. We're not taking him anywhere."

Cicero wrestled Aryana against the wall, one arm held across her chest and the other resting on her forehead. Aryana bucked and fought, but Cicero didn't budge.

"I would have called ahead, but you were in the engine and the heat affects your comms. Right? Right?" She widened her eyes and waited until Aryana nodded. "You know me, 'Yana. I wouldn't spring this on you if I had another choice. We need to take him to the Quay."

The man cleared his throat. "I apologize. If I'd known you had a Balanquin servant I would~"

Cicero turned on him, dropping her hand from Aryana's forehead to aim a finger at him. "This is my friend, my crewmate, and a damned fine engineer. She's not a *j'inklae* slave. Apologize to her. Her name is Aryana Barrien."

He swallowed a lump in his throat and nodded quickly. "I apologize, Aryana Barrien."

"Irias, find the Karezz somewhere he can be isolated. As long as you're on this ship, you do not have the liberty to move freely. If you want to leave your room, call for assistance and someone will escort you. Understood?"

"Yes. Sorry. Yes. I understand."

Irias led the man away. Cicero waited until he was out of sight before turning her attention back to Aryana. Aryana was still staring after the Karezz, her breath coming in ragged huffs. Cicero cupped her cheek and forced her to make eye contact.

"Let me take you to the mess. I'll get you some food, okay?"

"Mph." Aryana twisted away from Cicero's grip and walked away, but she went in the direction of the mess hall. Cicero followed her at a respectable distance, giving her the appropriate space. When she arrived, she sat down at the table and stared at her hands. Cicero went to the cupboards and dug around for something to eat. By the time she sat down across the table with two plastic cups of *m'iavdor*, Aryana had managed to calm her breathing.

Cicero pushed one of the cups to her. "I apologize for that."

"You would have warned me if you could have," Aryana admitted. Now that her adrenaline was gone, she was meek and contrite. She popped off the top of the cup and reached in to peel out one of the gooey rolls of dough. She put it into her mouth whole and chewed slowly. Cicero opened hers as well, but she used a two-tined fork to pluck hers out. "I apologize as well," she said when her mouth was empty again.

"Your reaction was merited."

Aryana smiled condescendingly. "Do you even know what the Karezza did to us?"

"No. But I know you don't talk about it with outsiders."

Aryana ate another ball of dough. "The Karezza saved us. Pelorum had two major republics. There was us, the Balanquin, and the Catarrh. We were rich and educated. They were smaller and less privileged. We had two centuries of peace, and the Balanquin took it for granted. The Catarrh spent that time building up a military force. They attacked us and we never even saw it coming. We were soft and trusting. We didn't know how to fight a war. So many of us committed suicide rather than fight. They were frightened of torture, imprisonment, pain. Some of us tried to fight. Our military was mostly ceremonial by that time, but some of the soldiers banded together and fought back."

Cicero said, "A Decade at the Battlements. I remember. Bauwerji Crow was one of the militia leaders."

Aryana nodded. "We didn't stand a chance. It was all we could do to just stay alive and defend ourselves, let alone striking back in any real manner. We were forced out into the deserts and struggled to find food or shelter. We wouldn't have lasted very long. I was born during the exile, so I didn't know anything different. But I did know that it was only a matter of time before we had to just give up."

She took out another ball and ate it, then licked her fingers clean.

"The Karezza found us by accident. One man in a scout vessel landed in the desert to repair his ship, and he met a Balanquin. She helped him get spaceworthy again, and he promised to come back with help. He kept his promise. Karezza warships blocked out the sun when they first arrived. For the first time we had hope. In under a year we managed to run the Catarrh out of our cities and reclaim our homes. We had victory."

Cicero stood up and went to the sink basin. She filled a mug with water and brought it back, along with a handful of napkins. Aryana thanked her with a nod.

"The Karezza offered to stick around to help us rebuild. They would be there if the Catarrh decided to attack again. We all welcomed the offer. We definitely needed the help. Our government was in shambles, our homes destroyed. The Catarrh had ten years to make themselves at home. And when the tide began turning, they did everything they could to make sure we came back to a disaster area. Even with the Catarrh run off, we still might not have survived if it weren't for the Karezza."

"And that's where things started going wrong?" Cicero asked.

Aryana nodded. "They created an interim government. Just to help reestablish the normalcy. They put themselves in positions of power and helped us get back to our lives. For a time we barely even noticed. They were necessary. They were a miracle. They made everything easy." She scooted her cup across the table with her fingertips. "My father was a patternmaker. He had to be retaught since the only sewing he'd done in ten years was mending whatever patchwork clothes the soldiers could find. He went to work in what we later learned was a sweatshop. His supervisor was Karezz. He made Karezz clothes. My mother was a surgeon. To the Karezza, that meant she knew how to sew. She had the table next to my father in the shop. But she didn't work the same hours as him."

Cicero said, "I think I can guess what happened."

Aryana stared at her and took a drink of her water. "It was nothing. It was just the cost of our victory. My mother's supervisor would take her away from her station so she could take a break. My father tried to argue, but they started giving him breaks as well. And if he fought back, they hurt his hands so he would lose income until they healed."

Cicero had balled her hands into fists. "I didn't know."

"We don't go around telling people that we turned ourselves into whore slaves. We traded an enemy that wanted us dead for one that wanted to keep us alive for their own purposes."

"So what changed?"

"Bauwerji Crow."

Cicero sat up straighter. "She's... never mentioned..."

"Like I said." Aryana shrugged. "She was working as a mechanic. One day she walked in on her supervisor raping a new hire. He was doing it in the hangar, where everyone could see. So Bauwerji picked up a wrench and used it until his skull was... well..." She picked up one of the dough balls and squeezed it between her thumb and forefinger. "She should have been executed for her crime. Killing a Karezz was the worst crime any of us could commit. But those women and men, they turned their backs on her. They chose not to apprehend her, which was also a crime. Bauwerji got into her *Biju Sprinter*, and took off for the Quay."

Cicero furrowed her brow. "The *Biju Sprinter*? That's a bracijera ship. And the distance between Pelorum and the Quay..."

Aryana nodded. "It almost killed her. She was unconscious and suffering from hypoxia when she arrived at the station. She was just conscious enough to ask for sanctuary from Admiral Reshef, and she granted it. That's why when the Karezza came looking for her, Admiral Reshef protected her. It could have caused a war between the Karezza and the Humans."

"No," Cicero said. "The Quay is too valuable. And Humans have too many allies that might side with them."

"That's what the Karezza were worried about. They didn't push the issue, and Bauwerji was allowed to stay under the protection of the Aphelion Project."

Cicero leaned back in her seat. "And after that, on Pelorum...?"

"Revolution. One of us had stood up against the oppressors, so the rest of us felt emboldened. Some of us went on strike. Others simply demanded permission to leave work and start businesses of our own. It was technically allowed under the new laws, but no one was willing to take the risk before Bauwerji took her stand. It was like something woke up in us."

"I can't believe she's never said anything."

"Who? Bauwerji? I didn't know you knew each other that well."

"We... we don't."

Aryana said, "I left Pelorum as soon as I could. I didn't want to spend another minute with those bastards. My parents paid for my escape. I hated leaving them behind, but it was better than staying to meet their fate. I still send them money sometimes. Father is still a patternmaker. Mother is... raising children." She looked away.

Cicero pushed her snack away, her appetite suddenly destroyed. She knew bits and pieces of the Balanquin/Karezza conflict, but the details were worse than she'd feared. When she hired Aryana, the girl had asked if there were any Karezz crew members. When Cicero said there weren't, Aryana politely requested that she never recruit any. The girl was skilled enough as a mechanic and engineer that she could safely make that kind of demand, so Cicero agreed.

"And I brought one into your home." Cicero stood up. "I'm sorry, Aryana."

"Where are you going?"

"I'm going to throw that *lysyi didko* out the nearest... no, I'm going to take off, get some altitude, and then I'm going to throw him out the window."

Aryana stood up. "Cicerone, no. Stop." She put her hands on Cicero's shoulders. "I know you, *ji'o*. You've respected me enough to never bring a Karezz onboard the entire time I've been here. If you decided to bring this one, then I accept there's a good reason for that. Is there a good reason?"

"I don't know if it's good enough. Given what I know now..."

Aryana said, "You knew bringing him here would break a promise to a member of your crew. Then the stakes must be pretty high. I'll make it work until we get to the Quay. I'll hide in the lower decks or the engine or something. It meant a lot, what you said to him about staying away from me. I have no doubt you'll enforce that."

"Especially now. Aryana, if he so much as looks at you, I'll have Se-Weoi rip his fingers and toes off, then his limbs, then his non-vital organs. And then I'll have him killed."

Aryana smiled. "Thanks, Captain."

Cicero nodded. "And if you want to lie and say he looked at you, that would be fine, too."

"Noted."

"I want to be off the ground in ten. Doable?"

"Eminently."

"Good. And that rattling noise...?"

Aryana waved dismissively. "Dealt with."

"Excellent. I knew I could count on you. And after this, I'll work on regaining your trust in me."

"Shouldn't be too hard."

Cicero winked and left the mess hall. Aryana gathered their cups of *m'iavdor* to put them back in the cupboard. She respected Cicero and, as much as she hated the idea of having a Karezza aboard, she knew that Cicero had used her best judgment. She also knew that the captain would never let that flat-faced mutt lay a hand on her.

Even so, the trip to the Quay would take just over five hours, and Aryana planned to spend every minute of it hiding in the engine room.

She finished cleaning up after her snack and retreated to her hidden sanctum.

CHAPTER FIVE

CICERO WAS surprised she had fallen asleep, only aware that she'd lost consciousness when it returned to her. She didn't even remember being tired. The last thing she remembered was being in the mess hall with Aryana hearing about the atrocities committed by the Karezza. From there she couldn't recall where she'd gone or when she'd decided to lie down for a nap. Her bed was impossibly comfortable. There was drool on the right side of her face. She reached up to wipe it away, but the movement caused her entire body to list to port.

She opened her eyes and discovered she was floating face-down in the corridor outside engineering. Nausea and panic wrestled for control of her mind. She stuck out her left hand to brace herself against the wall, but that caused such pain that she cried out and pulled the apparently wounded arm to her chest. It was then that she saw her right hand was smeared with blood. Not drool, then. She touched her face again and followed the stickiness up to a gash just below her hairline.

Alarms were ringing. Her vision swam as she righted herself, grabbing hold of the wall for balance and leaving streaks of blood behind. Once she could put her feet on the ground she pressed the bud into her ear and tapped it three times for ship-wide.

"This is Captain Drayton. I'm currently in the corridor leading to engineering. If you are conscious and uninjured, remain where you are. If you are conscious and injured, try to make your way to the Med Pod." She paused. "If you are unconscious, disregard this message." She laughed to herself and shook her head to clear the cobwebs. Oxygen deprivation, maybe. If gravity was failing then all life support systems were suspect. She pushed her way along the wall, her left arm still cradled against her chest, until she reached the hatch leading to the engine room.

Moving the heavy door was a trial even with two arms, but she somehow she managed to get it open. The heat that washed past her was scorching, hurting her eyes as she squinted inside. Checking the compartment was only a hunch, the vague awareness that she would be in that corridor for a specific reason, but even so she was shocked to see Aryana lying immobile on the floor. She called the engineer's name and, when she didn't respond, grunted as she pushed her way inside.

It took her a moment to realize that Aryana's position meant that engineering *did* have gravity. She stepped over the threshold and dropped to the ground. Her left arm took the brunt of her weight and she cried out in pain. Her shout echoed around the machinery as she waited for the initial burst of agony to fade enough for her to think. She was immediately drenched in sweat, her skin baking in the heat. She didn't know how Aryana stood it. The floor was too hot to touch, so she wrestled her way back onto her feet by hooking her right arm around a pipe.

"Yana," she said, "get up. I'm not going to be able to haul you out of here, so get on your feet. That's an order." She crouched next to Aryana, as the floor was too hot to kneel on, and touched her throat to make sure there was a pulse. "Okay. You're alive. And you're probably going to be a little bruised after this." She grabbed the collar of Aryana's shirt and began dragging her.

Five minutes later they reached the corridor. Aryana floated off the ground, and Cicero pushed the door shut to cut off the waves of heat. She was soaked from head to toe, and the blood seeping through the wound on her head threatened to turn into a faucet due to the pounding of her heart. As she was catching her breath, Kela Se-Woei swam around the corner. The Acapsian wore her nightclothes, which indicated it was later than Cicero thought.

"Kela. What time is it?"

"Seven past first bells," Kela said.

Cicero didn't know exactly what time she'd gotten back to the ship, but she guessed she'd lost something close to three hours. "We must be close to the Quay," she said. "The rest of the crew... where are they?"

"Unconscious. Some are injured. Not as bad as you are, though. What happened?"

"That was my next question."

With Kela's help, she rearranged Aryana's body to look for injuries. If the Karezz was responsible for this, she would find new and exciting ways to make him hurt. But other than the bruise on her temple and the burns from lying on the floor, there didn't seem to be any evidence of an attack.

"Can you get her to the Med Pod? She may have injuries that aren't readily apparent."

"What about you?"

"I need to find out what happened. I need to be on the bridge."

Kela said, "You need to be in the Med Pod with her."

"I'm fine."

Kela slapped Cicero's arm, causing her to see a wave of red. She fell against the bulkhead wincing with pain. "*Puw'sted j'hihian* whore *pulsated!*"

"Right," Kela said. "I'll help you get Aryana to the Med Pod, then hopefully Irias will be able to help you both out. Then I'll go to the bridge and see if I can work this *wadinor* shit out."

"I could order you to take her." Kela narrowed her eyes and Cicero flinched. "But I won't! I won't. You're cruel."

Kela shrugged and cradled Aryana's shoulders against her chest. "Grab her feet."

Cicero pinned Aryana's legs against her chest using her right arm. She and Kela moved through the corridors by walking on their toes, pushing off the floor like they were treading water in a swimming pool. They were crossing the cargo bay when Enatel Kaesa crossed their paths. He was Occamian, and he'd spent years on his family farm developing the upper body of an *akposee*. He took Aryana from them and easily held her in his arms.

"Do you have any idea what happened?" Cicero asked.

Enatel shook his head. "Last thing I remember, you brought the Karezz *di'oe* onboard. You don't think he did this, do you?"

"I don't know. But I want to speak with him as soon as possible."

Kela said, "As soon as possible is after you've gotten your arm checked out, Captain. You have a head injury. If this guy is dangerous, you'd be easy pickings for him."

"She's right," Enatel said. "Don't make me carry you. You know I could do it even if the gravity was working properly."

"Fine," she said, "just make it quick."

Kela said, "I'm going to check out the bridge. Should I stop by our guest's cabin to make sure he's still there?"

"Not yet. I don't want anyone confronting him alone. Where is everyone else?"

Kela said, "I saw Irias and Sery in the common room. Zennes is probably still in his cabin."

Cicero said, "Make sure the ship is on course and safe to fly. Then find everyone else and we'll meet up in the Med Pod. If I have to get examined, everyone else does, too."

"Yes, ma'am."

Cicero gestured for Enatel to lead the way. There had been crises like this in the past, attacks and other crews trying to take the ill-gotten gains Cicero had acquired fair and square. She sometimes acted as a bounty hunter, so from time to time their cargo was a criminal whose goons tried to free their boss from captivity. Her crew had proven themselves trustworthy allies in those times of need, strong enough that she quickly stopped worrying about the periodic scuffles.

Something about this situation, about Aryana's unconscious body in Enatel's arms and the memory loss and the utter crippling of their ship, combined to give her a feeling of doom. She would feel much better once Kela had checked the computers to see what exactly they were up against. Until then she would have to focus on getting herself back into fighting shape.

Cicero reset her own arm and used a mirror to mend the wound on her head. Enatel suggested a transfusion, but she didn't feel lightheaded enough to warrant it. Human blood was a precious commodity out in the hinterlands, so it was best to save it for when there was a real need. She wanted to save it just in case whatever they were facing wasn't over. Enatel wasn't much of a doctor, but he was the best they had at the moment. He made Aryana comfortable by strapping her to the bed and examined her injuries.

"It looks like bumps and bruises. A Karezz attacker would have done much more damage."

"Thank goodness for small favors," Cicero said.

The intercom near the door buzzed and Cicero floated over to respond. "This is the Med."

"I'm about to reinstitute gravity," Kela said. "Get somewhere and hold on tight."

Cicero drifted over to the unoccupied exam bed, while Enatel gripped the edge of Aryana's. The air in the room seemed to sway before pushing down on them. Cicero watched Enatel's legs drift to the floor as her own body relaxed against the plush cushions of her bed.

"Well done, Kela. Any word from the rest of the crew?"

"They're starting to wake up. I heard Zennes moving around."

She swung her legs off the bed and stood up. It took her a moment to get accustomed to gravity again. "I'm coming up to see what I can find out. Enatel, stay with Aryana. I don't want her to wake up alone." He nodded and Cicero left. She passed by the quarters on her way to the bridge, intercepting Sery as she came out of her quarters.

"Captain?" she said. "What the *th'wil* is going on?"

"I'm trying to find that out." She pointed at the Karezza's quarters. "Make sure that door stays closed. If anyone else wakes up, tell them we're working on it. Understood?"

"Yes, ma'am."

Cicero continued on to the bridge. Kela was at her usual station, but the monitor screens were logged in to view ship diagnostics instead of weapon systems. She glanced over her shoulder as Cicero came in and then went back to watching her screens.

"Good job getting us back on the floor," Cicero said. "Anything from the ship's records?"

"You're not going to like it."

Cicero said, "Of course I'm not. My whole crew was knocked unconscious and my ship is hurt. I just need to know how bad the situation is."

"It's bad. Very bad. We're off-course by about eighty minutes. I can figure out the right way to aim us so we're back on track, but that's not the most concerning thing. We were boarded."

Cicero's hackles rose. "What?"

Kela pointed at the screen. "An hour ago, we were intercepted by a... a ship I can't identify." Cicero noted that, but didn't interrupt. "We hailed them three times, but there was no response. According to this, I powered weapons. Engines were engaged for evasive maneuvers, but they hit us with something." She pointed at the screen. "Energy drain across the board. There was an explosion in engineering. I assume that's why you were heading down there."

Cicero nodded vaguely. She could remember moving down the corridor, being flung against the wall as they were hit by a particle weapon, but she couldn't tell if it was a true memory or something conjured by the report Kela was giving her.

"Whatever they hit us with next sent us reeling. We spent five minutes with no power. I assume that's when everyone was thrown around whatever room they happened to be in. We're lucky we weren't splattered against the walls since the inertial dampeners were on the fritz. They caught up and hooked up to us. There was an atmo balancing in the airlock, but other than that I can't find any evidence of the people who boarded."

Cicero moved away from the console. "The Karezz." She ran from the bridge, followed closely by Kela. Sery was still waiting where Cicero had left her. "Open the door! Kela, do you have a weapon?"

To anyone else barefoot and in nightclothes, the question would have been ridiculous. Kela, however, pushed up her sleeve and removed a small dagger. Sery punched in her code, checked to make sure Cicero and Kela were ready, and signaled it to open. Kela took a step back, but Cicero had an idea of what they would find inside.

The Karezza man was lying on the floor as if he'd fallen out of bed. His face was coated with blood that seemed to have come from his nostrils, eyes, and mouth. Sery crouched next to him and checked for vital signs. Cicero went to the foot locker and flipped up the lid. To her relief and, frankly, surprise, the precious box the Karezz had brought aboard was still there. Kela stepped back out into the corridor to examine the lockpad.

"Even if someone did board the ship while we were unconscious, they couldn't have gotten in here without the code. This hasn't been hacked. How did they managed to kill him?"

"He was the only Karezz onboard," Cicero muttered.

Kela and Sery looked at her with unasked questions on their faces.

"It means we have to get to the Quay. Now. Kela, get back to the bridge. See if the engines are in any shape to be pushed. I want us docking at the station in an hour."

"An hour?" Kela said. "Impossible."

"Make it as possible as you can, Kela. I have a feeling we're going to see that mystery ship again very soon. We're going to need the power of every race behind us if we're going to survive."

CHAPTER SIX

CORDWAINER LITTLEFOOT, the station's Medical Chief, was sitting alone at a table near the water feature of the food pavilion. Cordwainer sensed Bauwerji's approach and looked up, smiling as ze put her silverware down and rose to politely welcome her friend to the table. There wasn't much of a crowd so they had the little area to themselves. Bauwerji started to offer an apology but she stopped when she saw the ball of meat sitting on the doctor's plate. She wrinkled her nose and lowered herself into the other seat.

"Do I want to know what that is?"

"Pemmican with wild rice and salmonberries. Would you like to try some?"

"No, thank you." She sat down across from her friend. "Which restaurant served you that? I'll have them fined."

Cordwainer smiled. "I prepared this myself in my quarters. It's actually very good."

"I'll take your word for that." She had a packet of food from the Balanquin restaurant; a chunk of *waqin*cheese and strips of meat wrapped in leaves soaked in olive oil. "I'm sorry I'm late."

Cordwainer shook hir head. "I'm sure next time I'll be the one who is rushed with work and make you wait. No troubles."

Bauwerji was surprised by her friendship with the Human physician. It wasn't a relationship she'd sought out, and she was fairly sure Cordwainer hadn't manipulated events to make it happen. They were simply two people far from home who discovered almost by accident that they enjoyed one another's company. They were able to sit silently and enjoy a meal without being forced to make idle conversation. But when they did need to talk, both were willing to listen. It was one of Bauwerji's most treasured friendships.

They first bonded over a bracelet Bauwerji sometimes wore when she was off-duty. It was a handcrafted war souvenir, made from desert glass harvested from outside a cave she'd once turned into a fortress. Her lover at the time had made it for her, and Bauwerji wore it in her memory. Cordwainer mentioned it reminded hir of hir people's jewelry; she was Lakota-Human, from Earth, and ze showed Bauwerji some of the items ze'd brought from home. The beaded silver necklace so entranced Bauwerji that Cordwainer insisted she keep it. Bauwerji responded by buying hir lunch the next day, and a friendship was born.

Cordwainer was a gender-fluid androgynous Human. Hir skin was dark, hir hair light brown fading to gray. Ze was chosen for the lofty position of Medical Chief due to hir extensive knowledge of other races and their medical needs. Ze spent ten years on a station in Earth's orbit studying as much as ze could before even registering for the job. A lifesaving treatment for a Balanquin could prove fatal to an Acapsian, and basically everything that made the Karezza healthy would lead to a terminal diagnosis in every other race they'd encountered.

Being in charge also required good managerial skills. Human and Balanquin doctors couldn't even operate on a Karezz without risking contamination, and Ladronis respectfully refused medical intervention from anyone outside their race. Cordwainer had doctors who worked with hir for those special cases, and managing them called for skills ze hadn't learned in medical school.

Regardless, ze handled the various aspects of hir job with enough skill and grace that it appeared easy. Ze impressed Bauwerji every day with the respect ze showed for every patient regardless of species. It was something she wished she could learn from her friend. Ze thought about the Karezz soldiers on the station, specifically Constable Heely, and considered asking Cordwainer for advice on how to be more open and understanding.

She was just working out how to formulate the question when her communicator sounded. She held up her hand in apology, and Cordwainer nodded that it was okay. Bauwerji put the earpiece in.

"This is XO Crow."

Indira said, "Bauwerji, I know you're on break, but I think you're going to want to be at the docks for this. The *Sastruga* just hailed and asked for clearance."

Bauwerji fought the urge to smile. The *Sastruga* meant Cicerone. Indira knew that, and she would have known it was good news. So why did she sound so dire?

"Is everything okay?"

"I don't know. They're burning a lot of exhaust and the ship looks like it's been hit. They requested Medical and Engineering representatives on-hand when they arrive."

"I'm having lunch with Dr. Littlefoot. Should ze come along?"

"Absolutely. Yes, thank you. That will save me a call."

Bauwerji signed off and gathered up her food. She quickly explained what had happened and what was needed, and Cordwainer wrapped up hir food as well.

"Is that not Captain Drayton's vessel?"

"I'm trying not to think about that. Come on."

They hurried from the pavilion. The docks weren't far away, and the *Sastruga* would need time to navigate through the debris field, but still they moved quickly. Cordwainer was wearing a leather breechcloth and leggings under hir tunic, and ze gathered the material to keep it from tripping hir up. Bauwerji called up to the pilothouse and asked which slip the *Sastruga* was being directed toward. She and Cordwainer arrived with minutes to spare.

The medical team arrived as the ship was being hauled inside. They watched as the docking clamps swung around to draw the battle-worn *Sastruga* through the protective energy barrier and into a slip. The docking clamps were tall, mantid-looking constructions that automatically locked onto the nearest vessel and positioned it for a safe landing in one of the many berths that ringed the area.

As the ship was ferried to the end of its journey, Bauwerji analyzed the damage to the outer hull. Scars from directed-energy weapons ran down the starboard side. The engines seemed to be struggling to maintain full power; there was something resigned in the way their lights died when the docking clamps took over. Bauwerji felt a surge of dread as she envisioned everything that might have happened to the people within.

When they had the all-clear, Cordwainer motioned for the medical team to follow hir in. Bauwerji stayed far enough behind that she wouldn't get in their way, but she couldn't wait for an official report. Two crewmembers were already being brought out on hoverbeds, securely strapped down so they wouldn't tumble to the ground. As bad as they looked, Bauwerji couldn't help but be relieved when the hatch opened and Cicero walked out under her own power. There was blood on the collar of her uniform jacket and a salve glistened on her temple just below the hairline, but she was in otherwise good shape.

"Captain Drayton."

Cicero looked up. Her expression was tight with concern for her crew, but something around the eyes softened when she saw Bauwerji. "Executive Officer Crow."

"I'm glad to see you're not too badly injured." The subtext being that she had been extremely frightened that they would find her clinging to life when the ship arrived.

"My crew didn't fare as well." But her expression was warm, and grateful to know Bauwerji had been worried. She was a captain, so she knew some things couldn't be said out loud at moments like this. But she was also skilled at reading between the lines. "I'm grateful the station was here."

"So are we." She finally broke eye contact to look at the ship. "What can I do?"

"I think this is Dr. Littlefoot's domain. We can only watch and try to stay out of hir way." She touched her shoulder, and Bauwerji wondered if there had been another injury that was already healed before they arrived. "In the meantime, I want to meet with Admiral Reshef. This attack could have far-reaching consequences for every race in the Quay."

Bauwerji's concern came flooding back, and she nodded. "I'll escort you to the briefing room."

"Thank you." She touched Bauwerji's hand and softly repeated, "Thank you."

Bauwerji touched Cicero's hand, nodded, and caught Cordwainer's eye to let hir know they were leaving. Cordwainer nodded and then refocused on the task at hand.

"How bad?" Bauwerji asked as they set off.

"Bad," Cicero said. "My engineer, Aryana Barrien? She's been unconscious since the attack. We all lost consciousness for some period or another. It's hard to say, since the ship's systems were screwed with. But those of us who regained consciousness seem to be recovering well enough. I don't know enough about Balanquin physiology to know how bad it is that Aryana hasn't woken up..."

Bauwerji hesitated, but decided on the truth. "It's probably not good. Occasionally we'll enter a comatose state while our bodies heal. It's akin to hibernation."

"So she might still wake up?"

"On Pelorum, it would have been hard to say. But here, under Dr. Littlefoot's care, I'd say she has a better than good shot at recovery."

"Good. She's my second-favorite Balanquin."

Bauwerji smiled as she summoned the lift. "You still haven't said who it was that attacked you in the first place."

"No. Because we're not sure." Bauwerji looked at her, shocked, and Cicero shrugged. "My expert in these matters didn't recognize the ship. Now, they did board us. They fucked up our records. So there's a chance they also screwed with the scanners so they would look different than they really are."

They boarded the lift. "Do you at least know what they were after?"

Another hesitation. "Yes. We had a Karezz passenger."

Bauwerji tensed. "And is he aboard?"

"Not anymore. He's dead."

"So it's not all bad news."

"A passenger died on my watch, Bauwerji."

"I know," she said softly. "I'm sorry. But I'll not mourn him. If someone had to die..."

Cicero said, "Yes. I agree with you on that matter." They were alone in the lift, so Cicero reached out and took Bauwerji's hand. They had been lovers for almost three years, an unlikely match that Bauwerji continued to be surprised by. The first time she met Cicerone Drayton, her initial assessment was pirate, bounty hunter, rogue. But she also had a heart. She was compassionate and fiercely protective of her crew. She was still a scoundrel, and admitted as much if asked, but she was also kind. Bauwerji had never expected to find herself falling in love with anyone, let alone a Human, but Cicero was adept at stealing things that others called impossible.

"I am very glad you were not hurt any worse than you were."

"Thank you."

The lift doors parted and so did their hands. The majority of crewmembers aboard the Quay were aware of their relationship, but Bauwerji could sense that this was a time to be professional. Admiral Reshef was waiting for them and fell into step as they moved toward the briefing room.

"Captain Drayton. I'm glad to see you relatively well."

Cicero nodded. "Thank you, Admiral. Who else will be joining us?"

"The command staff. Ephor Wison, Selina Rogers, Nerea Paisian…" She looked at Bauwerji. "Constable Heely."

Bauwerji said, "If this is as serious as Cicero implies, then she'll need to be there."

Indira nodded gratefully at her pragmatism. "We'll record the meeting for Dr. Littlefoot since ze'll be preoccupied with caring for your crew."

"That's fine."

They entered the room and found the rest of the group was already waiting. The Council had been established early in the Quay's existence. In order to have a Human in charge of the day-to-day business of the station, the other races reasonably requested a vote in dealing with the larger issues. A representative of the major races was elected to sit on the Council. The Irikoan, Sautoriau, and Occamian didn't have a large enough population to warrant a place at the table. Cordwainer was the Human's representative, while Admiral Reshef was merely the facilitator of their meetings.

Jocia Wison, Ladronis, smelled of water and the spices she used to bathe. The Ladronis were practically amphibious, choosing to spend the majority of their time underwater. The few Ladronis homes she'd seen, constructs of twig, stone, and mud, seemed to be built around the basin they used as beds. Jocia also had a smaller basin near her door so she could wash her hands before entering or leaving her home. Whether she was trying to prevent the contamination of her home or vice versa, Bauwerji didn't know. At the moment Jocia's blue skin had a slight sheen that indicated she had recently bathed, though her pale yellow hair was dry. Her hands were folded in front of her as she waited for Indira to begin the meeting.

"Thank you all for coming so quickly," Indira said. "Most of you know Captain Drayton from the *Sastruga*. She's the one who requested this meeting, so I'll leave it to her."

Cicero nodded her thanks and looked at the gathered group. "I picked up a passenger recently. He had a story for me, one that I dismissed as soon as I heard it, but I was going to bring him here because it seemed like an easy gig. Instead, my ship was almost destroyed and several of my crew members have yet to wake up following an attack that left us utterly defenseless. I think the people who attacked my ship then boarded it and, when they didn't find what they were looking for, killed my passenger."

"What were they looking for?" Selina Rogers asked.

"If my passenger was telling the truth, a piece of an asteroid. It was a remnant from the beginning of the universe. From before any of our races evolved."

Constable Heely furrowed her brow. "I guess that would be valuable…"

"Whoever attacked my ship wasn't after the money. They were after something a lot worse. My passenger said that the rock contained the building blocks of life. Our life. The life of every race in this room, on this station."

Bauwerji said, "What would be the importance of that?"

Cicero took a deep breath and shook her head. "Again, just going by what my passenger said… but now I have reason to believe he was telling the truth. And he said that the genetic evidence on that stone could be used to wipe out all life in the universe by targeting individual races. If someone got their hands on it, they could sell a weapon of genocide to the highest bidder."

Bauwerji couldn't stop herself from looking across the table at Heely. To her dismay, Heely was already looking at her with an unreadable expression. If such a weapon existed, the Karezza would be capable of and more than willing to buy it and wipe out every Balanquin on Pelorum.

Indira said, "Where is the stone now?"

"It's safe," Cicero said. "The people who attacked our ship didn't get their hands on it, and I made sure it was in a safe place. You'll understand if I don't want to be too forthcoming with its location."

Heely said, "You don't trust us."

Cicero stared directly at her. "No."

Bauwerji said, "Assuming the people who attacked you will come back for another attempt at the rock, what do we do now?"

Cicero shrugged helplessly and held her hands out. "I'm open to suggestions."

Chapter Seven

Indira was obviously shaken by the news Cicero had delivered, but she gathered her wits and focused. The people around the table were looking to her for leadership. "First and foremost," she said, "we have to determine whether this technology could actually exist. Just because someone could theoretically use it to wipe out entire species, it's not going to do any good if they don't have the means to weaponize it."

Heely said, "We already have it. The Roadblock systems. Set it to Human or Balanquin, activate, and it stops that species in their tracks."

Nerea Paisian, the station's Paisian envoy, considered the statement before speaking. "Technically correct, although that is a much smaller scale than what Captain Drayton has postulated. Those are specific nets that are programmed to analyze a single person at a time. If it notes certain characteristics associated with the pre-set race, it activates the security protocol. For a weapon that actually seeks out and attacks the DNA of a specific race while leaving all the others unscathed... it would be a doomsday weapon of the highest magnitude."

Cicero nodded. "And what's worse, I think whoever attacked my ship already has a prototype. The Karezz who brought me the information and the stone was killed in his quarters. We were all injured and we lost our memories, but we're mostly unhurt. What if that was a side effect of the weapon? The genetic material on the asteroid may be the last piece necessary to fine-tune their weapon."

Bauwerji said, "So a ship could just pull up into orbit, hit a switch, and every member of one race or another on the planet below would die?"

"Essentially," Cicero said. "That's what the Karezz man was worried about. Given what's happened, it's what I'm worried about, too."

Indira said, "Okay. When Dr. Littlefoot has finished taking care of the *Sastruga*'s crew, I'll run all this by her to see what she has to say. Captain Drayton, you're certain that the asteroid is in a safe place?"

Cicero nodded. "For now, anyway. If the mystery ship comes here and attacks..."

"We'll be ready for them," Indira said.

Nerea said, "The Paisian fleet can be brought in to act as a blockade. I can contact them once this meeting is dismissed and have them depart immediately."

"Thank you, Nerea," Indira said. "We would be grateful for their help."

Heely said, "The Karezz fleet can be put on high alert as well."

Indira nodded. "Very good. They can coordinate through me."

"Typically that goes through the XO," Heely said.

"Now is not the time," Indira sighed. "The Karezz fleet can coordinate through me. If no one has anything else to contribute to the discussion..." She knew the Ladronis wouldn't offer to help, due to their pacifism, but she cast a glance at Jocia Wison regardless. The Ephor smiled regretfully, and Indira nodded to show she understood. "Then we'll adjourn. Constable Heely and Nerea, contact your people and have them get underway. Nerea, I would also like you to take a look at the *Sastruga*'s records."

Nerea nodded his head.

"I'd like to think we could defend ourselves against this mystery ship, but given what they did to the *Sastruga*, I'm not taking any chances. We're adjourned."

The group filtered out of the room, with Bauwerji waiting for Cicero so they could leave together. Constable Heely was one of the last to leave, and Indira stepped into her path.

"Stop."

"I have to stop. You're blocking the door."

Indira stared at her. "You're antagonizing Bauwerji. It has to stop."

Heely sighed and crossed her arms. "Bauwerji treats me like I'm *hi'fruzam.*"

"You're giving her every reason to continue. Make peace or just avoid each other. I would be happy with either choice. If this stone of Cicero's does bring trouble to our doorstep, I want to know I can count on the two people I trust the most. Should it become an issue, I think you know whose side I would fall on."

Heely grimaced. "If I was relieved of duty, the Karezz fleet might leave as well."

"I'm willing to take that chance."

Heely considered whether or not to call her bluff, then nodded. "Fine. I'll do my best to steer clear of her whenever possible."

"That's all I ask."

Heely stepped around the Admiral, and Indira turned to watch her leave. She'd been on-duty when they picked up Bauwerji's ship on sensors. A little Balanquin bracijera, all on its lonesome, almost too small to be picked up by their instruments. The only reason they were alerted at all was because it was moving quickly on an obviously plotted course. The ship had only barely survived its trip from Pelorum. Bauwerji was unconscious, hypoxic, starving, and dehydrated when they pulled her out of the ship. She regained consciousness just long enough to say one word: "Sanctuary."

Bauwerji was taken to the Med Center. While she was being treated, a Karezza cruiser arrived and demanded they hand her over as a prisoner of war. Indira was forced to make a choice without knowing what had truly happened. All she knew was that Bauwerji had allegedly killed her Karezz supervisor and fled the scene before she could be punished for the crime. Indira had seen the desperation on Bauwerji's face, even if it hadn't been apparent by the fact she'd jumped in a short-range ship to travel two thousand light years to find safety.

She refused to hand Bauwerji over and hoped the Karezza weren't willing to lose the friendship of the Aphelion Project over one person. In the end, she was proven correct; the cruiser departed without their prisoner. Once Bauwerji was awake and could explain what happened, Indira was vindicated. Bauwerji was granted sanctuary and began working for the Aphelion Project to earn her keep. Indira still considered it one of the wisest decisions she'd ever made.

Mara Heely had been a low-ranking member of the security force when Bauwerji arrived. She advanced through the ranks because she was a good constable, a hard worker, and she knew how to gain the favor of her superiors. The end result was unfortunate. She hated that her second and third in command were from warring races, but it couldn't be helped. They were both the best choices and the best at what they did.

Still, if Heely continued to act cruelly toward Bauwerji, Indira would have no choice but to replace her. Bauwerji was not the one causing trouble but, more importantly, Bauwerji also had nowhere else to go. If she went back to Pelorum she would be tried in a Karezza court as a murderer. Since she'd been required to give details of why she fled the planet to gain sanctuary, the Karezza would use that as a confession. She would be put to death for defending herself.

Indira sighed and disabled the lights in the briefing room. It was bad enough that they had a powerful enemy they knew nothing about. She didn't want to waste any more time than necessary dealing with interpersonal relations of those on her staff. Either Heely straightened up or Indira would find a new constable. As for the threat of losing the Karezza fleet... she'd called their bluff once before. She could only hope it would work a second time.

Bauwerji lay in bed with Cicero, holding the scoundrel's hands in both of hers. Her quarters were specifically designed for a Balanquin, meaning her bed was a platform suspended in one corner of the ceiling. Cicero usually hated it because she was always bumping her head on the ceiling if she woke up too quickly or needed to get up to use the bathroom. Tonight, however, she was cuddling too close to be claustrophobic. She had maintained her cool and calm exterior until the door was closed, and then she turned and fell into Bauwerji's embrace. The room was dark save for a small ovoid light-source above the bed, shining down so that Bauwerji's head partially eclipsed Cicero's.

"I thought I lost them, Bauwerji," she whispered against the material of Bauwerji's uniform top. "I thought I lost my whole crew. I had gotten them killed."

"Sh," Bauwerji said, stroking Cicero's hair. "Let me take care of you."

She had taken off Cicero's bloody tunic, leaving her in an undershirt. The blood had washed away easily enough, and now she ran her fingers over the pale pink skin of her lover. There were

Balanquin who found Humans difficult to look at; the hue of their flesh made them look like they were sickly. But Bauwerji found Cicero beautiful. She was like marble touched with just the slightest bit of fire. Warmed and darkened but not scarred. She bent down to kiss Cicero's shoulder, brushing her dark hair away to nuzzle her neck. She liked Human mating customs, too. The cuddling, the touching, the use of the mouth and tongue and fingers. Balanquin had a tendency to be very businesslike about their intimate affairs. Humans treated it with a near-religious reverence. A lover's body was something to be cherished, tasted, and explored.

Bauwerji extended her tongue and licked up to Cicero's ear, her hands moving over the other woman's back. Cicero lifted her head and Bauwerji's lips skimmed along her jawline until their mouths met. Cicero moved her hands to Bauwerji's face and touched it gently before moving to her hair. She lightly traced each braid, almost as if she was using it to read the history of the women each one honored. Bauwerji's tongue slipped into Cicero's mouth for a moment before retreating.

"I don't want to do this if you'd be uncomfortable."

Cicero's eyes were still closed. "I can feel my heart beating. I can feel yours. That's exactly what I need right now." She brushed her lips across Bauwerji's again. "I need to feel alive. I can't think of a better way. Can you?"

"No," Bauwerji said, nipping at Cicero's bottom lip. "But I confess that I'm not trying very hard."

Cicero smiled and tilted her head to capture Bauwerji's mouth. They repositioned themselves so that Bauwerji was on top. Cicero moved her hands over Bauwerji's clothes, finding catches and zippers and releasing them until she found flesh underneath. Bauwerji lifted her arms so her shirt could be removed, and Cicero sat up to press her face between the other woman's breasts. She cupped one in each hand, her thumbs over the nipples, and she moaned as she kissed the hard bone under the warm skin.

Bauwerji closed her eyes and stroked Cicero's hair. From keeping a watchful eye on her when they first met, to this. She remembered those first few hesitant days of friendship, the strained courtesy on both their parts. Cicero didn't trust someone who was in a position to arrest her. Bauwerji knew that sometimes there were extenuating circumstances that required lawlessness, but Cicero was a thief just for the hell of it.

As she got to know Cicero as a person, however, she came

around to a new way of thinking. She loved the freedom Cicero had. Her home was constantly in motion and she was always looking for the next port of call. Cicero's voice had picked up traces of accents from a multitude of races, though she denied having any accent at all if anyone brought it up. It was very clear to anyone with ears that she picked up a mixture of Balanquin, Paisian, even a bit of Ladronis which seeped into her voice from time to time. She was the only Human who could effortlessly pronounce Bauwerji's name correctly, although when it was pointed out, she insisted it was only because she was trying to be respectful.

For Cicero, the act of falling for a Balanquin was just one more aberration. Humans frowned on interspecies relationships. Bauwerji had heard that Earth still had rallies against it for one arcane reason or another. Some based it on religion, others said it was no different than having sexual relations with animals. Bauwerji bristled at that, but Cicero told her it was a tale as old as time. People were always trying to impose their own morality on anyone who was different. The discovery of aliens had just opened up whole new avenues of bigotry.

Bauwerji kissed the top of Cicero's head as the captain sucked her nipples. Such an exquisite thing, something so minor and yet Bauwerji had never considered it. Nipples weren't sexual in Balanquin culture. But oh, how Cicero had taught her to enjoy them properly. She bit her bottom lip and moved her hands down to touch Cicero's body.

Humans were vile creatures. War-like, aggressive, suspicious, xenophobic. They liked the fact they were isolated by technology, and they loved that other races relied so much on the Quay. In their eyes, it was a vulnerability they could exploit. "Do what we say, or we'll cut off access to your waystation, and if you don't like it, tough." Bauwerji disliked Humans. They were only one step above Karezza in her esteem. And yet... she supposed there was always an exception to the rule.

"Cicerone," she whispered.

Cicero lifted her head. Their lips brushed together briefly before they kissed.

"I love you."

"Bauwerji, I love you, too."

Bauwerji settled between Cicero's legs. She put her hands on Cicero's waist to draw her down against her thigh and began to gently thrust against her. The space between the bed and the ceiling meant that her shoulders were brushing against the smooth metal, but she didn't care. It made her feel like she was wrapped in a shell with the woman she adored. Cicero closed her eyes and lifted her chin, exposing her throat to Bauwerji's lips and tongue. She hooked her ankles behind Bauwerji and pressed her lips against Bauwerji's ear.

"Make me come..."

"Bauwerji put her hand under Cicero's head and made a fist in her hair. She pulled back as her other hand moved between them. She stroked Cicero to get her fingers wet, then extended her middle finger to pull her clitoris from its hood. Human and Balanquin were mostly similar anatomically, save for a few quirks. The most intriguing was that the Balanquin clitoris was more external than a Human's. Bauwerji stared into her lover's eyes as she stroked hers to full erection, fingers already slick with her juices as she pressed its tip against Cicero's folds.

"Yes," Cicero said, her voice choking off the end of the word. Bauwerji's clitoris was small at the tip but widened closer to her body. She arched her back and grunted when she felt Cicero squeeze her. There was no opening at the tip of her clitoris, no way for her to ejaculate, but moisture gathered around the base and transferred to Cicero's folds. She closed her eyes and focused on thrusting without losing her balance. A cramp threatened her right calf, but she soldiered through.

When Cicero came, Bauwerji followed her over the edge. She had been holding back her orgasm so Cicero could finish first, and the relief caused her to collapse in exhaustion on top of her lover. They murmured to one another, soft affirmations and repetition of each other's name as they caught their breath. Cicero lifted her head to Bauwerji's ear and whispered that she loved her again.

"I love you, too," she repeated.

Dr. Littlefoot's voice emanated from out of thin air. "Ladies. I'm assuming you did not intend to respond to my hail."

Bauwerji lifted her head and looked around until she spotted the communicator lying under a tangle of bedclothes. She freed it and said, "Apologies for that, Doctor. Did you enjoy the show?"

Cordwainer laughed nervously. "It sounded... enthusiastic, at least. I was attempting to contact Captain Drayton. Is she in a position to speak?"

"Here she is."

Cicero brushed her hair out of her face. "Any news, Dr.

Littlefoot?"

"Good news, in fact. Aryana is awake."

Bauwerji shifted off of Cicero in anticipation of her getting up. "That's wonderful. Is she... is she all right?"

"She had some burns that required grafting, but we took care of that while she was unconscious. Her wounds are bandaged up and salved. She's well enough for guests, and she asked for you specifically."

"Thank you, Dr. Littlefoot." Cicero had already climbed down the ladder and was gathering her clothes. Bauwerji followed her down. When she disconnected the call, she turned and cupped Bauwerji's face to kiss her lips. "Thank you, too. That was exactly what I needed after everything that's happened."

"I'm happy I could help."

Cicero smiled and brushed her hand over Bauwerji's. Bauwerji thought back to her life as a child, the peaceful world where joining the military was honorable but not considered dangerous. If the wars had never come, she would have stayed on Pelorum her entire life. If she hadn't become a fugitive, she would never have taken a position aboard the Quay. Everything in her life had to go wrong in order for her to be on the station when Captain Cicerone Drayton showed up.

Maybe she should stop thinking of those things as "wrong" and start considering them "necessary evils." She smiled at Cicero as she finished dressing and wished her luck with her newly-awakened crewmember. If the theories they passed around in the briefing room were anything close to fact, then they would need all the luck they could muster.

CHAPTER EIGHT

OF THE races inhabiting the Quay, the Paisian were the most alien in regard to Humans. They were the first to make contact with the upstart race. One of their ships was disabled and required extensive repairs to continue the journey back to their home planet. They would have been left adrift between solar systems if it wasn't for the small space station. The Paisian requested permission to dock. The Aphelion Project's commander sent the message on to Earth, but in those early days it sometimes took hours for a message to reach home. Then it would require committees, debates, and much consultation before they finally came to a decision. The commander knew the Paisian didn't have that long, so the request was granted.

The alien vessel had been docked at the Quay for seventeen hours when the Aphelion Project responded with a resounding negative. The commander sent back a single-word response: "Oops."

While the repairs were underway, the Human officers quickly learned that the Paisian were nothing like what they had anticipated. Each "person" was comprised of an entire host of small robotic creatures who joined together when necessary to form an individual. They were originally artificial intelligence created by a race which had since gone extinct, and which they rarely discussed with outsiders.

After their first encounter with Humans, they began assuming

Human shapes for their interactions. They called these creations "swarms" and gave each one a name to put their hosts at ease. They didn't quite understand Human naming trends, so they all used 'Paisian' as a surname. Nerea Paisian was assigned to remain at the Quay when its ship left, to act as an ambassador to the Humans and help with their nascent space station. Nerea was largely responsible for negotiating treaties with the other races in the area, and it also deserved much of the credit for helping the Quay become as strong as it was. It was capable of doing over thirty different tasks at once by detaching a swarm of fifty to a hundred nanoids and sending them off in a small swarm. The swarms it dedicated to each task varied in size according to the degree of difficulty and attention required. When the task was completed they would return to their host, reattach, and disseminate the information to the rest of the consciousness.

Currently, Nerea identified as male. Gender didn't really matter, as the individual pieces could mimic a female body just as easily, but he had existed long enough to enjoy a bit of variety. The various Paisian that made up the single entity called Nerea enjoyed working with other races. He liked the Balanquin for their steadfastness and strength; he liked the Karezza for their cunning; he liked the Ladronis for their music and spirituality. It was a joy to see them coming together for a singular cause. Though there were conflicts and disagreements to be sure, Nerea could see they were on a path to great understanding and cooperation.

That was in the future, however, and it would never come to pass if Captain Drayton's theories proved correct. Currently he had seven swarms dispersed throughout the station - monitoring repairs in the maintenance bay, arranging delivery for shipments from Pelorum and Acapsia, checking for flaws in the station's defenses, et cetera - but he knew he would need all the processing power at hand in case of an emergency.

One by one the swarms returned to him, alighting on his arm or shoulder before being absorbed into the whole. He catalogued the information delivered by each new arrival while waiting for the rest. It was sorted, filed, and earmarked to be sent to the appropriate work stations as soon as the full report was compiled. He was pleased to see everything on the station was operating at required parameters and their current deliveries were all on-schedule.

While his nanoids could give him a Human shape, they were utterly hopeless at complex things like faces or hands. Rather than forcing his fellow officers to interact with a mannequin, he had a series of pliable masks that gave the impression of a face. The masks fitted one over his head and the nanoids formed against its backside so he could blink, move his lips, mimic expressions, and so forth. His blunt and featureless hands were covered by gloves.

Once he was completely reconstituted, he ran a self-diagnostic to make sure everything was integrated properly. Sometimes the swarms malfunctioned or picked up viruses from interfacing with the tech of other races. He was pleased to discover there was nothing amiss this time. He was whole once more, and he adjusted the affectations that completed his uniform. He was a moderately attractive man, with short red hair and skin that was shaded blue-gray since Humans found pale white to be off-putting. He had once been told he resembled the Human actor Malya Trimitsu, but he couldn't see anything in his features to support the statement. Perhaps his mask had been designed with the actor in mind, but the nanoids behind the mask changed it just enough to give him a unique personality.

Once he was confident he'd reconstituted fully, he placed his hands on the pads next to his computer. Small pieces detached from his forearms and connected to the hardware. He didn't have to speak; the command was known by every piece of him as soon as it was integrated. The nanoids began their search of the *Sastruga's* records and downloaded every pertinent piece of information to his monitor. As he scanned them, he also requested any records taken while they were docked at Xibalba. The ship was constantly monitoring and recording information that no single mind could hope to process in any semblance of order.

Fortunately, Nerea wasn't restricted to a single mind.

As he examined the vast record of everything the little ship had encountered, he also called up the records of every race they had access to. The Paisian had been exploring longer than any other race, so they had the most comprehensive list. But the Karezza and Ladronis were just as informative. He crosschecked every unidentified ship that had made it into any vessel's official logs and compared them to the mystery vessel that had attacked the *Sastruga.*

He blinked behind his mask. It was an affectation, something he had noticed almost all binocular races and he assumed it in order to be less unusual to them. In this case it was a result of a surprising discovery. He ran through the incident once more and then reexamined the flagged reference material. He furrowed his brow, another affectation, and hailed Admiral Reshef.

"Nerea. Tell me you've found something."

"I believe I have, Admiral, though I'm uncertain what to make of it. Is Ephor Wison still in the pilothouse?"

The Admiral said, "No, she returned to her quarters to contact her people."

"I was under the belief that the Ladronis would not be assisting with the station's protection."

"No, no, they're pacifists. And I... respect that." Her tone said that while she did respect it, she also did not quite understand it. Nerea also found it unusual. There was no moral high ground in bowing down to an enemy. Crude aggression was one thing, but self-defense was often necessary.

Admiral Reshef continued, "Do you need me to bring her back?"

"No, I can call her myself. I know she requires her privacy. But I would like to discuss something with her as soon as possible. I've found a reference to the unknown vessel which attacked the *Sastruga* in a piece of Ladronis folklore. But the book in which it was found has been labeled as fiction-comma-children's. There is a possibility it is only a coincidental similarity."

"I'll let her know to contact you as soon as she's available."

Nerea said, "Thank you, Admiral. I shall contact the rest of the Paisian to engage their assistance while I await her."

He disconnected and opened a channel that would put him in touch with his homeworld. He missed being separated from the rest of his people. One day soon he hoped to visit and assimilate with them once more. He would share the knowledge he'd gained aboard the Quay, while they would impart any historic changes that had occurred on Pais while he was away. He could hardly wait. His hail was answered, and a portion of his mind was dedicated to the plea for assistance. Another part of his mind, a different swarm, was still analyzing the results of his research.

He read and reread the Ladronis text which mentioned a ship matching the one in Captain Drayton's scans. If it was accurate, then the ship was Wakerran. It was a race so ancient and so forgotten that even myths about them had been lost to the passage of time. He was surprised to find any reference at all in another race's history and accessed the Paisian records.

Curiously, very curiously indeed, he discovered that their records were sparse as well. The Paisian had been collecting and storing data for time immemorial for most mortals. If the Wakerran predated their memory then it must truly be an ancient race. A race which had vanished from sight for millennia only to reemerge now, when Cicerone Drayton was allegedly in possession of an asteroid that could explain the origin of every species currently calling the Quay home. It was more than curious and far more than simply alarming.

If the Wakerran had truly returned after eons, then the stone in Captain Drayton's possession was most likely authentic. And if that was the case, then every person aboard the Quay had every reason to be terrified.

From the time they were children, the Ladronis Weavers of Song had been taught that evil was found in discord and disharmony. They worshipped the Great Chorus, the belief that the universe was built upon music and melody. Music was a vital part of every race they'd encountered, which only strengthened their beliefs. The Ladronis rarely traveled from their home system, but visitors would often come to them. Those visitors brought music from their homelands. Some of it was highly objectionable, some was little more than sharp sounds over a hissing melody, but all of it contributed to the overall hum of the universe. Through it all they held strong to the belief that the antithesis of their religion was an inharmonious cacophony.

They were wrong.

Jocia Wison was the first Ladronis to leave their planet for an extended period. The Quay offered her refuge as a respected envoy, and a Karezza transport offered her passage to the station. She was told it would take five days to arrive, but she didn't truly appreciate what that meant until they were well underway. The first few hours of her journey went by without incident. After twenty-nine hours passed, she began to feel uneasy and sick to her stomach. By the third day she couldn't even bring herself to leave her quarters. The transport's physician examined her but couldn't find any physical reason for her sudden descent into sickness.

Jocia could have told them that. She knew her ailment was spiritual, and she knew that their religion had been wrong all along. Their enemy wasn't discord. Even in the most strident sound there was the chance it could resolve itself into something beautiful. No matter how grating a song there was always hope. She now understood the true threat to the Great Chorus.

Silence.

In her time aboard the Quay, Jocia had done much to ensure that none of her people would ever suffer the same affliction. She counseled transport ships so they would know how to prepare for a Ladronis passenger. She taught their medical staff how to recognize signs of aural distress while in the abyss. The maintenance crew of the station also consulted with her on ways to ensure that the station was never silent so the Ladronis guests would feel comfortable in any part of it at any time.

Still, even the most valiant efforts were nothing compared to the Great Chorus. Sometimes if she spent too long among the Humans and Karezza and Balanquin, she had to retreat to her quarters for a cleansing session of meditation. She would undress and sink into her pod, submerged to her shoulders as the speakers built into the floorboards played recordings from the Weavers back on Ladrona. It calmed her spirit and helped her get through the silences.

She had just come from a meeting with the rest of the command staff, though Cordwainer had not been there. In her still and quiet thoughts, Jocia allowed herself a smile at the thought of her lover. When Jocia arrived on the Quay, nearly catatonic from the silence, it was Cordwainer who had known how to bring her back from the panic. Ze had placed putty-like speakers in Jocia's ears and turned on a melody. It took some time for Jocia to be calmed, but once she was, healing came quickly. They were connected in that moment, and soon the relationship grew to love.

Her reverie was interrupted by the door chime. She sat up, toweled off, and draped herself without leaving the water. She answered the hail and looked up as Nerea Paisian entered the room.

"Brightening day, and soothing waters upon your shore," Jocia said.

Nerea inclined his head. "Your blessing is a kindness, Ephor. May I interrupt?"

"If it is necessary, of course."

"Of course."

She gestured for him to have a seat on the edge of her pod, but he refused with a gentle shake of his head. "I found a reference in what I believe is a Ladronis children's fable. I was hoping you could shed some light on its meaning for me."

"If I am able."

"The ship which disabled the *Sastruga* matched the description of a Wakerran vessel."

Jocia's expression hardened. "That is not possible."

Nerea gestured at her computer interface. "I could show you the comparison."

"Please do."

As he typed, she emerged from the pod and wrapped herself in a shawl. Her hands were shaking as she tied it shut. She couldn't allow herself to believe he was telling the truth, but he was Paisian. The idea he might be wrong was even more inconceivable. She padded barefoot across the room, leaving misshapen ovals of watery footprints in her wake. Nerea stepped aside so she could look at the screen. She recognized the Oxom writing, the simple phrases that indicated the story was for children. It was a horrible tale, something meant to frighten the young into behaving. She read the Wakerran ship description and glanced at the *Sastruga*'s sensor log.

Nerea sensed her distress and attempted to assuage it. "There is the alternative theory that it is someone who merely copied the Wakerran design from this book."

"Perhaps," Jocia said absently. "But I do not believe we can afford the luxury of believing that. If it was indeed a Wakerran vessel, then Captain Drayton is fortunate that anyone on her ship survived."

CHAPTER NINE

ARYANA WAS sitting up in bed, haggard and wan but apparently healthy. Her hair was center-parted and drawn back at the temples to create a ponytail while leaving her neck covered. She wore one of the skintight jumpsuits that helped monitor her vitals, but the sleeves had been peeled back to accommodate the bandages on each arm.

She looked up as Bauwerji entered and smiled politely, but her face brightened considerably when she saw Cicero behind her. "Captain," she said. "Dr. Littlefoot tells me that I have you to thank for pulling me out of the engine room. These burns could have been a lot worse if it wasn't for you."

"I'm just glad I got there when I did." Cicero looked up as Cordwainer joined them. "How does it look, Doctor?"

Cordwainer smiled at Aryana. "I would call her extraordinarily lucky, but getting knocked unconscious in the engine compartment is about as unlucky as it gets. Still, she has you as a captain, so I suppose she is still quite fortunate. The burns were moderately severe, but they didn't require surgery or skin grafts. Another blessing for you. Balanquin are very good at recovering from burns and heat injuries. I would prefer to keep her here on the station for follow-up care, but your doctor did good work. I'd be comfortable signing her care over to them if you have to disembark."

"It looks like we're staying where we are for the moment."

"What's wrong?" Aryana glanced at Bauwerji. "Are we under arrest?"

Bauwerji said, "And what reason would I have to place you under arrest, Captain Drayton?"

"Ignore her, she's delirious from the medication." Cicero's tone was playful enough that Bauwerji cracked a smile. "No. We're here as friends this time. Do you remember anything from before you were knocked unconscious?"

Aryana said, "Kela would know more than I would."

"I'm sure she would, but she was knocked unconscious as well. We all were. And none of us remember what led up to... whatever happened."

Aryana had been toying with the edge of her bandages, but she looked up at that. "What? Everyone on the ship was hurt?"

Cordwainer said, "Everyone has been checked out. You were the last to wake up, probably due to being in the heat for so long. You were dehydrated."

"That's not why," Aryana said. She averted her gaze again.

Cicero said, "So you do remember something?"

Aryana nodded slowly. "You came over the intercom and told us we had just encountered a vessel of unknown designation. You were going to try hailing them, but they hadn't responded to the first call. So we were to brace for evasive maneuvers. I was... ah..." She looked sheepishly at Bauwerji and Cordwainer. "I was talking to the engine to prepare it for a big job. Sometimes you have to sweet-talk the machinery to make it work right."

Bauwerji said, "Understood."

"Okay. I was in the middle of the pep talk when we were hit. Energy drain across the board. We lost artificial gravity. You called me on the intercom to ask if we could still evade the other ship, but the engine was toast. If we tried to move any faster than our minimum speed, we would've burnt it to cinder. Adrift and rudderless. You said it was best not to risk it and told me to get it back up to jogging speed. So that's what I started doing."

"Do you know why I was on my way to engineering?" Cicero asked.

"Internal comms were lost when the other ship hit us. I was reading a build-up in the plasma coils that could have caused an explosion. If you thought I was unaware of the situation, you might have been trying to warn me. I'm not surprised you didn't make it. Artificial gravity was trying its best, but I was still getting pretty seasick by the time we stopped spinning. Someone hooked up and boarded.”

Bauwerji said, “Did you see who it was?”

Aryana shook her head. “I assumed it was the Karezza coming back to get their man.” Her eyes widened. “He’s not here, is he?”

Cicero shook her head. “No. He was the sole casualty.”

“Small blessings. I heard the alarm that meant we’d been boarded, so I sealed off engineering so they couldn’t sabotage the ship. Then, I guess... I guess I just got knocked out when we lost gravity.”

Cicero started to say something, but she stopped herself. “You didn’t hear anything after the other crew boarded us?”

“Nothing I remember.”

“And you’re positive you sealed off engineering?”

Aryana nodded. “Protocol. Protect the engines at all costs.”

“Right. Okay.” She put her hand on Aryana’s. “We should probably let you get some rest.”

Cordwainer said, “There’s no reason for you to remain here, so you could move to quarters if you feel up to it. If you’re more comfortable staying, we have the room.”

“I’d like to stay.”

Cicero said, “I’ll be back to see you later.” She leaned over the bed and kissed Aryana’s hair. “And don’t worry about me leaving you behind. I’d never leave with an empty engine section, and I wouldn’t trust anyone but you down there. So you heal up quick.”

“Yes, Captain.”

They left Aryana with the doctor. Bauwerji waited until they were in the corridor before she spoke. “Something upset you about her story.”

“The engine compartment wasn’t sealed. I opened the door with one hand, because my other arm was dislocated. It was tough, but if the door was properly sealed it would’ve been impossible.”

“Do you think she’s lying because she didn’t follow protocol?”

Cicero shot Bauwerji a look. “Do you think I’m the kind of strict captain who would discipline her for not going by the book? Especially in that sort of situation. She could be misremembering. Or she could want so badly to have useful information that she just made something up to be helpful.”

“But her information was accurate, in regards to what happened during the attack. That was all information you attained after she was unconscious.”

"Right." Cicero reached up and pushed her hands through her hair. "I trust Aryana with my life. If she's lying to me, I know she has a reason. But I still want to know why."

Bauwerji stroked Cicero's arm. "Let me sit with her. Maybe I can draw out the truth. You're her superior and I'm a friendly stranger from back home."

"You have duties on the station..."

"My duty right now is to find out what happened to your ship. Miss Barrien knows something. It could be vital to finding out the whole truth."

Cicero kissed Bauwerji. "Thank you."

"Of course. I'll let you know if I find anything. Admiral Reshef will let you use my office in the pilothouse as a base of operations."

"Can I have some of your *chi'b'po?*"

"If you can find my stash."

Cicero said, "Darling, look who you're talking to. If I can't find candy in the office of the woman I'm fucking, then I don't deserve to call myself a pirate."

Bauwerji smiled. "The woman you're fucking?"

"The woman I love... to fuck."

"You are a *l'iall.*"

Cicero's grin widened. "Yes, but I'm your pest."

Bauwerji left her at the lift and went back to Aryana's hospital bed. The girl looked up as she approached, conflicting emotions of fear, worry, and doubt passing over her features.

"XO Crow."

"Please, call me Bauwerji. Not enough people on this station get it right, so I'd like to hear someone with the proper language try it."

Aryana said, "What do they call you?"

"Bowery."

Aryana grimaced and shook her head. "Sounds so guttural."

"Mm." Bauwerji moved a chair over beside the bed. "There's really not very much for me to do until we have an enemy to fight. I wanted to see if you wanted a little company. It's not often I get a chance to sit down with another Balanquin."

"Same." Aryana rearranged herself on the bed so she was sitting up straighter. "If you had some pips, we could play *podolor.*"

Bauwerji reached into the pocket of her uniform jacket and withdrew her identification pouch. She opened one of the small compartments and withdrew a plastic bag of pips that were red on one side and blue on the other.

"I should have known the great Bauwerji Crow would be always prepared."

Bauwerji smiled and poured the pips into her hand. "What do you know about the 'great Bauwerji Crow'?"

"Sorry. Only the rumors, to be honest. You were a member of the final military class to graduate in peacetime."

"I was. Our student body was standing in the courtyard when the Catarrh attacked. We lost a lot of good people that day."

Aryana nodded. "The Decade at the Battlements. Everyone knows those stories."

Bauwerji had a mental flash of those years. It hardly seemed like a decade, but she didn't know if it felt longer or shorter. Years of brutality and guerilla attacks against the invaders from across the planet's vast ocean. If only she'd known there was a crueler enemy in the future, one that would come from even further away, she doubted she'd have had the strength to keep fighting. In retrospect it seemed like a depressing and endless slog of war.

"I'm sorry," Aryana said, snapping Bauwerji back to the present. "I can tell that sent you somewhere dark."

Bauwerji shook her head. "It's fine." She continued setting up their game. "Besides, you saw just as bad. You were born during the Catarrh invasion, right?" Aryana nodded. "And you came of age under the Karezza regime."

Aryana's expression changed slightly, and she gathered her pips to stare at them in her palm.

"Aryana, look at me, young one," Bauwerji said, slipping into a more regional dialect of quinlitz that couldn't be translated easily. Aryana looked at her. "I know you had a Karezz on the *Sastruga*. I know what it's like to have one of those *sev'ro'min us wun* in a place I felt safe and secure. You know how I feel about Captain Drayton, but I'm disgusted she would do something so awful. She brought one of the bastards into your home. If you did something you're ashamed of, if you did something to the Karezz, you know I'll understand. I can take the truth and share it in a manner that conveys the information without revealing what you did. But we need to know. The station may depend on it."

Aryana looked at her hands. "I left the engine section. I made sure everything was in the green and I left to see if Cicero needed my help. But they found me first. They were Sautoriau soldiers."

Bauwerji furrowed her brow. "The unknown ship was Sautoriau?"

"No. They were just... um..." She made a gesture with her hand. "*Wa'ar cres n'u'r seq ken.*"

Bauwerji nodded that she understood the phrase. It meant disposable, hired for cheap so that it didn't matter if they died. The Sautoriau didn't mind being used or dying for their employers since the money was sent home to family and loved ones.

"They grabbed me. Everyone else was unconscious by that point." She suddenly looked away into the Med Center, scanning for evidence anyone was listening in. They were still using the dialect, so Bauwerji doubted anyone within earshot could translate. "They grabbed me and held me down. They called someone and a woman arrived. She was wearing some kind of suit so I couldn't see what she looked like, but I could tell she wasn't Sautoriau. She was tall and slender and wearing a mask so her face was just a blank."

Bauwerji said, "What did she say to you?"

Aryana swallowed a sizable lump in her throat. "She was looking for the Karezz. She said if I told her where she could find him, she would let me go. She said she didn't intend to kill him, but she would do it if I asked her to."

"I see."

Aryana wiped at her eyes. "My life was not in danger. I believed her when she said she planned to let me go. She hadn't hurt anyone else onboard, after all. She just knocked them out so she wouldn't be disturbed. That's why she knocked them out. If Captain Drayton or Kela had been awake, they would have fought back. People would have been hurt." She bit her bottom lip. "I had the choice. She said she would leave everyone on the ship alive if that was what I decided." Her voice dropped to a whisper. "I told her to kill him."

Bauwerji said, "I would have done the same thing."

"No."

"I would have."

Aryana blinked the moisture from her eyes. "It's not that I wanted to be his executioner. I simply couldn't bear the alternative. If he was alive when she left the ship, then it was because I had saved him. The woman had given me the option of being a killer or knowing I had chosen to save a Karezz. I thought I chose the one I could live with."

"You couldn't have. She didn't give you any valid options." She gave Aryana a moment to compose herself before pressing on. "Did you see how the Karezz was killed?"

"They tried to get into his quarters, but they couldn't get past the lock. They tried to make me do it, but I didn't know how. So finally she sent a message to her ship. There was a pulse of energy. It was nauseating and it made me feel like I was going to lose consciousness. Then they dragged me back to the engine compartment and told me they would hit us again with a stronger blast so I'd get knocked out like everyone else. I guess that's why I took so long to wake up."

Bauwerji nodded. "Do you know why they left before they got what they wanted?"

"I assume they were worried about being picked up by Regulators. Two ships hooked up like that out in the middle of nowhere... if a patrol had come by, they would have wandered over to see what was going on. I guess it was taking too long to cut through the door, so eventually they had to run to fight another day."

Bauwerji took Aryana's hand. "I'm sorry you had to go through that, Aryana-*ji'o*."

"Thank you. You'll tell Captain Drayton?"

"I'll tell her the parts she needs to know."

Aryana nodded. "I trust you. And if I have to be punished for what happened..."

Bauwerji shook her head. "You're not a murderer. You were simply given an awful choice. You said you decided on the one you thought you could live with. But I swear, you were bound to regret either outcome." She patted Aryana's hand. "I need to go tell Captain Drayton what you've told me. Can we put off the game for a bit? I'll leave you the pips so you can play solo for a bit."

"Of course. Thank you, Bauwerji."

"I am grateful I could hear your confession." She squeezed Aryana's hand as she stood up. "If you need to talk further, I'm certain Cicero will know where to find me at any hour. Don't hesitate to contact me."

"Okay."

Bauwerji let the girl's hand slide from hers and turned to leave the Med Center. She was well acquainted with 'unnecessary kills.' She'd taken more lives than was strictly necessary during every war she'd fought. Soldiers for the Catarrh, the Karezza, and the Cetidroi had all died at her hand even when mercy was an option. An enemy not killed when she had a chance could return later with murder in their own mind. She never envisioned herself as a murderer, but it was a philosophy she adopted out of necessity during the first year of the Catarrh invasion.

The surest way to end a war quickly: kill them all and save yourself time later.

CHAPTER TEN

"YOU MUST understand," Jocia said, "that we don't often discuss this with outsiders. It's not because we consider it a great secret but because it's just a silly myth."

They were gathered in the briefing room again. This time Cordwainer was present. Ze had been filled in about their earlier conversation. Jocia was uncomfortable being the center of attention, but she focused on the information she had to share.

"The description Nerea found was a reference to one of our song cycles. It's a tale passed down from generation to generation. Ladronis parents use story songs to teach their toddlers... well, many things. The same thing parents of other species use stories for, I suppose. One of the cycles is about the Wakerran, a fierce and monstrous race that existed at the beginning of time. They were vicious and cruel. The entire race was dedicated to warfare, they existed only to find more worlds to take over. They were a plague that comes in the night and scours the planet, they kill and gnash and~"

"Jocy," Cordwainer said softly, "you're singing."

Jocia looked at her partner and realized she had indeed picked up the familiar rhythm. "My apologies, Admiral. The point of the story is that they were eventually stopped by an unknown race. We called them *pri'zz'eari*. When I described them to Dr. Littlefoot, ze identified them as Seraphim. They are also called *ki'yoeh*, the *hee'j*..."

"Angelic beings," Indira said. "Powerful supernatural creatures."

"Yes. They banished the Wakerran to wander the far reaches of the uninhabited galaxy. It was meant as a warning. We should always be kind and compassionate to outsiders, lest we suffer the same fate. When the Cetidroi first appeared, we believed they were the basis for the myth. They were a powerful race that came from beyond where even the Paisian had traveled. They shared the same characteristics. But they identified themselves and ended that theory."

Bauwerji said, "We always suspected there might be other races where the Cetidroi came from. The Wakerran could be one of their neighbors."

Nerea said, "I found the cycle after Ephor Wison told me what to look for. The Wakerran were not only ferocious, they were nigh unstoppable. None of the races they chose to attack stood a chance at holding them back."

"This was, what, millions of years ago?" Heely shrugged. "We're all stronger now. Bigger and faster ships, tougher weapons..."

Bauwerji said, "How did bigger ships work out for you against the Cetidroi? I seem to remember the Balanquin bracijera ships were instrumental in winning that war."

Indira closed her eyes. "Bowery, is this really the time for this argument?"

Bauwerji sank back against her seat. "I apologize, Admiral."

Nerea said, "We all have far more advanced technology, yes. But it stands to reason the Wakerran are equally empowered. The *Sastruga* is a tough ship with a clever crew. They were left completely at their enemy's mercy before they could get a single shot off. I have no doubts as to the strength of our combined fleets, should it come to another war, but the Wakerran is a complete unknown. They killed a man through a locked door. The only reason Captain Drayton and her crew are alive is because the Wakerran chose to leave them alive."

Indira said, "So what can we do?"

"We can find information," Bauwerji said. "Aryana told me the Wakerran female was working with Sautoriau mercenaries. She had to hire them somewhere. Instead of just sitting here waiting for them to attack us, we can go on the offensive. If we find where she hired the Sau, maybe we can backtrack and find out where these Wakerran are coming from."

"Are you volunteering for that mission, XO Crow?"

Bauwerji nodded. "Absolutely. I want to be here to stand our ground if the Wakerran get this far, but hopefully we'll have enough warning that I can get back."

Indira said, "Good. Gather a crew to back you up. I'll find you a ship."

Nerea said, "The first vessel from the Paisian fleet will arrive in thirteen hours. They would be happy to serve as XO Crow's transportation for this mission."

"Excellent. Jocia, I want to know everything your song cycles have about the Wakerran. Constable Heely and I will listen to as many as you can dig up. Just try not to put us to sleep with the nursery rhymes, okay?"

Jocia smiled. "I will do my best."

"Then we're dismissed. Good luck with your mission, Bauwerji. Try to keep the wolves from our door, okay?"

"I'll do my best, ma'am."

Lalan Paget happened to be near the lift outside the Medical Center when Cordwainer Littlefoot emerged. Her presence there wasn't premeditated, though she admitted she would have camped out for an opportunity to interview one of the doctors. It was just sheer luck that she happened to be there when the highest-ranking physician on the station stepped out of the doors and moved quickly down the corridor.

The doctor seemed deep in thought and Lalan hated to interrupt, but she put aside her discomfort and approached anyway. She had been on the station for days, but she had yet to conduct any true research for her first story. It was daunting to be on the actual station, to sit in the pavilion and see members of so many alien races just casually walking past her table.

It was clear something big was going on. Everyone in command uniforms had a harried look on their face, and the crew of an unregistered ship had been rushed to Medical immediately upon arrival. Lalan turned on the recording device embedded in the collar of her blouse as she approached the doctor. Cordwainer was Human, like her, and Lalan hoped that meant ze would be more willing to talk. Hir skin was light tan, hir hair gray giving in to white around the temples.

"Excuse me, Dr. Littlefoot?"

Ze glanced at Lalan without paying her much attention. "I'm sorry, but I'm really rather busy."

"I know, I can only imagine. There's been a lot of activity around the station the past couple of days. I was hoping you could escort me up to the pilothouse so I could speak to Admiral Reshef about it."

"Admiral Reshef is the busiest of us all," the doctor said. "I'm sure whatever you need to discuss can wait. If you'll excuse me."

Lalan fell into step with Cordwainer as ze started to walk away. "My name is Lalan Paget. I'm a representative of the Home Press."

"Oh, right. I heard you were due. For a journalist, you've been doing a rather good job of keeping to yourself. Hopefully that doesn't mean you've been spying on us from a distance."

"Not at all. I was just acclimating to the station. I'm sure you can understand what it's like. Getting used to all the aliens. But it seems like there's a story waiting to be told. Is it true that the *Sastruga* was attacked by an unknown ship?"

Cordwainer said, "I'm certain Admiral Reshef wouldn't like me discussing private matters in a public forum."

"So the people living here on the station have no cause for alarm?"

"When there is cause for alarm, they will of course be alerted." Ze stopped and took a deep breath, choosing hir next words carefully. "People should not be alarmed. Cautious, perhaps. But that is certainly nothing new here on the station."

"Certainly not," Lalan said.

Cordwainer smiled, then offered her hand. "I have forgotten my manners. Cordwainer Littlefoot."

"Yes, I know." She shook hir hand. "I did extensive research before and during the journey out here. One thing about the trip from Earth, it gives you plenty of time to catch up on your reading."

Cordwainer nodded and scanned the corridor around them. "And once you're out here, it doesn't take very long to discover that there's only so much you can learn from reading. Do you know what happened to the last reporter assigned to the Quay?"

Lalan furrowed her brow. "I assumed his assignment ended and he went home."

Cordwainer shook hir head. "He had seventeen months left on his assignment. But he quit. He resigned from his post, sent back the money he'd already been paid, and declared he wouldn't be writing anymore 'propaganda' for the people back home to distort. The people on Earth don't want to know the harsh facts about what's really happening out here. They want to know everything is peachy, the aliens love and depend on us, and that we all get along a hundred percent of the time."

"And that's not true?"

Cordwainer looked at her with pity. "How could it possibly be true? There are six races permanently residing aboard this station. Humans can't even coexist peacefully with ourselves. Do you know Earth and Pelorum are the only worlds that still have intraplanetary wars?" Ze sighed. "The truth is, we're the young and embarrassing race that would probably have been wiped out by the Cetidroi if it weren't for the Balanquin people. Generations ago, our best and brightest managed to put a space station right where our neighbors needed it. But we're not essential to them."

"But the Quay is a vital position between several great powers. That has to count for something."

Cordwainer shrugged. "Imagine the universe is a vast campus with the greatest minds from history employed as professors. Einstein, Plato, Tesla, Archimedes, Diotima... they all wander back and forth between each other's classrooms to have deep conversations about the meaning of life. They walk along the same long path every day. Then, one day, without realizing the path was even being used, a member of the janitorial staff places a bench at the midway point between all the classrooms. Suddenly Albert and Nikola can have a seat if they get winded walking from one classroom to the other."

"So Humanity is... just a groundskeeper?"

"There's nothing wrong with that. Groundskeepers and janitors are vital. They keep the world from falling to ruin. They fix the problems that would never even occur to the great thinkers. But that doesn't mean the philosophers respect the contribution of the bench."

"That may well be," she said, "but the fact remains that it is still a hell of a bench."

Cordwainer smiled. "Indeed it is. And right now, the professors are extremely occupied with classes and don't have time to discuss maintenance issues. The analogy has fallen apart a bit, but hopefully you understand why I can't take you to see the admiral at this time."

"Of course. You've given me a lot to think about, Dr. Littlefoot. I hope we can speak again sometime in a non-professional setting."

"For both of us," Cordwainer said. "I would hate to continue this conversation with you as my patient."

"I would be lucky to have you as my doctor."

They shook hands and Lalan let Cordwainer continue into the Med Center. Once the doctor was gone, she stood and watched the rest of the crowd moving past her. A trio of Acapsian lingered near the elevator, deep in conversation. An Occamian came out of an office and smoothed a hand over his tunic before continuing on. She walked against the flow of the crowd to the nearest viewscreen and peered at the vista outside the hull.

The Quay was trapped between a sea of asteroids that could tear it to shreds, and the skeletal remains of a devastating war, but it stood steadfast in the darkness due to the dedication and skill of everyone aboard. Whatever crisis had arisen, she had faith that those in command were well suited to the task. In the meantime, this was Earth's front door. Humanity may be the groundskeepers of the Universe, but they still deserved what to know what was going on. They were owed the truth, even if it was frightening or if Humans didn't get to be the heroes.

Lalan was determined to be the one who pulled back the veil.

CHAPTER ELEVEN

EVERYTHING ABOUT the Paisian, everything they showed to other races at any rate, was contrived to make their allies comfortable. Swarms of Paisian could fill the empty shell of a ship with ease, or they could construct their vessels with miniscule passageways that even the most petite Balanquin couldn't squirm through. But they took design hints from the Quay and other vessels. Corridors, lifts, personal quarters, and seats were solely for the benefit of hosting other races.

Bauwerji had never been entirely comfortable with the Paisian. Everything about them was a false front. Their faces were literal masks, created for interacting with Humans and other races. When they were close enough, she could see seams and creases in their skin where the small nanoids had joined together. They could break off a tiny piece of their finger, leave it in someone's private room, and that piece could report back later. It was unsettling. They gave themselves names and strived to have unique personalities, but there was still something completely artificial about everything they did.

She knew her dislike of them came from prejudice, but she couldn't change her feelings. Nerea was fantastic at his job, and he was a valuable resource, but she couldn't think of him as a person. He was thousands of identities huddled together under one name. It was basically like interacting with a person-shaped ship operated by a crew she was never allowed to meet. She comforted herself with the fact that she hadn't picked up the Human term for them: Puzzlemen.

She was in the pilothouse as the first vessel from the Paisian fleet requested permission to dock. She moved closed to one of the monitors and watched as it was guided through the starship graveyard by one of the yeomen stationed behind her. The interiors of their ships may have pandered to Human conventions, but the exteriors were still strictly utilitarian; simple white rectangles with engines on the port and starboard sides, a secondary thrust mechanism perched on the stern, and a hatch. Nothing extraneous or decorative to be seen, no wasted effort to make it aesthetically appealing. And when it came to naming their ships...

"Paisian Vessel 4203-B14 is successfully docked," the yeoman reported.

Bauwerji thanked him with a nod and opened a channel to the Admiral to report the vessel had arrived. Indira exited her office and joined Bauwerji in the central aisle. She looked over Bauwerji's shoulder at the monitor.

"I've been in touch with their commanding officer. They're ready to leave as soon as you and your team are onboard. Have you figured out where to begin searching?"

"I have a pretty good idea. I asked some of my contacts where someone would go to pick up Sau mercenaries. Eight of them said one planet in particular, so that's where I'm starting the search."

Indira nodded. "Then you are relieved of duty until you return. Good luck, Bauwerji."

"Thank you, ma'am."

Bauwerji left the pilothouse and took the lift to the docks. She contacted her team and told them to meet her there. When she arrived, Jocia Wison was waiting by the doors.

"Officer Crow. I was just on my way to see you."

"I hope it can wait, Ephor. I'm moments away from shipping out."

Jocia fell into step beside Bauwerji and walked with her. "Actually, that was what I wanted to discuss. I would like to accompany you on the mission."

Bauwerji glanced at her. "You? But your people are pacifists. You know that if we find these people we're going to have to fight them."

"In all likelihood, yes. But I won't be the one pushing the

button to fire the weapons. But I believe I could play a vital role in the conflict to come, despite my reluctance to cause injury to others. The Wakerran only survived in the songs of my people. I could provide crucial information. Then there is the matter of the stone. Captain Drayton is keeping it safe for now, and I know you have feelings for her. But are you truly comfortable knowing it is being kept by a Human?"

Bauwerji didn't want to admit she had a point, but it was a frightening prospect. Humans had a way of lording the Quay over every other race without ever actually threatening to take it away. If they got their hands on a potential doomsday weapon, it could cause a rift that could only end in war.

Jocia said, "The stone would be safe with my people. If I am with you, I can report back to them as a witness rather than just sharing what I've gleaned from your reports."

"You have a point," Bauwerji said. "Okay. Tell Admiral Reshef you're coming with us and that I cleared it. We're leaving immediately so I hope you're already packed."

"I travel lightly. Thank you, XO Crow."

Jocia went to inform Admiral Reshef of her new status as team member as Bauwerji continued to the docks. Nerea was already on the docks with the captain of the recently-arrived ship, and he smiled when he saw Bauwerji approaching.

"Officer Bauwerji Crow. Please allow me to introduce Valdis Paisian."

Another Paisian, another bland mask that could be swapped out for another at a whim. She didn't know how she was supposed to trust a race who could change their identity like anyone else changed clothes, but at the moment they had no choice. The idea of one person called Valdis operating as the commander to a crew was actually false. There was only a swarm, and one group of them had arranged themselves in a Humanoid female shape and assigned itself a name.

"It's a pleasure to meet you, Officer Crow."

"Same." Bauwerji looked past her at the ship. "So that's it. Four-two-oh... whatever-whatever. I hope you don't mind if we give it a name that's easier to remember."

Valdis smiled. "Of course, Officer."

"Call me Bauwerji. And for the duration of this mission, the ship will be called the *Adedoja*."

Nerea said, "That's a beautiful name. What does it mean?"

"It doesn't translate well into other languages. It's the sudden cessation of a sound you didn't realize you were hearing."

Valdis considered it. "I very much approve of that name. In fact, I may keep it even after this mission is completed, if you don't object."

Bauwerji shrugged. "It's your ship. The rest of my team should be arriving shortly. I'd like to board now so I can enter the coordinates of where we're going."

"I can transfer the information from here."

"I know, but I also want to familiarize myself with the ship before we're underway."

Valdis nodded. "Oh. Of course."

Bauwerji thanked her and stepped past the Paisian to board the ship. Another Paisian in an unmarked uniform passed by. He looked up, nodded a greeting, and continued on. She knew he was made up from pieces of the same swarm that had formed Valdis, and he knew everything Valdis knew. Hive minds and shared consciousness. She shuddered and shook her head as she gathered her bearings and went toward the bridge. She would work with the Paisian and she would respect their contributions, but above it all she would be forever grateful that they were on the same side.

The ship departed the Quay soon after the last member of Bauwerji's specially-chosen team had boarded. She stood on the bridge and overheard a yeoman on the station guiding them back through the wreckage field. Once they were clear, the officer said, "Safe travels, Paisian vessel *Adedoja*." The name helped Bauwerji feel comfortable on the ship; the word reminded her of long cold nights during the Decade at the Battlements. Constant Catarrh attacks from dusk to dawn, so many distant bombings and so much chattering gunfire that she had to ignore them just to keep herself sane. But sometimes it would suddenly stop, the silence jarring and suspicious. She would always crawl to the entrance of whatever hovel they had taken refuge in that night to make sure no one was sneaking up on them.

Lalan Paget, the Human Home Press reporter, stepped forward to stand beside Bauwerji. Her long black hair was slicked back as if it had recently been wet, and the lights of the screen reflected off skin the color of wet sand.

"Why doesn't someone just clear out all this wreckage?" Lalan asked.

"Clear it out?" Bauwerji turned to look at her. "That's... brilliant. What a keen observation. We'll get a crew on it immediately when we return."

Lalan grimaced and crossed her arms over her chest. "Apparently the Balanquin understand sarcasm..."

"Working with Humans, it was a necessary requirement." She sighed. "Some of these pieces are too large to haul away, so they would have to be scuttled. But they're large enough to have the bodies of crewmembers trapped on board, so no one wants to destroy them until they've been searched. That takes time and effort, two things there isn't a surplus of out here.

"In addition to that, there are millions of tiny pieces that swirl around in between the larger chunks. Those tiny pieces are drawn to the gravitational pull of the larger pieces. If we take out what we can, the little pieces would still be causing damage. We've managed to corral everything into certain areas so people can get through, but getting close to the debris means you're entering a minefield. No one wants their ships to be shredded in an attempt to recover corpses. It's not viable or recommended.

"And thirdly, the pieces we can salvage can be used for cheap repairs at the Quay. It's one of the reasons we're so heavily trafficked. We're convenient, and we have a junkyard within reach. If something is damaged or breaks down, there are enough wrecks out there for us to find a replacement bit with very little effort." She looked at Lalan. "Are those enough reasons, or shall I continue?"

"No," she grumbled. "My question has been answered."

Bauwerji smiled brightly. "Great to hear it!" The smile collapsed as she faced forward again, dropping her hands to link them behind her back. "If you have any other pointless observations, ask Valdis or Nerea. They can dedicate entire swarms to your interrogation. I don't have the luxury of disconnecting the portion that has to speak with you."

Lalan scoffed and shook her head. "You're the one who asked me to join this team, Officer Crow."

"Every Home Press reporter we've had on the station has been an Aphelion mouthpiece, but you're new. I can convince you to tell the truth. Dr. Littlefoot told me that she had a conversation with you, and you seemed like you could be a good ally. That doesn't mean I have to like you."

Lalan laughed. "Damn. You're cold. You just flat out admit you hate me?"

Bauwerji sighed. "I don't know you well enough to hate you. But I'm not planning to become your friend, and I don't plan on that changing any time soon."

"So what is it? Humans? You think we're beneath your attention?"

Bauwerji nearly let it go, but the opening was too good. "Yes, I do. Humans can be clever and they can show ingenuity, but on the whole, you're an embarrassment of a race. You can barely be trusted to treat each other with respect, so what hope does a Balanquin have? You make hobby of ingesting poisons that are so fatal and so prevalent that you have to make laws restricting its use. And you *still* use it. You are a self-destructive, capricious, unpredictable race who would choose a comforting lie to a protective truth. I look at you, Miss Paget, and I see a child from a race of children."

Lalan grimaced. "Well, as you said yourself... Without these 'children,' you wouldn't have the Quay. So..."

"The Quay was completed thanks to Paisian and Acapsian input and technology. The Balanquin prevented the Cetidroi from blowing it to pieces."

Lalan worked her hands into fists and tried to control her breathing. "We're not janitors."

Bauwerji wondered where that comparison had come from. "No, I never said you were. You're the local animals that we didn't bother to evict when we moved in."

Lalan huffed. "Well, I'm sure the leaders of the Aphelion Project will love to know your stance."

"I'm sure they will," Bauwerji said. "But I don't speak for my people. Hell, my people disown me. My views are my own." She turned to face the journalist. "But know this. If your people decide to go it alone, they'll find it a very solitary existence. If the Karezza don't kick you off the station and take it for themselves, the Paisian will disable everything that makes the Quay habitable before they leave. You wouldn't have the opportunity to begin a fight you would definitely lose, because you would be forced to scurry back to that pollution-ridden ghetto you call a planet with your tails tucked between your legs. How overpopulated is it now? Do you really think any country would take in a few hundred Human refugees arriving in one big flotilla?

"I'm not threatening you, Miss Paget. I'm just laying everything out for you. Your survival depends on our support. I don't hold that against you. But that does not mean I have to like Humans. I will do my best to treat you as an individual and judge you based on your own merits. At the moment you are just another Human in my eyes. Hardly worth my time."

Lalan said, "I'm sure Admiral Reshef would love to know your prejudice against her people."

"She knows. And she is also an exception. She's proven herself to be a smart, resourceful, capable officer. If she told me to step into space without a protective suit, I would trust that she knew what she was doing. Prove yourself to me and I'll grant you the same benefit of the doubt."

"So the Quay is a meritocracy."

"As it should be. As everything should be."

Lalan said, "You truly believe that?"

"Pelorum is a meritocracy. Or at least it was before the Karezza came in and took over. I would like it if the Quay was one as well, but you know how you Humans cling to their antiquated ideas."

"Well. I suppose the only thing I can do is try to get into your good graces."

"You can start by questioning the officers I brought with me."

"Where are they?"

"Not in this room."

Lalan took a deep breath. "It's good to know bitchiness isn't solely a Human trait."

Bauwerji smiled without humor. "No. But damned if you haven't tried to perfect it. Goodbye, Miss Paget."

Lalan looked as if she was about to say something else, but decided against it. Instead she turned and left the bridge.

Bauwerji sighed, her posture relaxing.

Nerea smiled. "You could have given the child a break."

"What would that have accomplished? Treating her as I did means that she'll be trying twice as hard to impress me. She'll be doubly sure that she won't make an idiotic neophyte mistake. That's all I want from her on this mission."

Nerea shook his head in amusement as he faced forward again. "Creatures like you would never be able to exist as a swarm."

"Thank God. Millions of my neighbors knowing my secrets and innermost thoughts? I'd rather kill myself."

Nerea looked at Valdis, but neither Paisian said anything.

CHAPTER TWELVE

THEIR DESTINATION was a city called Karakoz, the capital of a world called Tunzha. The planet had a heavy Karezza population and, ordinarily, Bauwerji would chop both her legs off before setting foot on the surface. But the times were desperate, as Humans were wont to say, and she didn't have the luxury of shunning a city so renowned for its mercenary trade. If the Wakerran hired out Saus to do her dirty work, odds were good she'd hired them here. The Karezza weren't terribly strict about what kind of business happened on their worlds, so long as they got a cut of the profits.

She watched on a monitor as they approached the planet. Karakoz was located on the planet's smallest landmass, an island shaped like a palm frond in the eastern ocean. Ships of every design hovered in atmo above the planet like fat flies bumping against a window on a sunny day. The *Adedoja* joined their number. There was nothing suspicious about a Paisian ship among the thieves and brigands gathered there, but Bauwerji could almost sense the ships around them trying to subtly shift out of their way.

Once the ship was settled in orbit, Captain Valdis cleared Bauwerji for departure. She called her team to the shuttle. Her team consisted of several Aphelion Project soldiers: three Acapsian, two Human, and a Paisian. She had also asked Dr. Littlefoot to accompany them on the mission on the off chance they caught up to and captured the Wakerran. She had no idea how they would subdue a completely unknown race, and she hoped the good doctor's expertise would give hir the upper hand in any confrontation.

Cordwainer was actually the first to arrive at the shuttle. Ze took the seat next to her on the shuttle and strapped hirself in. Once the buckles were secure ze pulled on the harnesses to make sure they were taut. Bauwerji watched with quiet amusement until she couldn't stop herself from chuckling.

"Are you going to be okay?"

"I am. What?"

Bauwerji laughed. "Have you ever been this far from Earth before?"

Cordwainer said, "I've... yes. I took a tour of the neighborhood about a year after I arrived on the Quay. Three weeks to explore the home planets of every race. I wanted to actually see the people I'd spent so long studying. See how they live."

"Did you ever leave the ship?"

"I, uh... it was the rainy season on Acapsia, so it was advised that I remain aboard. And Ladrona is... it's just... they're n-not unfriendly, but they aren't particularly keen on strangers, so I felt it was best that I–" Ze shook hir head. "No. I never left the ship."

Bauwerji laughed and reached over to take Cordwainer's hand. "It's going to be fine. If things get too rough, I'll protect you. It's just like the Quay, but with fewer uniforms and more Karezza faces."

Cordwainer said, "Yes, about that... will you be okay with that?"

One of the Aphelion soldiers arrived. Bauwerji watched him sit and fumble with his harness before she answered.

"I'll be fine. I've gone on this sort of mission before."

"Yes. But this time you'll be walking into the lion's den. A Karezza planet. I know you deal with them all the time at the Quay, but this is their turf. There are millions of them here."

"Not in Karakoz. There are only a few thousand there." Cordwainer didn't smile at the lame attempt at humor. "No. It doesn't concern me."

Cordwainer said, "Good. I'm glad. If I may ask, why did you inquire as to my state of mind? I thought I was hiding it well."

"From most, maybe. But not from your lunchtime companion. I can read you very well, Cordwainer."

"Thank you for your concern."

"Sure. I like you more than I like most people. And you got a

Ladronis to fall in love with you. You must be something pretty special. She'd forget her pacifist ways and kick my ass if I let anything happen to you."

Cordwainer smiled and relaxed against her seat. "I will try to relax."

The rest of their team boarded and Bauwerji contacted the captain to let her know they were ready to disembark. The shuttle was pushed away from the *Adedoja*'s artificial gravity, pushing them back against their seats and then seeming to pull them forward against the straps of their harnesses. Their arms and legs drifted up. Bauwerji was so well-trained at fighting the initial surge of nausea that she barely even noticed it anymore.

The trip from the *Adedoja* to the surface took a little over forty-five minutes. Bauwerji released Cordwainer's hand so she could bring up a map of Karakoz on her screen. The docks were on the northern side of town, with people-carrier tracks branching out in every direction like veins to a heart. Karakoz, like so many cities in the Karezza empire, was almost entirely populated by criminals. She figured at least two-thirds of the ships they passed were carrying stolen or illegally-appropriated designation numbers.

The skies above Karakoz were thick with storm clouds and pollution. Streaks of thick black clouds broke across the nose of the shuttle as they approached the ornate docking system. Bauwerji requested permission to land from the port authority and received approval within seconds. Whoever cleared them for landing probably believed the ship ID was fake, but simply didn't care. A constable in a port city like this could do his job and get killed for the trouble, or he could look the other way and get rich off bribes.

The city had grown up like mold around a large river and its three tributaries, the mass of buildings sprawling in tight clusters over the gray-green land. When they landed, Bauwerji and the rest of her team traded their Aphelion Project uniforms for the drab orange shifts that were in fashion on planets like these. The less attention they drew to themselves the better.

Bauwerji added a red-and-black checkered scarf that could double as a shawl, pulled the wide end up over her head, and ducked her chin behind the mantle she had created. She might not have any issues strolling around a Karezza planet, but a lot of them considered the Balanquin lower-caste creatures. She'd rather avoid any unnecessary distractions while they were on business.

Cordwainer also donned a scarf that would hide hir face.

Karezza got along with Humans just fine, but ze was fine-featured and appeared frail. The Karezza were known to treat people weaker than them like novelties, and sometimes their games resulted in bruises and broken bones for their unwitting playmate. The shawl and scarf helped bulk hir up a little so she looked sturdier at first glance. Bauwerji checked to make sure everyone else was suitably attired, then opened the hatch and led them out.

"Baardwik, Marinos, you stay here and watch the shuttle. If you see anyone coming or going with Sau mercenaries in tow, contact me immediately."

The officers nodded and moved to take positions where they wouldn't be obvious. Bauwerji led the remaining group out of the docks and onto a street crowded by vendors and a flood of people in every gender and every color trying to remain inconspicuous. Bauwerji touched the stunner at her belt to remind herself it was well within reach, in case it became necessary.

"Do we have any idea what we're searching for?" Cordwainer asked.

"Sau mercenaries, and anyone who was looking for the same thing a few weeks ago."

Cordwainer said, "How do we know it was a few weeks ago?"

"Because Sau are lazy, stupid, and easily distracted. They wouldn't stay on a job longer than a few weeks and, if they did, they would take whatever they'd earned and moved on to the next job. Trust me, the men who attacked the *Sastruga* had been hired sometime in the past month."

"It sounds like we'll be working backwards against nearly impossible odds." Ze looked at the crowd around them. "Hundreds of Sau could have been hired from this port just in the past day."

"Possibly," Bauwerji admitted. "Does Earth have chenchurus? Small heads, big heavy arms with claws on the end?" Cordwainer thought for a moment but then shook hir head. "They're blind beyond three feet in front of their faces so they're not very good at hunting. But they have a wide reach and they're fast. They feel vibrations from other animals in the ground, so they wait for something big and predatory to walk by. Then they just follow along behind it until it finds something to eat, and it uses its big arms to steal the prey."

"We may be blind, but we can be smart about where we look."

Bauwerji nodded with a smile and scanned the streets. Twin alleys stretched out to their left and right, covered passageways that broke off into open-air taverns. Every table was filled with people hunched over their drinks or otherwise engaged in furtive conversation. Bauwerji split up the crew, sending one to the right while she led her group down the leftward alley. Humans would have called it 'the sinister' choice, a moniker she had little trouble believing at the moment.

Almost immediately after leaving the main drag, someone pressed against her side. He was Karezz, wall-eyed and string-haired. His skin was pockmarked and ashen enough that she could see a tracing of veins through his cheeks. "Hey, pretty lady. Want to live in someone else's skin? Want to see what it's like through Acapsian eyes? Huh? How about it? The pill is cheap but the experience is priceless."

"Maybe another time."

His focus sharpened as he took note of her heavy brow and the color of her skin. "Hey. You're Balanquin. Pretty little Balanquin. You want to make real money? Couple hours of your time, feel real good for you. Lots of Karezza willing to pay for Sensuite vids of pretty Balanquin girls. What do you say, you want to get fuc~"

Before Bauwerji could clear her weapon to shoot the man in his face, breaking their cover, his eyes suddenly rolled back in his head. His knees turned toward each other and Bauwerji had to grab him to keep him from collapsing into her. She stared at his now-slack face and then saw Cordwainer was holding a small jet injector.

"Neurorelaxant. It'll give his brain a much-needed rest, and he'll be good as new - which isn't saying much - in about twelve hours."

Bauwerji blinked in shock.

Cordwainer shrugged. "I thought things might get confrontational. This draws much less attention than gunfire or knifeplay."

Bauwerji said, "I changed my mind, Dr. Littlefoot. *You* protect *me* from here on out."

Cordwainer smiled and helped Bauwerji move the smut peddler to a horizontal surface along the edge of one building. The doctor took an extra moment to arrange his limbs so it looked as if he had just fallen asleep while Bauwerji looked to see if anyone had noticed their altercation. She'd heard about the Sensuites he mentioned, of course. Karezza on the home front were jealous of their kin living on Pelorum. Not because of the adventure or thrill of living on another planet, but because those soldiers were able to rape any Balanquin citizen they wanted. So some of them recorded Sensuites of the experience and sent it back to Karezz. Those types of vids were, of course, wildly illegal. But there was little to be done to stem the tide of them.

"The lovely gentleman should wake up with a hangover but nothing more serious," Cordwainer said. "He may find his wallet a bit lighter, however."

Bauwerji looked and saw that Cordwainer had emptied the man's pockets onto the ground. Already an Occamian had crouched to sort through the offering.

"That's devious, Dr. Littlefoot."

"Thank you. Are you all right?"

"Let's just keep looking."

They moved on through the crowd. No one seemed to notice or care that one of their own had just fallen unconscious in the middle of the street, but Bauwerji doubted it was an uncommon sight on these streets. A con man, a thief, a smuggler... if he got knocked out, most people assumed he had it coming and minded their own business. Bauwerji moved on, and soon the vidirector was out of sight and out of mind. She spotted a tavern with a healthy number of Acapsian inside, so she sent the Acapsian officer inside to inquire about hiring Sau.

"Officer Crow."

The voice startled her enough that she reached for her weapon again, but she recognized Valdis Paisian's voice. "How the hell are you... oh, *dedevosjej vai q'am.*" She reached up and felt around the curve of her ear. As expected she felt a small metallic structure attached to the lobe. It was a piece of the Paisian captain stowing away on her flesh. She shuddered violently at the idea of carrying a spy around on her body.

"I am well aware of what those words mean, Officer Crow, and I am quite offended."

"Well, then maybe you shouldn't..." She was trembling with rage. "Do not violate my body like that again, am I clear?"

"Extraordinarily. I apologize for the intrusion." The swarm lifted off her ear and buzzed toward Cordwainer. The doctor had been watching Bauwerji with concern, but then ze clapped a hand over hir ear and gasped in surprise.

"Quell! Oh... Captain. I... yes." Ze looked at Bauwerji. "Of course."

Bauwerji reached up to massage her ear, wishing she could wash it.

"Captain Valdis said that a vessel matching the one seen in the *Sastruga*'s records has just been spotted entering this sector."

The violation was almost forgotten as the meaning of hir words set in. Bauwerji looked up at the sky as if she could see the ship approaching. "Looks like I was right about the Sau getting bored. They must have done a runner, and now the Wakerran needs more."

"Should we go back to the docks?" Cordwainer asked.

"No, we're going to stay right here. If the Wakerran bitch wants a new crew, we're going to give her one."

Cordwainer's furrowed brow smoothed out as ze realized what Bauwerji was saying. "Oh, no."

Bauwerji grinned. "Welcome to the criminal life, Dr. Littlefoot. You're gonna be a mercenary."

CHAPTER THIRTEEN

KAREZZA HAD two smells. Solitary, they were pungent but bearable. In a crowd, the stench became overwhelming and pervasive. Bauwerji had only been able to ignore it since their arrival on the planet because they were outside. Once they entered the tavern she was grateful for the scarf covering her Balanquin features. She tucked the cloth tighter around her nose and breathed through the meager filter it provided as they moved to the bar.

Cordwainer hurried to keep up with her as they moved through the crowd. Ze leaned close to Bauwerji's ear as she looked warily around them. "Officer Crow, are you certain you know what you're doing?"

"Rarely, but it's gotten me this far." She knocked her knuckles on the bar to get the tender's attention. He was a *zohish*-Occamian, his milky eyes swimming into focus on her. He had a smashed-in snout and a fringe of yellow-orange hair framing his unlovely features. "A ship just landed. They're going to send out a scouting party to find mercenaries. Get word to your people on the dock and pass word that they're going to want to come here and talk to us."

"*Wn h'y deameli uhu'ciye irotliq?*"

Bauwerji put down a credit and pushed it across the bar to him. "Tell them we know where the rock is and we'd be willing to share that information for the right price."

The tender looked at the coin, looked at Bauwerji and the crew behind her, and plucked up the credit. "*Af'see cu aragtle belunamy.*"

"Good man," Bauwerji said. She took a full mug of liquor off the bar before its intended customer could take a drink. She hoisted it in a toast to the tender and nodded at the back wall with her head. "We'll be waiting in that booth over there."

She led her team through the bar and claimed a seat where she could see the entrance. The stink permeated the cloth and tried to drag her back to the streets of her home planet after the occupation. She tried for years to believe it was a tenable situation, something that would eventually become acceptable. She heard stories of superiors forcing themselves on Balanquin workers, of the Karezza who crushed any attempts to unseat them from power. She was so tired of fighting she allowed herself to believe it was lies and propaganda. Then her superior took a shining to her, and she realized just how true all the stories were.

She and Cordwainer sat together on one side of the booth. The rest of their team sat across from them with their backs to the door. Due to her size and the colorization of the skin she had showing, several Karezza in the bar were trying to get a closer look at her. She didn't feel wary of their attention; if anyone made a move she was fully capable of protecting herself. She had killed one Karezz rapist and one more would just be a new notch on her belt.

One of the men weaved through the crowd and put his hands on the table. He leaned forward and stared hard at Bauwerji. When he spoke, his words were quinlitz.

"My friends and I have a matter to settle. I say you're Balanquin. They say none of your kind would be stupid enough to walk in here, even with a group of *gu'whon brisi.*"

Bauwerji tugged down the scarf covering her face. The Karezz man's smile widened. "A treat!" He reached across the table. Bauwerji offered him her hand, and he took it. She pressed down between the fine metacarpus and dug in before smashing his hand down to the table.

"The last Karezz who put his hands on me found himself brainless and leaking blood on the floor of my hangar. I don't like the idea of killing another one of you owl-faced pricks, but after a murder, mutilation seems like a much smaller crime. If you reach for me again, I will spend a good long time deciding just how many of your fingers to leave you with."

He tried to pull his hand away, but Bauwerji kept her grip a second longer than necessary to prove her dominance. When she let him go, he started to cradle the hand against his stomach but stopped himself before showing the pain. He spoke again, shifting to chelseet.

"You told Anioin that you were offering to sell your services."

"You couldn't afford me," she said, also in his language.

"Karezz don't pay Balanquin. We take. You remember that, pretty lady. If my friends and I decide to make use of you, we will have you."

Cordwainer watched him walk away, and then looked at Bauwerji. "Please put the scarf back on."

"It doesn't matter," Bauwerji said. "He'll tell his friends there's a Balanquin on-site, and soon everyone will know anyway. It's not like the scarf was doing me any good against the stench anyway." She looked at Cordwainer. "Do you still have the Paisian in your ear?"

Cordwainer winced and reached up to touch hir ear. "I do. While I admit, it's a touch unsettling... I don't think it merits your reaction."

She looked out over the sea of Karezza faces surrounding them. "When the Karezza took over Pelorum, they set themselves up as our superiors. Just to help us get back on our feet. Their leaders may have had the best of intentions, but the people who took over simply saw us as... drudgers. People they could treat as less than people. We were little more than animals in their eyes. But apparently that was all they needed."

"What do you mean?"

"I mean they raped us. Every chance they got. A few of us complained when it first started, but those people were quickly and quietly let go from their jobs. They had to find another Karezza who would hire them, but by that point they'd been proven to be troublemakers. You either learned to live with it or you found a way to live without working. I decided I would rather have a cock in my mouth every once in a while than risk living on the fringes again. But that doesn't mean I consented."

"No, of course not," Cordwainer said softly. "Bow... Bauwerji. I am so sorry. I had no idea."

"We don't really broadcast it. Admiral Reshef knows. That's why she's so fiercely protective of me. I owe her everything. It would have been so much easier for her to turn me over when the Karezza showed up looking for me. Aphelion values their friendship more than the Balanquin. But she stood up for me."

"The Karezza made you a fugitive because you were raped?"

"Oh. No, because I killed my rapist before I fled the planet. I wasn't lying about the fate of the last Karezz to touch me."

Cordwainer's eyes widened. "Oh. I see. Now that I have all the information, I'm surprised your reaction to Valdis Paisian violating your body wasn't more pronounced."

"The day isn't over yet. I still have to survive a trip back to the Quay aboard a Pissant ship."

Cordwainer said, "There is a chance our meeting will be successful and you'll leave this planet aboard the ship of an unknown enemy with the ability to cause genocide at the press of a button."

Bauwerji smiled. "With any luck. At least that way I'll get a look at who we're dealing with. I want to know who attacked my friend's ship."

Cordwainer started to say something, then winced and touched hir ear. "Captain Valdis, please, adjust the volume. A group of Sau have received your message. They're on their way."

"Get yourself out of sight." She nodded to the Aphelion soldiers to do the same. "I don't want anyone getting recognized."

"I wish you fortune, Officer Crow."

"Thank you, Dr. Littlefoot."

Ze slid from the booth and quickly blended into the crowd. Not long after Bauwerji was left alone in the booth, the Sau mercenaries appeared. They walked to the bar, spoke to the Occamian, and he pointed them toward Bauwerji's booth. The Sau were broad-shouldered and more muscular than any other members of the race she'd had the misfortune of encountering. Their skin was a sickly green, their eyes black and ringed with a pale yellow shell of bone. The skin of their lips was thin and molded to the bones of their jaw.

The one who reached the table first spoke without preamble. "I am Othieno. This is Juma, Masilo, and Melesse. We speak to you on behalf of the future leader of this galaxy. We grant you permission to join our ranks in clearing the path for her dominance in this and every sector of space."

"You boys don't beat around the bush, do you? Aren't you going to buy a girl a drink? Woo her a little before you offer her a job?"

"We require mercenaries, not intimate relations. We were told you have information that our esteemed leader considers valuable. For that, you are considered valuable in her eyes."

"Always nice to be wanted," she said.

One of the other Sau stepped forward. "You are a Balanquin in a Karezza bar. May I ask you a question?" She shrugged indifferently. "Are all of your holes sore at the moment, or is there one they didn't use?"

Bauwerji threw the still-full mug at the bastard's head. It shattered against the bones of his face and his friends stepped away from the explosion of broken glass, too shocked to react properly. Bauwerji took advantage of their momentary distraction to rise from her seat and disarm Othieno. She pressed the barrel of his weapon against the thin skin under his jaw.

"Take another step and I'll blow your boss' head off. Then I'll give you some very sore holes."

"Leave her be," Othieno grunted.

Bauwerji said, "We started this civil. We're going to end it that way. Your friend speaks rudely to me again, and we'll end this with brains and blood all over this bar. Which do you prefer?"

"I was moments away from ordering them to wait outside." He nodded at the door. The other Sau hesitated, then drifted away.

Bauwerji waited until they were gone before she took the gun away from his skin. He rubbed at the indentation the barrel had left and carefully lowered himself into the booth opposite her.

"The information you claim to have. Can you prove its validity?"

"I got the location from the captain of the *Sastruga*. She's Human. She has a Balanquin engineer, and she's the one who told me who you guys were."

Othieno nodded slowly. "And why are you offering to help us?"

Bauwerji looked out at the bar, scanning its patrons until she found the man she'd threatened before Othieno's arrival. "See these Karezza? You're telling me this rock I have can kill each and every one of them at the press of a button and leave the planet intact? That's something I'm extremely interested in. My planet was taken from me. I spent years fighting a war to free my people and, when we won that war, we were immediately enslaved by these shovel-faced assholes. I want to take my world back by any means necessary."

Her intention was to make Othieno believe her intentions, so she was forced to draw from very real feelings. She hated the Karezza. She wanted them dead. Saying it out loud made her blood boil and made her ashamed, but she needed to sell herself as a mercenary. She glared at the man seated across from her. She made sure he could see the very real hatred in her eyes.

"I can't do anything with the rock, but your boss claims she can make my dreams come true. For the right price, I can get her the rock. All she has to do is promise me that she'll use it against the Karezza instead of the Balanquin. Give me an answer or I walk out of here and find the next highest bidder."

Othieno considered for another moment before he nodded. "Very well. I'll take you back to our ship, but heed this warning. If you are being untruthful, if you cannot deliver the prize my commander has been searching so desperately for, then she will not be pleased. And she will take out her displeasure on you in ways that will make these Karezza look kind by comparison."

Bauwerji shrugged and scooted out of the booth. "What are we waiting for? Let's go meet the new boss."

As she followed Othieno and his crew out of the bar, she scanned the crowd until she spotted Cordwainer watching them. The doctor nodded, and Bauwerji forced herself to look away before any of the Sau became suspicious. She didn't know what awaited her on the mysterious Wakerran ship, but anything that got her out of the Karezza-infested bar had to be a step up.

CHAPTER FOURTEEN

CORDWAINER WATCHED from a distance as Bauwerji met with the Sau mercenaries, quietly relaying the situation to Valdis. Though the Paisian captain assured hir that she could see everything with the nanoid sensors, Cordwainer found it comforting to give commentary. It made hir feel useful when otherwise ze would just be a carrier for the swarm.

Cordwainer touched hir ear and opened a channel to the soldiers at the dock. "Officer Crow is leaving the tavern now. Presumably she's heading toward the docks, being escorted by four Sau men. Don't engage and don't allow yourselves to be seen."

"Acknowledged, Doctor."

Cordwainer abandoned hir stool and moved to follow Bauwerji, but a broad Karezza man stepped in hir way. "Where are you going, little Human? My friends and I have a bet on whether you're a malekind or a femalekind."

"You lose," Cordwainer said. "Kindly move out of my way."

The Karezza put his hand on Cordwainer's shoulder to keep hir from moving. His other hand moved toward hir waist. "It'll be quick. And I can make it fun, no matter what I find."

Cordwainer reached for the jet injector ze'd used on the vidirector, but someone grabbed hir arm before ze could get into the pocket. A second Karezza crowded hir from behind as the first stepped forward to pin hir between them.

"It'll be quick and fun, I promise," the first one said. "At least my turn will be."

Cordwainer recalled what ze knew about Karezza anatomy. There was a pouch just underneath their ribs where chyme and digestive fluid accumulated before moving on through the digestive system. Ze turned hir left hand sideways and cut it hard against the Karezza man's side. Ze felt the sac burst under his skin even before he grabbed his side and backpedaled against the bar. Cordwainer jabbed hir elbow back and did the same thing to his friend. Both men bent in half and clutched their stomachs.

"Sorry, gentlemen," ze said, "but I'm afraid your time would be better spent finding a physician. The acid currently flooding your abdomen is quite corrosive, but it's not fatal for another few minutes."

The first man grimaced and, despite his obvious pain, reached for hir again. Cordwainer grabbed the nearest mug from the bar and smashed it against his face.

"I could have stunned you, but that would have prevented you from seeking medical attention. The choice is yours. I won't be a murderer, but you can choose to let yourself die. Decide if your life is worth saving." Ze looked to make sure his friend was staying down, then slipped through a crowd that suddenly parted to allow hir through.

The Sau had surrounded Bauwerji for the walk back to the docks, but Cordwainer managed to keep up with them without much trouble. They were nearly out of the bazaar when Bauwerji suddenly slowed her pace and slipped between the two men bringing up the rear of their convoy. She moved straight for Cordwainer and growled a quinlitz word that vaguely translated to "prevaricator" before slamming hard against Cordwainer's shoulder. They both tumbled, but Bauwerji sacrificed herself to cushion the doctor's fall.

"Get away from him." Othieno grabbed the back of Bauwerji's collar and hauled her up. He swung his boot at Cordwainer's head, purposefully missing but close enough to frighten hir. Ze scrambled to hir feet, blocking hir face with both hands as ze backed away. The Sau bared his yellow teeth. "Move along, fellow. Move along."

Cordwainer held hir hands up apologetically, ducking hir head and hurrying back through the crowd. Ze ducked around a corner and pressed against the wall. Over the hum of the crowd ze could hear their voices carrying.

"Who was that? An ally of yours?" Ze heard the clap of palm against the smock Bauwerji wore as she was roughly patted down. "Did he give you a weapon? What was that all about?"

Bauwerji said, "Z.. he was a thief. I've been waiting for you long enough that I got bored, so I played a few games. That Human cheated me. I decided to recoup my losses before breaking orbit."

Cordwainer reached for hir pocket and found hir folder was still there. Whatever Bauwerji's intention was, the Sau believed her lie. The group continued on. Cordwainer waited a few seconds before ze stepped out of the alleyway to continue pursuing them. Ze didn't dare follow them onto the docks with no concealment, so ze remained outside as Bauwerji and her escorts vanished inside.

"Brightening days," ze whispered, quoting an ancient Ladronis blessing, "and soothing waters upon your shore. Be safe, Officer Crow."

Yahri-class vessels were literally junk, Occamian refuse haulers that once carted trash from planets to be destroyed on an outer planet. When one of them could no longer fly, it was easier to just leave it adrift and find a new ride home. Scavengers like the Sau scooped up the derelicts, cobbled together engines and life-support systems that provided the bare minimum of comfort, and used them as disposable transports.

Bauwerji wasn't surprised to find the Sau were using one of the junkers. They entered through a hatch in the side, and she saw that the interior walls of the ship's stern had been stripped away to form a sprawling hangar. She skirted that area and moved toward the bridge. Othieno arrived first and contacted the dock master to be cleared for takeoff. Bauwerji glanced at the console in front of him and saw an alarming amount of systems were in the red. Energy signatures on the leeward hull were flashing red and yellow. Atmo leakage. Every system was running at full power, churning along hard and hot just to keep the ship in one piece. If they pushed the engines an inch farther than necessary, the whole works might shudder apart and fall to pieces.

"I don't suppose you offer cabin service on this cruise."

"Be quiet and sit down."

Bauwerji didn't like the idea of strapping herself to this tin box, but she also didn't trust the artificial gravity. Better to be tethered than be thrown against the walls and ceilings on their way out of the atmosphere. She found a seat and settled in, pulling the harness down across her chest and fastening it to straps that hugged her abdomen.

"I hope your boss has a nicer ship than this."

Othieno ignored her. The rest of the Sau took their seats as well. The engine gurgled and smoke lifted from seams along the floor as the ship lifted out of its berth and took to the skies. Bauwerji smelled a distinct odor of burning rubber and melted plastic as they banked to the south and gained altitude. She wrinkled her nose and looked for a source of the stink, but it seemed to be coming from everywhere.

"This thing is sound, right? I don't have to hold my breath once we're out of the sky?"

"You'll be fine," one of the Sau said, mumbling 'weak Balanquin' under his breath in *xibili*.

She thought about responding to him but decided it would be more valuable to make him think she couldn't understand their language. "Well, that sounded flattering."

He sneered at her.

On the screens she watched as they cut through clouds, and soon the polluted brown air gave way to the emptiness of space. Breaking through the atmosphere was relatively easy, but she felt as if she had dropped a few pounds as the ship began relying on its own gravity. The Paisian ship that had brought her here from the Quay was lost amid the other traffic orbiting Karakoz. Othieno seemed to be a skilled pilot; anyone who could provide a comfortable ride in a bucket of *trez* deserved at least a little respect.

"Your boss is going to a lot of trouble to get this rock," Bauwerji said. "She doesn't really believe it can do what the rumors say, does she?"

"You don't? You were willing to steal it."

She shrugged. "I'm smart enough to know when something is a hot commodity. I learned a long time ago that if something sounds too fortuitous, it's most likely a falsehood."

"You're Balanquin," he said. "Does that mean you believe in *abjijet seri*? The Heavens and the Earth conversed, thunder roared and the land shuddered, an argument between the two great beings resulting in life bursting forth to silence them?"

She grimaced at his dismissive tone. She wasn't particularly religious, but she didn't like outsiders mocking her planet's primary religion. "I'm a Balanquin who fought for a decade against people who sucker punched us by destroying half our military with their first strike. We were rescued by people who took over every facet of our daily lives and proceeded to turn us into slave labor in our own homes. I don't tend to give religion much thought one way or the other."

He smirked. "Sau believe that life began as an accident, and we should simply enjoy the miracle. Looking for meaning or depth is just a waste of time."

"Well, sure." She looked at the Sau beside her. "Who would want to believe this guy was made on purpose?"

He showed her his teeth.

"Well, whatever you believe, that rock will prove all these silly myths are barely worth the stones they're carved into. We're all just junk, trash left behind after a big explosion."

"The cenancestor," Bauwerji said. "I've heard that theory. There was a race out here in the cosmos somewhere, they got blown up, but their DNA got left behind on the shrapnel of their planet. Those rocks ended up flying through space until they landed on Ladrona, Pelorum, Earth, Okoan… then evolution took over. So we're all cousins."

He nodded. "Basically so. That rock contains genetic material that is the base for every race we've ever encountered. Probably some we haven't."

"What about the Paisian?"

Othieno laughed. "Who knows where the Puzzlemen came from? They were probably here when God was still shedding his first skin."

"I think it's *ji'juntea*. But if your boss is willing to pay for shit, then I'm more than happy to bulk up my bank account."

Othieno turned on a monitor and spoke in a language Bauwerji had never heard before. Seconds later the stars were obscured by a massive ship materializing directly in front of them.

"Red darkness," Bauwerji cursed.

"Through the veil," Othieno said.

The ship was curved on the bottom, featureless save for two engines on either side. They were coming upon it at a sharp angle that made the ship look as if it was listing to starboard. A slit opened on the edge and Othieno corrected their positioning as he guided them to the bay. The *yahri* ship shuddered as it entered the ship's gravity field and something clattered behind her. One of the Sau got out of his seat to investigate it as Othieno set the ship down. He turned to his men.

"Stay here. We still need to find more men, so we'll be heading down to the planet again once this one speaks with the boss. Try to fix anything that got shaken loose on this trip."

Othieno gestured for her to get up and follow him. Bauwerji unfastened her harness and let him lead her out of the ship. The air in the hangar was thick and smelled disgusting; she fought her nausea as Othieno walked to a door which led deeper into the ship. He gestured idly at a row of masks without slowing down to take one himself.

"The Wakerran apparently have a unique atmosphere. They dial it down for us, but you might need a little more help."

Bauwerji thought about refusing on principle, but she grabbed one of the masks as she walked past them. She was determined not to use it unless absolutely necessary. Othieno was already in the corridor, and she hurried to catch up with him.

The corridor was so wide she couldn't touch the curved walls with her arms stretched out to either side, but the actual walking surface was so narrow that she could only walk directly behind Othieno. She saw several circular portals, but there was no clear way to open any of them. The air was filled with a constant hum that she was startled to realize was speech. It seemed to be using the same language Othieno had used to announce their arrival. She couldn't tell if it was a live monologue or a recording, but either way something about the voice made her skin crawl.

When they reached the end of the corridor Othieno directed her to stand beside him on a platform that was slightly wider than the hall. He pressed his palm against the wall and they were lifted at great speed. Bauwerji wished for something to hold onto but settled for gripping the air mask with both hands. The ride was quickly over, and she steeled herself to prevent her legs from buckling as she stepped out into what looked like an amphitheater. The far wall was a web of screens showing various areas of the ship. The back wall was a gelatinous mass of oily matter that seemed to be breathing. Bauwerji moved away from that toward the mechanical nest in the center of the room.

"The Socigines," Othieno said, "I bring you information."

The nest, which rested on a metallic cup that looked like half an egg, was occupied by a purple-skinned woman with wires running over her lap like snakes. The wires ran from the base of her nest to shining brackets embedded in her skin. She was rotund rather than fat, and her spindly arms were crossed over her bosom. Her hands were oddly shaped, with long curved digits on either side of the palm. Her face was obscured by a black mask with white lenses over the eyes and what seemed to be a first-generation translation matrix strapped in front of her mouth. Still, the fact she seemed to be plugged into her ship wasn't the most startling thing about her.

The most startling thing was that Bauwerji didn't recognize her race.

She had been prepared for that, due to Cicero and Aryana's accounts, but the reality was still unsettling. As an officer on the Quay, even the minor races passed through once or twice per season. Aphelion Project species made up the majority of the permanent staff, but with smugglers and pirates and private convoys, the cruises and the tourists, she thought she'd seen every race capable of space flight. But none of them matched this woman's coloring, none of them even came close to her likeness.

The woman stared at Bauwerji for a long moment before a voice emanated from the mask. "Balanquin. I have met Balanquin before, but you are a different colorization."

"Most people don't notice that."

"I like knowing things about the people I meet. Your skin is gorgeous."

Bauwerji forced a smile. "Thanks. Yours is... unique."

"You have bared your teeth at me. I've heard this is a gesture of friendliness and peace with you. Our kind consider it a threat, a show of force and strength. I do not want you to feel threatened, Balanquin. This should be a very peaceful first encounter."

Bauwerji stopped smiling.

"I am the Socigines."

"Is that a name or a title?"

"It is how I am identified."

Bauwerji said, "Okay. Bauwerji Crow. I hear you're looking for a stone. You attacked some friends of mine looking for it, but you had to leave empty handed."

The lenses over the Socigines' eyes flashed pink and lavender, implying they were somehow organic. She leaned forward and the wires trailed across her skin. Suddenly Bauwerji was reminded of a spider crouched in the center of its web.

"You have it?"

"Not on me. I think it's time we talk about price. What are you willing to exchange for what I know?"

The Socigines glanced at the Sau. "You promised her payment."

"It's kind of how things are done in this section of space, ai?" Bauwerji said.

"How unfortunate. Misunderstanding. We do not wish to exchange currency for what you have. We want it. We will take it. And then we will do away with you the same way we destroyed those who didn't give us what we wanted."

Bauwerji sighed. "That's unfortunate. I guess I'll be heading back to the surface now." Othieno stepped between her and the door. Bauwerji looked at the Socigines. "You just threatened to kill me for information. That's not exactly good incentive to tell you anything."

The Socigines swayed in her nest. "We do not require you to speak your knowledge, Crow. The information is in your head and I shall read it as one would read a book."

Bauwerji said, "Okay. I hope that was enough time, Valdis."

"It was suitable, Officer Crow."

The voice came from the air around them, causing Othieno and the Socigines both to cringe and look for someone to attack.

"That's Captain Valdis," Bauwerji said. "She's Paisian. A few of her pieces were hitching a ride on a Human I'm traveling with. I tackled her when we were still on the planet and gave Valdis permission to hop onto me. It sickened me to do it, but hey... needs must, as the Humans say. I needed to get her on this ship by any means possible. While we were talking, she was taking control of your computers. It's her ship now. And I bet she's already sent alerts to every ship in orbit around Karakoz."

Othieno let loose a fearsome battle cry as he lunged at her, bringing his gun up to fire. Bauwerji had anticipated the attack and stepped out of the way. She grabbed the gun, twisted, and heard the bone of his finger snap as it was caught inside the trigger guard. He howled and fell to the side, and Bauwerji kicked him in the stomach. He crumpled to the ground and Bauwerji sidestepped his falling body to approach the Socigines.

The lenses now flashed darker red and crimson. "You may have control of the ship, but the Sau aboard will never let you leave alive."

"I don't know about that. Hey, Othieno. Are you still conscious?"

He growled in response, sitting on his knees with muscles tensed in preparation to launch himself at her. "I will disembowel you."

"Why? We're allies now."

He laughed.

"I'm serious. You failed her and let me onto her ship. You're the reason this is happening. So if she deals with me, what makes you think she'll keep you around?"

"If I take care of you, she'll give me a chance to fix things."

Bauwerji scoffed without taking her eyes off her enemy. "She strikes you as the reasonable sort, ai? Wanna take a chance with her or with me? I can take you to the Paisian vessel, get you back home. Far as I know you haven't done anything worth arresting you for. Well... petty black marketing, but I'm willing to overlook that in exchange for your cooperation."

"I... you're... it..." He looked between Bauwerji and the Socigines.

"She's taking advantage of you," the alien woman hissed.

Bauwerji said, "Of course I am. You're a Sau mercenary. You came to Karakoz looking for replacements so you can end your contract with her, and you work with whoever is giving the best deal. The deal I'm offering is that you get to go home. Once you're there, hop a ship and get back to whatever you're doing. Settle down and start farming. The deal she's offering... g'hin, I don't know what her eye colors mean, but they can't be anything good. You know her better than I do."

"Othieno... don't listen to her."

"What do I have to do?"

Bauwerji smiled. It was always nice to make new friends.

CHAPTER FIFTEEN

BAUWERJI STAYED well away from the Socigines' nest. She had no idea what it was capable of, and she didn't intend to find out by testing it. "Are there any defensive measures I should know about?"

The Socigines chuckled. "Do you honestly believe I would tell you?"

"I wasn't asking you."

Valdis said, "*I'm reading high energy levels being diverted to her position. Some of it is life support, but I believe the bulk is defensive. Disabling... now. It is safe to approach.*"

Bauwerji moved closer. "You might want to tell me how to get you out of that thing. Otherwise I'll just start cutting wires and hoping for the best."

The woman reached up and began to unfasten the wires herself. "I am surprised, Bauwerji Crow. You gave my men a convincing argument to get here."

"You heard what we said?"

She tapped one gnarled finger against the side of her head, then indicated the screens. "I see everything. Monitor everything. They would not have brought you here if I hadn't agreed. You would truly shun the opportunity to regain your planet from those who stole it?"

"And become worse than they are? No thanks. We're not genocidal." The final wires fell from the Socigines, and Bauwerji motioned at Othieno. "Secure her. Captain Valdis, we're bringing a prisoner over. I'm not sure what she's capable of, so you might want to go overboard on the security measures."

"*Understood, Officer Crow.*"

Othieno had moved close enough to bind the Socigines. He had one foot on the metallic shell of her nest, his torso exposed as he reached to bring her far arm closer to the other. The Socigines hissed and brought her leg up from the mess of wires that covered her lap. There was a bony extrusion rising from her knee and she buried it in the Sau's stomach. He shrieked in pain as she reversed her hand, grabbing him at the wrist and bending it until the bone snapped.

"Oh, *mi'I'tajo'k*," Bauwerji cursed.

She ran forward and grabbed Othieno's shoulder to haul him off the woman's bone weapon. Blood spurted from the gash just below his ribs, green and gelatinous, as he collapsed. The Socigines threw her bulk forward against Bauwerji, turning herself into a projectile. Bauwerji was hit by the woman's shoulder and could do nothing but hold on as she was thrown to the floor. The alien pinned her down and brought one of her clawed hands up.

"You will regret not taking my offer."

Before she could bring the claw down, however, her weight was lifted off Bauwerji and they both began floating. Bauwerji pushed aside her disorientation, grabbed the alien's arm, and snapped it as easily as Othieno's had been broken. The Socigines howled in pain and confusion as she swung her other arm around. Her hooked thumb caught Bauwerji's side and buried itself in the meat just above her hip. Bauwerji bared her teeth and jerked away, tearing her flesh to escape the claw.

"*Apologies, Officer Crow,*" Valdis said. "*I had to disable to gravity. It was the only offensive gesture I could think of.*"

"You did fine, Valdis."

She pushed her foot off the floor and propelled herself toward the Socigines. The alien was cradling her broken arm, but she lashed out with the other hand. Bauwerji caught it, the claws still dripping with her blood, and pulled it around behind the Socigines' back. The gravity was slowly restored, dropping them all to the ground as gently as possible. She kept it pinned there and looked over to where Othieno was floating limply beside the nest.

"Othieno? You still conscious?"

There was no response from the Sau.

"I could use some backup, Valdis."

"*We're docking now. Aphelion forces are facing resistance from Sau forces, but we should reach the bridge in short order.*"

Bauwerji finished securing the Socigines' hands. "Take all the time you need. Dr. Littlefoot and the forces on Karakoz…"

"*They're already aboard the Adedoja.*"

Bauwerji reached down and touched the wound in her side, wincing. "Tell Cordwainer I'm going to need hir expertise."

"*Ze will be notified.*"

The Socigines said, "What is your intention with me, Balanquin? You cannot honestly hope to imprison me, and you must know that there are others of my kind waiting to take over should I fail."

"One monster at a time," Bauwerji said. She got up, ignoring the pain in her side where the Socigines had stabbed her and walked to Othieno. She wasn't entirely sure how to check a Sautoriau for vital signs, but the amount of blood he'd lost and the slack expression on his face indicated it would've been a lost cause anyway. "Sorry about that, Othieno. Looks like our partnership was short-lived."

Bauwerji chuckled without humor, then grabbed at her side with a grunt of pain. All she could do was wait for the Paisian crew and the Aphelion officers to dispatch with the rest of the mercenaries. If she could spend that time without moving, speaking, or breathing too deeply, she had a feeling she would survive her wound. She only hoped they would move with expediency, because the pain was definitely getting worse with each passing second.

She had suffered worse, though. She applied pressure to the wound and watched the Socigines as she cast her mind back to the Decade at the Battlements. No medics, no clean hospitals to tend to their wounds. Their training hadn't prepared them for the quick and dirty medical care they would be getting in the field. Soldiers were cut open during sandstorms because, while infection was a real threat, a spur left inside a body would definitely lead to death.

The Socigines glared at her, the lenses of her mask flashing different warm colors. The mask looked as if it had been made from skin or hide. Bauwerji could see the basic shape of the woman's face underneath it. Not clearly, but enough to determine she didn't look like any other race frequenting the Quay. The last time anyone had encountered a completely unknown race, it resulted in the Cetidroi war. She was reluctant to revisit that part of history.

"I admire your restraint, Balanquin," the Socigines said. "Were I in your place, I would not hesitate to rid my planet of its scourge."

Bauwerji said, "I'm sure there are a great many differences between us, Socigines."

The woman chuckled softly, a sound like feet shuffling in dry leaves. "I wonder if your leaders would echo your sentiments. They might welcome me as a hero if I made them this offer."

"I wouldn't be so certain of that. We trusted outsiders once before, and the result was our current situation. I doubt even our myopic leadership would be quick to accept help from someone we didn't know. The Balanquin will finish this war on our own, without incurring further debts."

"Noble. The cemeteries of every world I've ever been on are filled with noble souls."

The doors parted and Bauwerji turned to see a squadron of Aphelion soldiers pour into the room. Once they were out of the way, Cordwainer pushed through and hurried to Bauwerji's side.

"Nice to see you again, Doctor. Sorry about how rough I got down on the planet."

"I knew you had something up your sleeve. Or clinging to your ear, as it turned out."

Bauwerji winced as ze began probing the wound. "I couldn't exactly call out to Valdis and tell her she could jump aboard again."

"It was very brave of you to allow it to happen. If you need to talk~"

"No." She said it firmly enough to convey that the topic was closed, and Cordwainer accepted with a slight nod. Bauwerji looked down at her wound as Cordwainer smeared it with a pale blue paste. She hissed through her teeth as it frothed and began burning away any potential bacteria. "She did that with her thumb. If I'm infected with some damn ancient virus now..."

Cordwainer said, "The antibiotics I'm using should kill anything she might have transferred. I'd like to keep an eye on it for a while, though."

Bauwerji nodded. Her attention was grabbed by the Aphelion soldiers securing the Socigines in a hard plastic shell. There was a hiss as the interior of the pod was filled with a sedative gas. They waited to make sure it was working before one of them activated the magnetic field along the underside of the shell to transport it to the ship. Bauwerji noticed one of the men was holding the Socigines' mask and realized the alien's face would be visible.

"Hold a moment." She gestured for Cordwainer to help her

stand. Cordwainer took her hand, supported her back, and walked her over to the pod. The porthole was fogged around the edges from the sedative, but the alien woman's eyes were still struggling to remain open. The skull was flat along the top, with a ridge running between the eyes to a pair of mandibles that opened to reveal a tangle of vine-like appendages extending from the mouth.

Bauwerji resisted the urge to shudder at the sight. "Looks like not all of us share a common ancestor, huh? I don't remember any of my relatives fucking a mole crab. Get her out of here."

The large black eyes drifted shut as the pod was propelled forward to the exit. One of the soldiers remained behind to give Bauwerji a situation report: they had engaged eighteen Sau mercenaries on the ship, and they were all now in custody or 'incapacitated.' Bauwerji thanked him and leaned heavily on Cordwainer's shoulder as they walked off the bridge.

"What are we going to do with the ship?" Cordwainer asked.

"The *Adedoja* should have towing capabilities. It might make our trip back to the Quay a little slower than normal, but it'll be worth it in the long run."

Cordwainer had to turn sideways when they reached the corridor, shuffling along the narrow walkway as the walls bellowed out to either side of them.

"Are you certain that's wise?" ze asked. "I thought the entire point of capturing the enemy here was to prevent her from reaching the Quay."

"It was. But we're in control of the ship now, and the Karezza and Paisian fleets should be there to keep an eye on it. The fact is, we need this ship even more than we needed the Socigines. She was right when she said the threat wasn't eliminated by capturing her. There are likely other Wakerran ships out there. It'll be nice to know what weaknesses they have when they show up."

"You believe we will have another war."

Bauwerji said, "I'm from Pelorum. War is inevitable. The only thing we can do about it is prepare ourselves and hope the next one ends as quickly as possible."

She hoped she sounded confident. She hoped the ship would give up its secrets and give them the upper hand necessary to send the Wakerran running when they finally showed up. Because the truth was that every war she'd fought was against an enemy even stronger and more implacable than the previous. She was terrified that their luck was going to run out and, if she was right, there was a very good chance that the Wakerran would be the enemy that finally bested their combined might.

If that was the case, she was determined that she would go down fighting.

CHAPTER SIXTEEN

THE ADEDOJA had been on high alert since Captain Valdis revealed Bauwerji was aboard the Wakerran vessel. Tensions only heightened when a squadron was sent to take over the other ship. The soldiers who hadn't gone on the mission were stationed in the corridors. Jocia Wison and Lalan Paget were asked to remain in their quarters unless summoned.

Jocia was more than happy to remain where she was. Her room had been altered and reconstructed to fit the needs of a Ladronis occupant, which meant several basins full of water and hanging vines. The temperature was also hot and humid, a mixture that she couldn't quite achieve at the Quay no matter how she tried. She had been kneeling in front of her prayer pool since Cordwainer left, eyes closed and hands resting in the cold water.

"We are all parts of the Great Chorus," she whispered. "Our hearts beat its rhythm, our blood whispers the tune, and our breath carries it into the empty air. The song echoes in every curve of every world. We are all notes in a song that began long before we were born and will continue long after we return to dust. Cordwainer Littlefoot is a precious note in your song. Ze is... a fleeting whisper of a note, and ze lingers in your mind long after the echo has faded. Ze is gentle and flowing, and hir melody is relentless. Ze is calming and bright." She laughed and her voice cracked. "I loved the song before I met hir, but I never truly heard it until I put my head to hir chest and listened to its harmony. The Great Chorus is stronger with hir in it. Protect hir. Keep hir in your song. Of this I beg you, and for this I sing."

She continued the prayer until she heard the chimes indicating someone was at her door. She lifted her hands from the basin and let the water spill from her palms. It formed thin curtains between her fingers before she finally brought her hands up to her face and patted the remaining wetness on her cheeks. She stood and gathered the robe around her legs to respond to the summons.

The swarm of nanoids outside her door was barely larger than a loaf of bread. It hovered at eye level and had a rudimentary representation of a face.

"Brightening day, Captain Valdis. Is there news?"

"The team is on their way back. Dr. Littlefoot wished for me to inform you that ze was uninjured."

Jocia smiled and swept her hand from left to right in front of her heart. "Are we still on high alert?"

"Indeed we are. But Officer Crow requested your presence when the prisoner was brought onboard. She seemed to believe you might be of assistance."

"It is the entire reason I came. Am I needed now?"

Valdis said, "If you wish I can escort you to the hangar now, and we will await the team together."

Jocia nodded and dried her hands before she stepped out of her quarters. As they walked, Valdis detailed everything Dr. Littlefoot and Bauwerji had done while off-ship. It sounded so thrilling and dangerous. Try though she might, she couldn't imagine her lover being in the midst of such danger. She looked down and saw her hands were shaking at the thought.

"You seem distressed, Ephor Wison."

"I'm quite alright. Thank you." She folded her hands into the folds of her robe. "You said Officer Crow is injured, but recovering?"

Valdis zipped along the corridor, bobbing slightly as if taking steps. "Yes. Dr. Littlefoot tended to her wound and she should make a complete recovery." The swarm turned to face her again. "Are you sure you wouldn't like more time to prepare?"

"No. I feel any preparation would only delay our meeting, and tensions are high enough as it is. The Wakerran introduced herself in an aggressive manner, but there's no reason our first contact has to be adversarial. I asked to come on this journey to present a friendly face."

Valdis buzzed softly, a contemplative sound. "I suppose it is bad enough that she will awaken in a cage. This might be our only chance to stave off another war."

The thought chilled Jocia to the bone. She remembered the Cetidroi invasion; massive ships rolling across every system and taking whatever they pleased. The Karezza fleet couldn't match their strength, and even the Paisian seemed out of their depth technologically. Representatives from the Aphelion Project came to Ladrona and pleaded for assistance against their common foe. The Ladronis fleet was hardly formidable, but ships and soldiers could help create blockades to slow the Cetidroi advance. The governments of Ladrona refused. To even stand on a battlefield was to soak your feet in bloodshed. They were warned that the Cetidroi wouldn't respect their beliefs, but they refused to budge.

The war was finally won by the Balanquin and their small bracijera ships. They were fast and maneuverable enough that the Cetidroi weapons couldn't lock onto them. They disabled enough systems to make the Cetidroi vulnerable. The Karezza, Paisian, Occamian, and Acapsian ships were then successful in forcing the invaders into a retreat. The Aphelion Project never held the Ladronis' refusal against them, but Jocia felt a certain amount of shame that they'd done nothing to protect their neighbors. It was one of the deciding factors that led to her leaving home and taking a position as ambassador on the Quay. She wanted to bring her people out of their cloister and into the light, to show the rest of the universe they weren't cowards who expected others to fight their battles.

She had both anticipated and dreaded this day, the moment she would be called upon to stand before a monster and attempt to reason with it. The Wakerran not only utilized violence, it seemed to revel in it. She had read Aryana Barrien's report and knew that the death of the Karezz on Captain Drayton's ship was unnecessary and cruel. His life had been dispatched as carelessly as someone might have swatted a fly. What common ground could she possibly find with a person such as that?

"The ship arrived ahead of schedule. We should go directly to the holding cells. Officer Crow reports the creature calls itself the Socigines. Whether that is a title or a name, we can't be certain."

Jocia stepped onto a lift that carried her and the swarm down to a level which required the captain's voice code to access. As the doors parted, she explained she created the entire section as a series of antechambers with multiple checkpoints and fail-safes to ensure no one could bypass it on their own.

"We have no idea what this person is capable of, but the swarm I had aboard her ship gave me some idea of her technological knowledge. I believe this will suffice as a prison, but I will monitor her continuously for signs of escape. Hopefully the extra measures and vigilance will suffice."

"One can only hope," Jocia said.

A few minutes later the lift opened again. A second Paisian - in reality just another piece of Valdis' swarm - led the procession of soldiers escorting a hovering metal shell. Valdis opened the cell and directed them to place the prisoner inside. Jocia took a step back as the shell passed her, folding both hands behind her back.

"Where are Cordwainer and Bowery?" Jocia asked.

Valdis said, "Dr. Littlefoot thought it prudent to take Bauwerji directly to the infirmary. The XO protested, of course, but she will appreciate the effort when she heals without a scar."

The soldiers finished with the pod and stepped out of the cell. Valdis reinforced the energy barrier that isolated the prisoner and, via remote, vented the gas keeping her unconscious. Jocia found the courage to step closer to the barrier so she could see the alien woman's face through the pod.

"She's fascinating. Insectoid, but there's something familiar about the shape of the face." She traced the shape of a jawline, tilting her head to one side. "I-"

The eyes snapped open. Jocia took a step back, her shocked gasp caught in her throat as she covered her mouth with the hand she'd raised.

"Ladronis," the woman said.

Jocia took a moment to ensure her voice wouldn't waver. "Brightening day. My name is Ephor Jocia Wison. I am an ambassador-"

"You are the weak child the Aphelion Project chose to interact with me. Why? A futile attempt to put me at ease? You sent a soldier first."

"Officer Crow was sent as a response to your violent acts. The Aphelion Project knew you might have to be subdued."

"And now the soft hand. Appealing to my gentler instincts? Will you sing me a song, Ladronis? Hum in my ear and soothe my warrior heart?"

Jocia said, "That's the intention. We want to prove that we are willing to negotiate. To reason with you and your people. There is no reason for us to be enemies."

The Socigines laughed. "And yet, there is no way we can be friends."

"Why not?"

"This corner of the galaxy teems with life, doesn't it? Balanquin, Human, Karezza, Acapsian. You believe that makes you special. You're nothing but bacteria. A mold in the forgotten corner of a washbasin that hasn't been used in years. You grew and spread because no one thought to check your evolution. But you have been noticed, by races older than you. Stronger and smarter than you. Races that see no value in your continued existence and shall do everything in their power to wipe you out. Your days are numbered, Ladronis." Her eyes scanned across the room outside her cell. "When we have the stone, we will have the means to scrub your planets clean as easily as you would kill the mold in the washbasin."

Bauwerji Crow had entered the room in time to hear the end of the tirade. "Good luck finding it from behind that wall."

"Balanquin," the Socigines said. "You look as if you have healed well."

"I'm on the mend." Bauwerji glanced at Jocia. "How is the negotiation going?"

"It's... um..."

Bauwerji shook her head. "Never mind." She focused on the Socigines. "We're not going to keep you awake just so you can mock us and babble about your grand schemes. Valdis is going to spend the trip back to the Quay digging around in your ship, and Cordwainer is going to knock you out again so ze can dig around in your anatomy. Ze's already got full-body scans from the pod you're in. Ze said it won't be necessary to vivisect you, but I'm trying to talk hir into it. Just for fun."

The Socigines smiled. "I saw your blood and now you wish to see mine."

Bauwerji returned the smile. "Pretty much. So enjoy your nap."

The gas began filling the pod again, and the Socigines smiled. "I shall sleep, Bauwerji Crow, but I want you to consider your rank. I want you to think of who your people sent to respond to this threat. No Admirals, no Generals. Not a warship, but the first vessel that was available with a small contingent of soldiers. Look around yourselves and think about the military force you left in check when you came looking for me. Then consider that my people have done the same thing."

The Wakerran's eyes drifted shut, but she forced them open again.

"Run your tests. Dig through every secret my ship has. Cut me open and dig through my intestines. It won't do you any good in the end." She smiled as her head drifted forward. "You will all be destroyed in time no matter what happens to me. In the end, I am nothing but a scout. When you face the full might of the Wakerran fleet... you... will tremble. Enjoy the last days of your lives. There are not... many of them... remaining."

The last word faded as the Wakerran succumbed to the gas. Bauwerji took a deep breath and looked at Valdis and Jocia.

"What now?" Jocia asked, her voice meek.

"Now we take her back to the Quay. We spend the trip finding out everything we can about her and her vessel. She can threaten us all she wants. We've never backed down from a fight, and we're not about to now."

She turned and walked out, and the Valdis constructs followed her. Only Jocia remained behind, watching the woman on the other side of the energy barrier. Bauwerji could talk as bravely as she wanted, but the measures they'd taken just to contain one Wakerran proved how frightened they were of her. She couldn't begin to imagine what would happen if they faced a fleet of these creatures.

Her hands suddenly felt dry. She rubbed them together, also becoming aware of the silence around her. She needed her basins, her songs, and the comfort of the Great Chorus. She hoped somewhere in the combination of the three she found some measure of peace.

CHAPTER SEVENTEEN

THE APHELION forces were on high alert. Admiral Reshef made an announcement asking everyone to please remain in the residential areas until further notice. Selina Rogers was already in her quarters when the *Adedoja* returned with its prize in tow. She had been entertaining one of her clones in bed, a male derivation of herself that she'd enjoyed several times in the past, but she excused herself and turned on one of the screens so she could watch its approach.

James, her masculine clone, sat up as well. He watched as the ship was towed into view. "It certainly doesn't look like much."

"It doesn't look like anything we've seen before," Selina said. "That alone makes it intriguing."

James moved to sit behind her and began massaging her shoulders. Selina used a palm control to adjust the camera position so she could watch the ship's progress. During the Cetidroi war, the Acapsian government had discussed a possible alliance with the newcomers. New technology was a tempting prospect. Their leaders had been drooling over what they might discover. In the end, they voted to stay with their current allies to fend off the invasion. It had been the wise choice in the long run, but this was a different matter. This was one ship. She could negotiate an alliance before any shots were fired, build a friendship. Then, if the Wakerran decided to attack later, she could convince them to take a more peaceful path.

She could save countless lives.

Her clone's hand moved down to her breast to tease the nipple. Selina arched her back at the touch and reached back, resting her hand in James' lap. He was hard, and she traced the length of him with her thumb and forefinger. It was so fantastic to tease her other-gendered self, to see how she would have developed with a different set of chromosomes. James moved his hand between her legs. He had the same fascination, even though he was the one crafted rather than born. Selina knew there was heavy narcissism involved in making love to herself, but every other race had maxims about truly loving yourself. Some were more literal than others.

Her communicator chimed and she checked to see who was calling. She saw Admiral Reshef's name and smiled. She turned around and pushed James down onto the mattress. He put his hands on her hips and guided her to his lap, easing her down as he slipped inside of her. Selina sighed and closed her robe around her chest and directed the call to her screen as she clenched her muscles around his erection. The screen came to life with the image of Admiral Reshef in her office.

"Hello, Admiral."

"Miss Rogers," Indira said. "I hope I'm not interrupting anything."

Selina rolled her hips. "Not at all. I was watching the *Adedoja*'s triumphant return on my monitor. Quite an accomplishment Officer Crow managed to pull off."

"Very true. That was actually why I was calling. I was hoping you would be joining the rest of the council at the docks for the ship's arrival. The Wakerran may currently be our enemy, and at last report she was being kept unconscious, but I would still like for us to be there as a symbolic gesture."

"Of course, Admiral."

"Excellent. They're being guided through the debris field now. Our yeomen estimate arrival in eleven minutes. Do you think you'll be finished fucking by then?"

Selina's face stretched into a smile. "I believe so, ma'am."

Indira allowed a smile of her own, eyes dropping down briefly before she disconnected the call. Selina chuckled and began moving her hips freely, lifting and dropping down, fingers splayed on James' flat chest. She looked down into his eyes, still almost identical to hers despite the difference in gender.

"I believe she is of your persuasion, James. If I sent you to her, and you fulfilled her needs, would you report back every... intimate... detail...”

“If she allowed me to share,” he said, “of course.”

Selina closed her eyes and dragged her hands down his chest. She only let him climax after she came, trembling as he throbbed and filled her. All clones were sterile as a matter of convenience; no sense in a woman facing a paternity suit because her male copy couldn’t keep it in their pants. Sometimes she wondered about it. The child would be her DNA entirely, sired by her and carried by her, and a complete reproduction of herself. The possibilities were almost worth the punishment that would come from tampering with the clone’s makeup.

When they were both finished, she let him slip out of her and crawled to the side of the bed. She dressed in her standard uniform and put up her hair. She turned back and ran her eyes over James’ body.

“You were a fantastic companion, James. I shall miss you when you’re gone.”

He smiled back. He would be leaving on the next shuttle to Acapsia, most likely never to return. It was a shame, but there would be another clone eventually. An Alex Rogers or Sabra Rogers, a Jeremy or a Diana. She was sure whatever version of her visited the Quay next would have his or her own interesting quirks that she would enjoy exploring.

She left and walked to the docks. Admiral Reshef, Constable Heely, and Nerea Paisian were already waiting, representing the Quay’s council. Also present were Captain Drayton, Engineer Barrien, and two other crewmembers from the *Sastruga* she hadn’t been introduced to. Selina assumed they had been invited because of their encounter with the Wakerran. Indira looked over at Selina as she joined them.

“I hope you didn’t rush through anything, Ambassador.”

Selina grinned. “Not at all, Admiral. Everything was completed satisfactorily for all parties.”

Captain Drayton looked rested and calm, but the Balanquin engineer seemed jumpy. She watched Indira and Selina’s interaction before snapping her head back toward the dock. The *Adedoja* was going through the final docking procedures. Indira motioned for a group of soldiers to move forward. Selina noticed the soldiers were made up of a variety of species; most likely an attempt to render the Wakerran’s genocidal weapon ineffective.

The ship was cleared and the soldiers moved in. As the prisoner was secured, the crew disembarked. Bauwerji's uniform tunic was torn and smeared with blood, indicating an adventure had occurred. Excitement and danger, how fun! She resisted the urge to smile and ruin the dour mood everyone else had adopted.

Bauwerji and Valdis were the first to reach the station's representatives. Indira said, "I hear congratulations are in order, XO. Well done."

"Don't celebrate yet, ma'am. The Wakerran gave us reason to believe the threat is far from neutralized. I'll give everyone a full briefing once I've changed out of my uniform."

Indira nodded and watched as Cordwainer joined them. "And Doctor, I want a full report of the Wakerran's vital signs. I want to know what we're dealing with."

"I'll put together an official statement."

Indira started to say something else, but she was distracted by the soldiers returning with the hovering pod. She moved closer and the rest of the group did the same. Selina was no soldier so she forced herself to stay behind Constable Heely just in case there was any danger. Constable Heely put a hand on the glass and leaned close for a long moment before wrinkling her nose.

"Ghastly. Bauwerji, you had that thing inside of you? You might want to disinfect your whole insides."

Bauwerji ignored her and watched as Indira tilted her head to look at the alien through the glass porthole. Despite the circumstances, Indira seemed awestruck by what she saw.

"Amazing," she whispered. "The Quay hasn't had a true first contact situation since the Cetidroi. And before they arrived, it had been decades. This is a historic day, folks."

"Let's hope this introduction goes smoother than it did with the Cetidroi." Bauwerji stepped to one side and motioned for the *Sastruga*'s engineer to come closer. "Aryana... is this the woman who attacked your ship?"

The young Balanquin looked, then took a quick step back. "No."

The tension immediately tripled. Indira said, "What do you mean it's not?" Indira asked.

"The woman on the *Sastruga* was slender. She was wearing a mask that completely hid her face, but even so... This couldn't possibly be the woman I saw."

Bauwerji turned to the soldiers. "Lock down that ship

immediately. I don't want anyone on or off it until we've searched every square inch." She looked apologetically to Indira. "Admiral, we swept that ship for life signs before we set out, and countless times since then. If there was anyone else onboard, we would have found them."

"Assuming you knew what you were looking for. I'm not holding this against you, Officer Crow. But if there is someone else aboard~"

"We'll find them, ma'am."

Bauwerji started to go back to the ship, but Indira stopped her. "The security officers can conduct the search. You need to change clothes."

Bauwerji looked as if she wanted to argue, but at last she nodded. Indira gestured for Constable Heely to take over. The Karezz touched a device in her ear and began herding her people toward the ship. Selina looked at it again and thought it had become more ominous in the past few seconds. She stepped out of the way as Indira and Bauwerji moved away from the docks, deep in discussion about security measures they would need to keep the Wakerran in custody.

Selina took the opportunity to look through the glass at the Wakerran. The woman was still unconscious, her eyes closed except for a sliver. She looked hideous, just Human enough to look Wrong. Selina found herself physically nauseated by the sight but she didn't look away. She had no idea when she would get another chance, and her people would want to know as much as possible about this new arrival. Moments like this were why she had come to the Quay in the first place.

But oh, how disgusting the creature was! The disgusting mouth-pieces hanging free from its mandibles, and the seam down the center of its face that made it seem as if it could split in half at any moment. Her skin crawled and her body seemed desperate to be away from the thing. And yet... and yet, the potential value in this monster was too great to ignore. The ship. The weapon. If the woman were to wear a mask, perhaps it would be enough for a summit.

Selina had a mental image of shaking the woman's hand. The thought nearly made her vomit, and she put a hand to her mouth.

She felt an itch at the back of her skull, as if ants were crawling on the inside of her skin. She took a step back but rocked forward on the balls of her feet to end up closer to the pod. She was staring directly into the beast's face when its eyes opened wide and stared back at her.

Selina Rogers, Acapsian. Riches and wealth and power. Prestige shall be yours. Your people will benefit greatly from this alliance. We shall become great friends. Your ambitions will be ours and we shall strive to achieve them. Together. To the great benefit of both our races. The Acapsian and the Wakerran shall form an empire that stretches across the vastness of space until the obstacles standing in our way are but footnotes in our history.

Images filled her mind and crowded at the edges of her consciousness. She saw herself eating with the Wakerran, food slithering from their mouths over her chin and down the front of the Wakerran's shirt. She saw herself lying in bed with Wakerran on top of and underneath her. Their repulsive mouths closed on her nipples, covered her mouth, slid between her legs, and she shook with pleasure and revulsion. When the images dissipated, Selina pulled away from the pod, unsure of what she'd just experienced. Her hands were shaking and she felt pale, the nausea growing until it was all she could think about. Someone put a hand on her shoulder and she jumped away from it before she realized it was Jocia Wison.

"Are you all right, Miss Rogers?"

"I'm... fine." The security officers were moving the pod away, seemingly unaware of the fact its occupant was awake. Or... was she? Selina suddenly wondered if she had imagined everything. She patted Jocia's hand before stepping away from her. "I'm just a little ov-overwhelmed by all of this excitement. Perhaps I should go lie down for a bit."

"Perhaps that would be wise."

Selina smiled and smoothed down her robes. She refused to think about the bizarre images she'd conjured up. At the time, even with the queasiness, there had been something appealing about the scenarios. She looked away to where the guards were walking the pod to its eventual new home in the holding cells. She could still hear the Wakerran's voice in her head... though that was impossible. She'd never heard the alien speak.

She swallowed the sizable lump in her throat and closed her eyes until her mind calmed, then she hurried off to her rooms. She didn't care if her peace of mind came from food or fucking; she just needed comfort and calm and those were the best ways to get it.

She just hoped another encounter with James could erase the lingering images of the Wakerran from her mind.

CHAPTER EIGHTEEN

LALAN PAGET was unnoticed as she left the ship, though she understood why everyone had more important things on their minds. She moved to one side of the group and activated the camera on her lapel. She would move without argument if anyone shooed her away, but she couldn't pass up the opportunity to record this historic moment. Constable Mara Heely and Ambassador Rogers both looked at the Wakerran through the glass porthole of her pod, and Bauwerji seemed to be giving a report to Admiral Reshef. They were speaking too quietly for her to hear over the hum and chatter of the docks.

The Balanquin engineer from the *Sastruga* also looked at the Wakerran, and whatever she said caused a new flurry of activity. Soldiers returned to the *Adedoja* and Admiral Reshef ordered a lockdown of the dock area. One of the constables finally noticed Lalan hanging around and ushered her toward the exits. When she looked back she saw Nerea and Valdis both breaking up into smaller swarms which floated back toward the ship.

"Can you tell me what's going on?" she asked the man escorting her to safety.

"They think there might be another Wakerran onboard."

"If they take this much precaution for one, I can't imagine how dangerous a second would be."

The security officer said, "Let's hope we don't find out."

He left her by the lifts and went back to see where he was needed. Lalan took out her camera and held it in front of her face. She hit record, activated the stabilizer, and dropped her hand as the screen reflected her image back to her.

"This is Lalan Paget from the Home Press, reporting to you from the Quay. It's been an eventful few days here on the station, beginning with the arrival of an independent vessel called the *Sastruga*. The ship's Human captain, Cicerone Drayton, claimed they were attacked by a vessel that couldn't be identified. Further investigation revealed that the ship matched one found in the Ladronis' mythology. It was the ship of a race called the Wakerran, urban legends, monsters from prehistory..."

She could see past her camera as she continued speaking. Bauwerji was following Dr. Littlefoot toward the lifts, and Captain Drayton was walking with them. Cicero looked distraught, her brow furrowed as she worried her lip with her teeth. Bauwerji reached out and touched the other woman's shoulder and said, "I'm fine. Cordwainer patched me up. I just need to heal."

"It could have been so much worse," Cicero said.

"But it wasn't."

Lalan nudged her camera to follow her. "Three people who are intimately connected to this historic moment are coming through right now. Dr. Cordwainer Littlefoot, Officer Bauwerji Crow, and Captain Cicero Drayton. I'm filming a report for the Home Press and I was wondering if~"

Bauwerji reached up and covered the camera's lens with her hand. "No."

"The people of Earth deserve to know if there's a threat on their doorstep."

"And they will," Bauwerji said. "But we don't need fearmongering."

Lalan said, "I'm only telling them what's happening."

"How long does it take a message to reach Earth?"

"Seventy-two hours, unless it's priority."

Bauwerji said, "Then they don't need minute-by-minute news. Just hold off, okay? Admiral Reshef will tell you when you can send your reports."

"That sounds an awful lot like censorship."

The lift had arrived, but Bauwerji stepped away from it. "Humans are reactive creatures. You're giving them something they can't possibly react to. They can't leave Earth. They can't fight back.

They would simply be bouncing around your little planet looking for an outlet. Is getting an exclusive really worth causing that back home?"

Lalan said, "Have you ever been to Earth, Bowery?"

Bauwerji snorted and shook her head. "No. I came from a war zone. I have no interest in visiting another."

"And what happens if the Wakerran destroy the Quay? What then?"

"What if they do? Would Earth really benefit from getting a heads-up from you?" She stepped onto the lift with Cordwainer and Cicero. "The less Earth knows, the happier they'll be."

Lalan put her hand on the lift door to keep it from closing. "Better to be blindsided? Caught off-guard in a sneak attack? How did that work out for your people? How many of your friends died in the first attack by the Catarrh?"

Bauwerji looked homicidal, but it was Cicero who stepped forward. "Do you need a Human to say it to you? If so, listen carefully." Her voice was calm and measured. "There's nothing Earth can do. There is no defense they can put up against these bastards. If the Wakerran get past the Quay and the combined fleets of the Paisian and Karezza, then Earth will be torn apart in less than a day. I have family back there. I assume you do, too. I would rather let them live their last few days in blissful ignorance than fear they can do nothing with."

"Agree to disagree."

"We don't have to agree. But know that the next time you use emotional blackmail against my girlfriend like that, I'll teach you some manners. I'm not a member of the Aphelion fucking Project and I can do whatever I want to you. Don't make me get creative."

Lalan tried to maintain her bravado, but the look of sheer determination in Cicero's eyes was difficult to counter. She looked at Bauwerji. "I apologize, Officer Crow."

"Just be smart about your occupation," Bauwerji said. "If you upload without authorization, your credentials will be revoked. Aphelion and the Home Press won't pay to have you shipped back to Earth so soon after your arrival, which means you would effectively be a prisoner here on the Quay with no way to pay for it. You would owe for your lodging and food. The debt would be crushing in only a few days. Your entire life would be wrecked. I'm not threatening you. I'm just enlightening you to the truth, see?"

"I understand."

Bauwerji nodded and touched Cicero's arm. Cicero looked at her and, after a moment of silent communication, she stepped back. Bauwerji looked at Lalan. "Earth does deserve to know what is going on here, but in their own time."

"And you get to dictate that?" Lalan said. "You and the rest of the Aphelion Project?"

"If Earth doesn't like it, they can come out here and face the risks with the rest of us."

"We're here. Cicero, me, Admiral Reshef... we're here now."

Bauwerji said, "How many Human lives were lost when the Cetidroi attacked? Do you know how many Balanquin were killed? Because I do. Don't make this a battle, Lalan, please. Don't turn the command staff of this station against you on your first damned story. Even if you keep your credentials, this posting can be a very lonely place if the people in charge don't trust you."

She stepped back and the lift doors closed before Lalan could think of anything else to say. She looked back toward the ship, which was still teeming with activity. She chewed her lip and tried to think of what she would have done if she was still on Earth and heard news about the Wakerran threat. Bauwerji was correct; there was nothing Humanity could throw at the attackers that the Quay didn't have. There was nothing they could do but watch in horror as death moved slowly through the solar system.

Lalan looked down at her camera, stabilized it, and hit record again. "This is Lalan Paget reporting from the Quay. For the time being... nothing important happened today." In her peripheral vision she saw another set of soldiers moving forward to assist with searching the Wakerran ship. Under her breath she added, "And I hope to God it stays that way."

The Sautoriau mercenaries were each processed by Mara Heely's forces and separated into isolation rooms. Each one was scanned and cleansed of weapons or virulent diseases that could be spread through the Quay's systems. They were ordered to change out of their uniforms and put on bland jumpsuits provided by the Aphelion Project. Heely oversaw the processing and chose one of the men at random to be taken aside into her preferred interrogation room. She had a headache, and she reached to rub two fingers against the base of her skull in the hopes she could stave off any symptoms that might come with it.

She hated dealing with Sau. There weren't a lot of them, but the few who made it to the Quay seemed to cause enough trouble for a whole parade. She didn't like painting an entire species as worthless thieves based on the actions of a relative few, but it did seem as if the Sautoriau who made it off their planet did so for the sole purpose of causing trouble elsewhere. Other races looked to the stars and saw mystery and adventure. Sau looked up and saw potential victims and purses that needed to be emptied.

Heely herself had been born on the Karezza home planet and left because there were just too many damn people around. Her family lived in a tower connected to five other towers by walkways above the street. The streets were full of barely-moving bodies, a stream of Karezza inching along the ground with their fellow pedestrians pressed against their fronts, their backs, crowded on all sides. There was barely any room to breathe on her home planet.

Then one day they found another world. A world with vast deserts and cities where they could settle and spread out. Pelorum, home to the Balanquin and the Catarrh. All the Karezza had to do was defeat one race to earn the favor of the other. Since first contact was made with the Balanquin, they received the Karezza military's help. The Catarrh were defeated and the Karezza offered to stick around to help with the aftermath of the war.

It was supposed to be a colonization. The Balanquin were supposed to accept their new neighbors and, if Karezza intelligence and advancement meant the Balanquin became subservient, that was their own fault. She idly reached up to rub the back of her skull as she remembered the promises their first wave sent back. The Balanquin were stalwart and tireless workers. They could be used for the construction of a second Karezza planet. A new colony would lessen the strain back home, and both worlds would be able to flourish and thrive.

If only their people on Pelorum had been able to fight temptation. A few more years and the Balanquin would have been too cowed to protest any... indiscretions their superiors might take. It was all ruined because a few horny Karezza chose to rape a few noisy Balanquin. And because of Bowery Crow. Fucking troublemaker. On the frontline for every war the Balanquin had ever fought, and she'd drawn first blood against the Karezza. Heely would never forget that, and she would never come to terms with the fact Bowery Crow was now her coworker. Her superior officer.

The security officer who had searched the Sautoriau prisoner cleared his throat. She realized he had been standing beside her for a while, and she shook her head to dismiss her ruminations.

"The room and the prisoner have both been cleared, ma'am. It's safe for you to enter."

"Safe for me," she said. "Not for him."

Heely tried not to wrinkle her nose as she entered the room. Sautoriau men had a distinctly sharp odor about them that assaulted her Karezz senses. The room's filters would diminish it somewhat, but it took some time before the reek wasn't noticeable. She stood in front of the table and stared at the man's ghoulish visage.

"You're in the system as Kei Masilo. Is that accurate?"

He lifted his chin and narrowed his eyes at her. His tongue pressed between his teeth.

"Attractive. How long were you in service aboard the Wakerran ship? We know it was long enough for you to get bored. You were looking for replacements. So three months? Four? Sautoriau get bored quickly, but you have to work long enough to earn a good amount of mazuma. Four months sounds about right for someone with your record."

Masilo said, "You are a fan of my work. Woman who appreciates artistry."

Heely laughed. "Artistry? You call what you do art? Confined eight times in the past four years. You're hardly a mastermind. You're a grunt. Ground-level muscle who gets left behind while those in charge run free with the loot. Your employers hire you so they have someone to dump when things go bad. The correctional officers stop long enough to secure you, and they're gone." She smiled. "That's why every constable and guard lets you go. We all know you're nothing."

He glared at her. "I have nothing to say to you, Karezz."

"Oh, you have plenty to say. I want to know about your former employer. The Wakerran woman."

Masilo leaned back and crossed his arms over his chest.

"Loyalty to the person paying you, is that it? Consider this. The Wakerran is in custody now. The Paisian are infesting every program on her ship. That includes her coffers. The Aphelion Project is now in control of whether or not you get paid. Which I suppose makes us your employers." She put her hands down on the table and looked into his eyes. "How many Wakerran are on that ship?"

For a moment it seemed as if he wasn't going to answer. Finally, he said, "Just one. She's Socigines."

"Yeah? What's that mean?"

"Explorer, scout. I mean, technically, it means 'the eyes from which we look and see,' but simpler. She's the only one on the ship."

Heely said, "We have a report from someone who was awake when you took over the *Sastruga*. She says your boss was a slender lady who could move around easily." She nodded toward the wall. "That woman who was loaded off your ship couldn't walk by herself very well. She was top-heavy and leg-weak. Someone boarded the *Sastruga* and I want to know who it was."

"Or I don't get paid?" He shrugged "Or maybe I walk away without helping you. Maybe I don't get paid, but next employer knows they can trust me. I keep my mouth shut."

Heely said, "Or I drag you to the next room, tell your friend that you refused to help, then shoot you in the face before I ask him the same questions."

"The Aphelion Project is too moral for that," Masilo chuckled.

"The Aphelion Project wants to prevent another war. One Sau death to save countless Humans or Paisian or Ladronis lives? I may get scolded. But I won't suffer for it." She leaned closer. "No one cares if a Sau dies. That's your entire business model. One gets killed, there are six more on Karakoz waiting to be hired." She unfastened her holster. "Make your choice, Masilo."

He looked at her weapon and then back at her face. "There are four of them."

"Where are the other three?"

Masilo gestured vaguely toward the door. "Out there."

Heely furrowed her brow, then slowly realized what he meant. "We didn't capture the ship that attacked the *Sastruga*. There are three other ships out there."

"The Socigines is one person. Four bodies. One consciousness. Four ships. You catch one. Other three on high alert. Other three probably already on their way here to get their fourth back."

Heely unfastened the straps holding Masilo to the table. "Get out of here. You're free."

"What about my payment?"

"You'll get more work."

Masilo cursed in Sauto as he shoved his chair back. He rounded the table and Heely threw herself at him. He called her a bitch in his own language and shoved her away. As she stumbled, she pulled her weapon and shot him in the face. The security officers were through the door before his body hit the ground. Heely spun on them, teeth bared and eyes flashing angrily.

"He slipped his bonds. Who the *k'il* strapped him down?" The men spluttered, but she waved them off. "Never mind. He gave up what we needed before he tried to escape. I need to speak with Admiral Reshef. Our troubles may only be just beginning.

CHAPTER NINETEEN

ADMIRAL RESHEF was in her office when Constable Heely brought her the bad news. She immediately called a meeting of the council, trying to think of what she would say when they arrived. Her position wasn't elected, but it might as well have been. She was appointed by an Aphelion Project committee on Earth, and then she was presented to the other races of the Quay for approval. She remembered the months of waiting as she was judged by aliens she had never met and, if they didn't like her, never would meet. She tried to continue her life on Earth without checking her screens on a daily basis, hoping against hope there would be an answer.

Then one day it came. She was confirmed. The first thing she did was run to the bathroom and throw up, horrified at what she'd gotten herself into. She would be the highest ranking representative of Humanity on the shores of a vast and still unknown sea. She would be the one making decisions that could affect their entire planet. And the decisions she made on the Quay also affected the Balanquin, Paisian, Acapsian. If she made the wrong choice at a crucial juncture, the Quay would cease to exist. Humans would be cut off from the greater universe. The other races would be crippled, having grown accustomed to the station's presence.

Her job was to prevent an unending wave of disasters from crashing onto Earth's shores. If she failed, Earth wouldn't stand a chance.

She was standing by one of the three floor-to-ceiling screens in the conference room. The screens showed live footage of the Quay's exterior. It was supposed to prevent claustrophobia, but she found it relaxing to watch the balletic spin of asteroids, comets, and ship debris. It was hypnotic. Watching it made the turmoil in her mind seem a little less insurmountable.

"Ma'am."

She turned to see Bauwerji standing behind her. "How long have you been here?"

"Not long." She touched her side. "Cordwainer fixed me up, good as new."

"Glad to hear it. It's nice to have some good news for a change."

Bauwerji said, "What's the bad news?"

Indira briefly summarized what Heely had learned during the interrogation. She raised an eyebrow when Indira said Masilo had been killed attempting escape. She turned her head and looked at the constable.

"Odd that he was able to slip out of the restraints."

"Apparently he wasn't secured well."

"Right."

Indira sighed. "I agree with you. It's sketchy at best, but we have bigger issues right now. We'll discuss her official statement when we have a chance to breathe." She sighed. "What's your opinion on this new development?"

Bauwerji thought for a moment. "Even if there are three other ships out there somewhere, we need to keep the fleet here at the Quay. The rest of the council might suggest moving them to defend their own systems."

Indira said, "Shouldn't we consider that? We don't want to look like we're only defending Earth at the expense of everyone else."

"Let's say we did send the fleet out. Where would we send them? The Wakerran could come from any point on the map. We would have to completely surround Pelorum and Acapsia and Pais. It would render every squadron worse than useless. We keep everyone here and send them out as needed if the Wakerran ships are spotted. We know what they look like now, so we have something to look for."

Selina Rogers stepped into the room, scanned it for Indira, and walked directly over to her. "Is it true? There are more Wakerran ships out there?"

"So it would seem," Indira said. "We're considering our

options."

"There's only one option that I can see," Selina said. "Capitulation."

Nerea Paisian overheard the suggestion. "That does not seem to be a plausible solution to our current predicament."

"No one wants another war," Selina said. "We have no idea what the Wakerran are capable of."

Bauwerji said, "Not yet. But we have one of their ships, and one of their scouts. Given enough time we can get a good sense of what we're up against."

"Or we can simply call a truce," Selina said. "We give them what they want."

Cicero had been lingering on the sidelines, hovering near the wall to keep out of everyone's way. "You can't be serious. What they want is the means to cause genocide on a planetary scale."

Selina said, "They're attacking us because they don't know anything about us. Ignorance goes both ways. We respond to their scouts with violence, they'll react with violence, and we all get caught up in the crossfire. The whole universe burns because we went into the meeting with guns blazing. Instead we make a peace offering. The stone. We show them that we're willing to compromise."

Cordwainer cleared hir throat. "It might not be as crazy as it seems on the surface, ma'am."

Indira said, "Explain."

"We have a Wakerran now. We can examine her. Find out her genetic makeup." Ze turned to Cicero. "If we also had the stone, we could find a way to create a prototype of the weapon they're threatening us with. We hand it over with the stipulation that it can be used against them. Mutually assured destruction."

Constable Heely said, "Appeasing them with the threat of future violence. It's a valid plan of action."

Cordwainer looked distinctly uncomfortable to have the Karezz woman agree with hir, but ze said nothing. Ze folded hir hands on the table and looked at Indira.

"So the options we have right now are fighting a war I doubt we can win, or threatening them and hope they don't call our bluff."

Jocia said, "The third option is surrender."

Heely snorted and shook her head. "Leave it to the Ladronis to come up with that one."

"It is an option," Jocia said. "I did not advocate it."

"Yes. But if you were given the choice, you would bow your head and let these Wakerran cut it off."

Jocia took a deep breath before responding. "I would not choose to begin a war, you are correct."

Indira pulled out her chair and sat down. "Whatever choice we make is going to have far-reaching consequences. War or not, the Wakerran are out there now. We have to deal with the fact there's a new and aggressive race kicking up dirt all around us."

Heely said, "All the more reason to react aggressively."

Bauwerji muttered, "*Qiar*, you are such a fucking Karezza."

"Perhaps we should follow the Balanquin example. Drop our trousers and bend over so they can fuck us whenever they please."

Indira snapped, "Constable Heely. That was entirely out of line."

Heely smirked and waved her hand dismissively. The red of Bauwerji's face had deepened to a new shade of scarlet, and Indira watched her for a long moment to make sure she wouldn't launch herself across the table at the constable.

Selina Rogers was barely concealing her smirk. "I think that's actually a decent idea. Sexual experimentation with a new race~"

"Just be quiet," Bauwerji said.

Selina arched an eyebrow, but she didn't continue.

Indira said, "We have to show the Wakerran that we don't want to fight, but we're also not going to passively hand ourselves over to them. We're also not going to hand them the means to destroy any race that pisses them off." She tapped her fingernails on the tabletop and looked at Cordwainer. "As much as I hate this idea, I think we only have one course of action that keeps everyone safe."

Nerea said, "I don't believe handing over the rock to the Wakerran will be prudent."

"Nor do I," Indira said. "We don't do that part of the plan, but we do the rest of it. Captain Drayton has the stone, and we have a Wakerran in custody. Ze can create the weapon the Wakerran hope to produce. Would you be willing?"

Cordwainer tensed. "It... would be a violation of every ethical code I've ever taken. But if it prevents planetary genocides, I could convince myself I was working toward a greater good."

"I think it's the only thing we can do at this point. We could greet the Wakerran peacefully, but we make sure they know we won't be easily defeated."

Bauwerji said, "It's a brutal course of action."

"They killed the Karezz man on the *Sastruga* in cold blood just to prove they could. I highly doubt playing nice with these people will have any dividends. We need a show of force without actually drawing blood. This weapon is horrendous, but it's the best option we have." She saw the conflict in Cordwainer's eyes. "Just because we have it doesn't mean we'll ever use it."

Jocia said, "That's what the Mars colony said about the cobalt bomb. And what America said about the atomic bomb. Twice we created weapons as fright tactics, never to be actually used. Twice we became monsters and learned to live with it. You're asking Dr. Cordwainer to be instrumental in creating a third weapon."

Indira tried to put as much apologetic sympathy into her voice as possible. "I could make it an order, if that would make it better."

"Just following orders," Cordwainer whispered. It had been hir idea, but it was obvious the reality of being asked to follow through weighed heavily. Ze looked down at hir hands.

Heely said, "Don't worry about it, Doc. I'm sure when every Human has been wiped out by these *vekju*, you'll sleep well knowing your morality is intact."

Indira said, "Constable Heely, I am about to revoke your speaking privileges for... all time. Be silent and do not speak again unless I address you. Is that understood?"

"We need to take action."

"Perhaps we should simply lock the Wakerran people in a room and shoot them in the face one at a time," Bauwerji said.

Indira slapped her hand down on the table. "Bickering children! My god! Perhaps the Wakerran don't need a doomsday machine to destroy us, because we'll do it ourselves. Bigotry and hatred and pacifism in the face of creatures whose only goal is to kill us because we're seen as an accident of biology. I will not sit idly by and allow the Wakerran to destroy this sector." She jabbed a finger at Cordwainer. "Dr. Littlefoot, I can tell you're conflicted about this, so I'll make it easy. You will create the weapon or I will have your resignation by the end of the day." Cordwainer nodded. "Captain Drayton, provide the doctor with the stone."

Cicero looked at Cordwainer and opened her mouth to speak.

"I swear, if you refuse to hand over the rock, I will kick you off my station without the benefit of a spaceship."

Cicero closed her mouth, then nodded. "As you say, Admiral."

Indira stood up and moved to where Mara Heely was standing. "Stand up straight, Constable." Heely did as she was told. She was a few inches taller than Indira, forcing the admiral to lift her chin to look into her eyes.

"If you ever again speak so crudely to any member of this staff, *any* member of this staff, I will have you arrested for verbal cruelty by your own people. I will have your career and I will ensure you never again get another respectable job. Am I understood?"

"Yes, ma'am."

Indira turned and scanned the faces in the room. "I don't want to be the Quay commander who ordered the creation of a weapon that could cause genocide at the push of a button. But I also know we're up against a foe that is technologically more advanced than we are. I know how that story ends, and it isn't pretty. Look." She pointed at the screens as a piece of particularly large debris floated past. "We're surrounded by remnants of a fleet that stood up against the Cetidroi and lost spectacularly. The devastation from that war was incalculable for every race seated around this table. If there's a way to prevent the first shot from ever being fired, I'm going to take it. And if that means people are still alive to consider me a monster... then I... I supposed that's an outcome I can live with."

She turned her back on them and walked out of the room. She didn't know if she could truly live with what she'd suggested, but it was the best option in a swarm of bad ones. The only thing she knew for certain was that even if everyone survived the coming days and weeks, the Quay would need a new commander. Even in victory she couldn't imagine remaining in charge after the choice she had just made.

Cordwainer hurried after her. "Admiral. Please, wait one moment. I've made my decision."

Indira stopped. "Oh?"

"I will do it."

Indira closed her eyes. "I'm very sorry to hear that, Dr. Littlefoot."

"As am I. Captain Drayton requires use of her ship to retrieve the stone. While she is away, I will examine the Wakerran for... for ways to utilize what I learn from the rock. The task may be insurmountable and deplorable, but you have my word that I will try to the best of my abilities."

"I'd expect nothing less of you." She turned and finally looked at the doctor. "You're a good person, Cordwainer."

"I feel the same way about you. Hopefully history will remember us in the same light."

Indira managed a weak smile and nodded. Cordwainer departed and Indira continued to her office. She pulled out her chair and turned it so she could face the screens behind her desk. Since the end of the Cetidroi war, their yeomen had gotten preternaturally skilled at navigating the graveyard of ships that enclosed the Quay like the rings of Saturn. Now they were joined by an intact fleet of Paisian and Karezza warships, guns at the ready and full of soldiers prepared for another battle.

She could live with her decision if it meant she wouldn't add to the field of death she saw every time she looked at the screens.

CHAPTER TWENTY

THE DOCK master informed Cicero that her ship was ready for departure; all the major repairs were finished and the rest could wait until she retrieved the stone and brought it back. She expected that her crew would have dispersed, but a quick search at one of the station's interfaces revealed they were all currently in the pavilion near the Sensuite theaters. She approached from the upper deck so she could see them before they saw her, and she spotted them gathered around a table near an Occamian eatery. Six people she trusted more than anyone else in the galaxy, Bauwerji excluded.

Irias Vuule was a Ladronis who left his people because of a rage that he couldn't quell. He liked to fight, and he never did well turning the other cheek. Cicero liked having him around because his anger was tempered by a pacifist's mind. He thought out every act of violence and only followed through if he found it absolutely necessary. It made him a trustworthy ally in some of the tense confrontations she'd had with clients.

Currently Irias was eating a piece of *cudommine* from the Occamian restaurant, licking the sauce from his middle finger. Across the table, Kela Se-Woei was watching him intently. She was Acapsian, and her kink for eating was well-known among the crew. Irias and Zennes had a friendly rivalry when it came to her affections, and Cicero knew for a fact that she had taken both of them to bed with her on several occasions.

Enatel Kaesa was sitting beside Kela trying to ignore Irias' display. As far as she could tell, the Occamian was asexual. He seldom spent the night in any room but his own, and when they stopped off-world he never partook of the local "nightly companions." Beside him was Sery Aranic, the only trustworthy Irikoan she had ever met, other members of her crew included. Sery's loyalty extended to the rest of the crew, Cicero herself, and no further. She would lay down her life for the people of her ship, but the rest of the world was fair game.

Zennes Dainai was the only one besides Aryana who was missing. He was also Irikoan, but nowhere near as reliable as Sery. She assumed he was in the Sensuite and decided she wasn't going to wait for him. Kela was the first to see her coming and tapped the table to alert everyone else. The chatter died down as she pulled a chair over.

"Uh-oh. I don't want everyone to stop having fun just because the boss arrived."

"It's all right," Enatel said. "Irias was just tickling Kela's sensitive bits."

Kela grinned. "And doing a fine job of it, I must say."

Irias licked his lips and leaned back in his seat. "What say you, Captain? Or more accurately, what say the Admiral?"

"I don't know how many details I'm at liberty to share, but there is a plan afoot. It involves getting the rock back from where we stashed it."

The group's good humor faded. Kela said, "Are we sure that's a good idea? We all know how dangerous that thing could be."

Cicero sighed. "Apparently we're taking the stance that the weapon will be created no matter what we do, so we're going to make sure we have it first. I want to know if you're all comfortable with that."

Looks were exchanged around the table before attention focused on Cicero again. Enatel said, "Depends on what you mean, Captain."

"We've taken a lot of jobs for some very bad people. We can only assume what they've done with the merchandise we delivered. This time we have the unfortunate benefit of knowing exactly what they want the rock for. It's the final piece they need to create a doomsday device that can wipe out an entire species."

Kela said, "A species that crippled our ship and killed a man in cold blood. Will many tears be shed if the universe is rid of them?"

"True. But once the weapon has been created, there won't be any going back. It can be altered to target any race. Sau mercenaries causing too many problems? Take out the species-killer, problem solved forever. The Karezza cold war with the Balanquin stretching on too long? Pick the one you like the best and don't worry about writing a treaty. We'll be giving the Aphelion Project unprecedented power. The power to play god."

Sery said, "You suddenly don't trust Aphelion?"

"I trust the people of it, sure. Admiral Reshef. Bauwerji. But I wouldn't trust any corporation as vast as Aphelion with something this powerful. That's the option I want to give you. We're not beholden to the people in charge of this station in any way, shape, or form. That was the promise I gave when you signed on to the *Sastruga*. We're free of affiliation. They're letting us leave the station to retrieve the stone. We don't have to actually come back."

Kela said, "Are you serious?"

"If any of you have qualms about what we're doing, yes."

Irias said, "All things considered, Captain, cutting off all contact with the station would affect you far more than it would any of us. You may not be tied to the Aphelion Project, but you definitely have connections here it would be painful to sever."

"I know. That's not the issue here. My loyalty is to my crew first."

Zennes arrived from the Sensuite, his skin still smelling of oils and scented incense. He was the polar opposite of Enatel; he took any and every opportunity to engage in carnal pleasures. His tastes were very particular: he liked men and women of any race who was willing to be with an Irikoan. He gauged the tone of the table as he took a seat beside Sery.

"What have I missed?"

Cicero briefly caught him up. "If we do this, it could be some time before we're welcome back at the Quay. We might never be allowed to come back. That would be a trial, but it's doable. We would have to rely on a lot of disreputable shipyards for repairs and stopovers."

Kela asked, "Does the Aphelion Project have a chance against the Wakerran without this weapon?"

"I don't know. But I know Admiral Reshef isn't entertaining any other options so long as the stone is available. Maybe if we took that away, she would be forced to come up with a plan she could actually live with." She leaned back. "Look, it's a big decision. We would be fugitives from most of our allies. Not exactly a new prospect, sure, but we've always been able to rely on the Quay. If we do this, we can forget that security. We don't have to make a decision right away. We'll go, we'll get the stone, and then we'll vote on what we do next. Sound good?"

The crew nodded. Enatel said, "What about Aryana? She gets a vote, surely."

"She does. But seeing as she was personally victimized by the Wakerran, I wanted to bring this option to her privately. She may have an emotional response, and I know she wouldn't want that put on display. Not even to you lot." She stood up. "Enjoy the rest of your stay. It'll take a few hours for a pre-launch check, but once we're clear I want to go as soon as possible."

"Aye, captain."

She plucked a piece of food off Irias' plate and popped it into her mouth, holding eye contact with Kela as she chewed. Kela took a deep breath and smiled pruriently. The captain winked at the Acapsian and left the crew to discuss their options. She ascended to the highest walkway, where the screens were programmed to show a stretch of the Kuiper belt. She rested her hands on the railing and stared at the screen as if it was the window it was meant to emulate.

Seven billion kilometers straight ahead, give or take depending on the current orbital status, Earth was silently spinning along. The planet where she was born and took her first steps. The planet where her family still lived, though every member had probably disowned her long ago. In the years since she escaped the world, returning had never appealed to her. She knew that her destiny lay in the stars. She was born on Earth, but born into the universe.

But if she made an enemy of the Quay and the Aphelion Project, she would never be allowed to go back. Choosing to stay away was one thing; being banned was entirely different.

Something made her turn away from the spinning rocks. Through the crowd she saw Bauwerji, the wholly unexpected love of her life, striding her way. Bauwerji saw her as well and graced Cicero with one of her rare smiles. Cicero pushed off the railing and moved to meet Bauwerji halfway. The flow of pedestrians continued around them as they stopped and gripped each other's hands.

"I would have thought you'd be busy in the pilothouse right now."

"There's not a lot to be done. We're always prepared for some sort of disaster, so the yeomen are well trained to respond if something happens. Besides, I can run really quickly when I have to. I wanted to be sure I came down to see you off. I wasn't sure when you would leave."

"We have a bit of time." She took Bauwerji's hand, guiding her to the railing so they weren't blocking traffic. "Can I ask you something serious?"

Bauwerji nodded.

"Can you live with what Admiral Reshef is proposing? Killing an entire race?"

"We'll be killing four members of a race," Bauwerji corrected, "and hoping the rest take it as a message to stay away."

Cicero said, "It will be a genocide, Bauwerji. Cold-blooded murder."

"If we use the weapon, it will be because they are attacking us. They've already attacked us. Whatever we do when the Wakerran show up, our response will be justified."

"You're not answering my question."

Bauwerji sucked her bottom lip into her mouth and ran her tongue across it. "During the third year of the Decade at the Battlements, I was leading a group of soldiers through a valley in search of food. We hadn't eaten in... days, at least. Maybe a week. We were looking for food. We rounded a rock formation and spotted a Karezza troop in a wrecked transport. They were waiting for reinforcements to help them repair the ship. They didn't see us. We could have snuck back out of sight and hidden until they were gone.

"Instead, I ordered my people to attack. We used the rocks as cover and we killed every soldier in sight. We raided their camp, took their supplies, and set the engines to explode by remote control. Then we waited. When their reinforcements showed up, we waited until they were in range and..." She mimed an explosion with her hands. "We killed at least seven Karezz that day. We didn't give them a chance to engage or fight back. We didn't wait until they spotted us, or try to escape. We just took them out."

"That was different. That was war."

"This is war," Bauwerji said. "The Wakerran want us eradicated, but they're not interested in a fair fight. They're coming to wipe us out. This weapon is atrocious, I admit, but it puts us on equal footing with our enemy. I'm not going to lose any sleep about using it if things get that far."

Cicero nodded slowly, not in agreement but in understanding.

"Okay. I should go make sure my ship is ready for departure." Bauwerji had put her hand on the railing, and Cicero covered it with hers. "Whatever happens, Bauwerji, I want you to know that I love you."

"I love you, too."

Cicero stepped closed and kissed Bauwerji. She thought maybe her destiny hadn't simply been space, traveling the stars, seeing other worlds... maybe her destiny had simply been to get far enough away from Earth to meet a Balanquin. The Balanquin currently in her arms, holding her tight as they kissed goodbye for what might have been the final time. Cicero didn't want to release her, but finally she did. She brushed her nose against Bauwerji's cheek and breathed deeply. Her skin still smelled like desert sand and sun after so many years away from Pelorum, and she found the scent intoxicating.

"Bauwerji..."

"What are you going to do?" Bauwerji asked.

Cicero opened her eyes and saw Bauwerji staring at her. She might not know details, but she certainly knew something was up.

"Come with me," Cicero said.

"I can't. I need to be here in case something happens." She put her hand on Cicero's, not tight enough to keep her from moving, but a definite presence. "Cicerone. Don't do anything you'll regret."

"That is exactly what I'm trying to avoid, Bauwerji." She kissed her lover again, then brushed her hand across the braids on the side of Bauwerji's head. "I know this honors the women in your family, but maybe they could watch over me for a little bit?"

Bauwerji said, "They've been watching over you since I made you the guard of my heart." She took Cicero's hand to kiss the knuckles. "Whatever action you take, I only ask that you make sure it's the one you can live with."

"I will."

"And I trust you." She touched the back of her hand to Cicero's cheek. "I should go."

"Me too."

They parted and walked in opposite directions. Cicero didn't look back, and she sensed that Bauwerji didn't, either. She put in her earpiece and tapped it to call Aryana.

"This is Captain Drayton. Report to the docks. We're shipping out as soon as possible."

CHAPTER TWENTY-ONE

BAUWERJI WATCHED the *Sastruga*'s departure from the pilothouse, eavesdropping on the yeoman who directed Cicero through the debris field. She was still thinking about their goodbye. Something had been left unsaid between them, some large conversation that was supposedly hidden under the actual words being said. Bauwerji was rarely good at picking up on cues like that from Humans. She found it difficult to understand much of anything Humans did, in fact. They were crude and aggressive creatures. Impulsive. Frustrating.

The first time she met Cicero, it was because the *Sastruga* had been detained for suspected smuggling. Security forces detained her crew, but Bauwerji wanted to meet the captain herself. They were introduced to each other in a small room rigged with monitoring equipment. Captain Drayton was suave and bemused by her incarceration. Bauwerji was sick of dealing with egotistical pirates and wanted to make an example of their latest capture.

"This meeting is being recorded," Bauwerji said.

"You're Balanquin, right? I have a Balanquin engineer."

She ignored her, pulled out the seat, and lowered herself into it. "I'm XO Bauwerji Crow. I'm the second-in-command of this station. State your name for the record, please."

"Cicerone Drayton, Human, from Earth, Barysaw, Belarus. Ever heard of it?"

"I have not."

"You have beautiful eyes."

Bauwerji glared at her. "Captain Drayton, you're being accused of carrying contraband from Okoan to Ladrona. How do you answer these charges?"

Cicero put her elbow on the table and cupped her chin. "My ship was hired to move cargo from Solivislad Dea on Okoan to a temple on Ladrona. I operate under the auspices of Blind Assurance. The law protects me if I remain ignorant as to what I'm carrying, which I was. If you really want to punish someone, it will have to be the person who hired me to take that equipment to Ladrona in the first place. Are you queer?"

Bauwerji furrowed her brow and tried not to show she was thrown by the question. "To punish those who hired you, I would have to know their names."

"And that information is protected under the Covenant Act. I am not at liberty to reveal the identity of my clients to anyone, even the Aphelion Project. But I would really like to know if you're interested in female companionship. Most Balanquin are pansexual, right? But I know from experience that a lot of them lean toward one gender or the other."

Bauwerji stood up. "If you're not interested in helping us, then there's no need for this to continue." She almost left, but then she added, "Regardless of gender, I'm not particularly fond of interspecies fraternization."

"So you've never been with a non-Balanquin."

"I've..." She sighed and looked away; her hesitation had already provided enough of an answer.

Cicero smiled. "Let me take you to dinner."

"No." She opened the door. "There will be a guard outside. If you choose to be helpful, he will get in contact with me."

A few days later, the *Sastruga* was cleared and permitted to leave. Bauwerji was surprised when she went to the pavilion and saw Cicero sitting outside one of the Balanquin restaurants with a plate of *shauv* in front of her. The meal was only half-eaten, and the Human was definitely daunted by the idea of finishing. Bauwerji ordered a glass of *ch'ko* and carried it over. She poured half the contents over Cicero's plate and then sat down.

"It's more palatable with the sauce."

Cicero smiled sheepishly. "It wasn't terribly bad without it."

"I've never met a Human able to stomach it dry. There's no

shame in using the seasoning. I think it tastes better with the sauce, to be honest." She looked at the half-eaten plate. "I got a very comprehensive lesson in obscure Ladronis religious ceremonies today."

"Is that so?" She tried a bite of her food with the sauce and gave an approving nod. "What brought that up?"

"You did. During the interrogation you mentioned that you had been hired to deliver this contraband to a temple."

Cicero narrowed her eyes and pretended to think. "Did I?"

"So I brought it up with Ephor Wison, our envoy to Ladrona. I described what we found on your ship and told her where you claimed to be going. She said there's a very small sect on the lower landmass of her planet. They use that equipment to add to the Great Chorus. The larger governments think the music they produce is disharmonious, or something to that effect, so they banned it. The argument could be made that, while you were breaking the letter of the law, you were doing something that was essentially, morally right."

"Hm. I mean, that certainly sounds plausible."

Bauwerji said, "At any rate, we couldn't prove malicious intent. Your ship has been cleared for release for over three hours. I would have thought you'd be halfway to your next confidential job by now." She reached across the table and picked off a piece of the *shauv*. She popped it into her mouth and chewed. A bit spongy still. She added some more sauce.

"You weren't the only one thinking about our encounter in the interrogation room. I thought maybe I'd given you the impression I was only interested in you as an exoticism. I didn't want to have dinner with you just because you were Balanquin. You're a tough, high-ranking officer on a station where your people make up... what, five percent of the population?"

"Three," Bauwerji said. "On a good day."

Cicero said, "I'm in a profession where ninety-nine percent of the people I deal with have never seen a Human before. I get treated like... well, I think you can imagine how I get treated. I was inspired when I saw you. I wanted to know more about you. I only brought it up in a romantic context because I... well... because you're also really gorgeous."

Bauwerji fought the smile, but it spread across her face anyway.

"What did you say your first name was?"

"Bauwerji. Most non-Balanquin can't say it properly, so they just call me Bowery."

Cicero said, "But that's not your name. Say it again? A little slower."

"Bah-wahr-j-yee."

Cicero repeated it. Bauwerji corrected the pronunciation at the end, the complex "-rji" suffix that gave so many races trouble.

"Bauwerji," Cicero said.

"That's close."

Cicero shrugged. "I guess I'll have to practice. Over dinner?"

"You don't give up."

"No. Not easily."

Bauwerji sighed and closed her eyes. "I suppose one meal would be fine."

Cicero grinned. "Fantastic."

Years later, Bauwerji was running over the much different conversation they'd just had. Cicero wasn't just saying 'until next time.' She was saying a final goodbye, just in case it had to be their last. Maybe she was anxious about the current climate. Maybe she thought the Wakerran would show up and lay waste to the station before the *Sastruga* came back. Or maybe she was going to do something incredibly stupid.

She was aware of someone moving to stand beside her. She knew without looking that it was Admiral Reshef.

"The *Sastruga* is away, ma'am. Captain Drayton gave seventeen hours as an estimated time of return."

"Excellent. Keep me apprised." Indira remained where she was.

"Was there something else?"

"I don't know, Bauwerji. Was there?"

Bauwerji started to deny it, but she sighed. "Just concerned, ma'am. About the general state of things."

"Understandable. It's a very stressful time. But no matter how busy things get, if you need to talk, my office door is open."

"Thank you."

Bauwerji felt comforted by Indira's offer. One thing she'd never had during any of the other conflicts she'd fought was a commanding officer she could trust. She knew she could be honest, open, and vulnerable with the admiral without sacrificing her respect. Joining the Quay had been her only option at the time. Now she was certain it had saved her life. Being part of the station's crew gave her a purpose, yes, but it also gave her a family she could count on in moments of strife.

She was moments from surrendering, from going to Indira's office for a nice long conversation about Cicero, when her communicator chimed.

"This is XO Crow."

"Officer Crow," a male voice responded. "This is Constable Merspeth from the detention center. It's the Sau mercenaries we took into custody from the Wakerran ship. They're... they're all asleep, ma'am."

Bauwerji frowned. "It may be their sleep cycle, Constable."

"No, ma'am, you don't understand. They all just... lost consciousness."

She was moving toward the lift. "All at the same time?"

"We checked the surveillance logs. The same time, down to the second."

Bauwerji signaled to Indira. "I'll be right down." The Admiral hurried from her office and met Bauwerji at the lifts. She explained what she had just heard.

Indira said, "Sau don't have mutual sleep cycles, do they?"

"Not that I'm aware of. To be fair, I'm not exactly an expert in Sautoriau biology." The lift arrived. "Do we have one of those aboard, by chance?"

"I'll check with the resident biologists, but I wouldn't be too hopeful. I'll check while you're in the detention center."

Bauwerji nodded and stepped into the lift. A few minutes later she was delivered to the holding cells, where Merspeth was waiting for her. She started walking toward the cells, and Merspeth filled her in as he fell into step beside her.

"The mercenaries were processed, numbered, and locked in their cages at fifteen past the hour. The guard on duty noticed the lack of movement. We checked the monitors after we established every single prisoner was asleep."

Bauwerji said, "Were any non-Sau prisoners affected?"

"No, ma'am. We have an Occamian and a Human incarcerated and they're both still wide awake. And everyone on duty is conscious as well."

Bauwerji had reached the first cell with an affected prisoner. He was sitting at the desk next to his bed, slumped forward with his head on the table and one arm dangling by his side. Bauwerji continued on to the next cell, where the Sau seemed to have fallen while standing in the middle of the room.

Merspeth said, "If you have any theories, ma'am, I would be

open to hearing them."

Bauwerji shook her head slowly. "If there are four people operating as one entity called the Socigines, then it stands to reason they're linked somehow. Telepathically would be my guess. If that is the case, then it stands to reason the Socigines linked themselves to the Sau mercenaries as a way to keep them in check. Easy to stop a mutiny if you're pulling the puppet strings of the people in your employ. She might have cut the strings to prevent any of them from talking to us."

Merspeth said, "But could she do that while she was unconscious?"

"Maybe there was a timed delay. If she didn't send them any signals after... what, twelve hours? Less? Then the failsafe kicked in and they all just went to sleep." Her communicator chimed again. She resisted the urge to sigh as she activated it. "XO Crow."

"Bauwerji, this is Dr. Littlefoot. I thought you would want to know our guest has woken."

"How long ago?"

"She was playing possum for a while. Ah, feigning sleep. But her vital signs indicated she was alert, and she gave up the ruse when we confronted her. I would say she's been conscious for fifteen minutes."

Bauwerji looked at Merspeth. "Fifteen minutes?"

He checked his watch and nodded. The Sau mercenaries had all passed out fifteen minutes ago. "Is she still being exposed to the knockout gas?"

"Yes, ma'am. But it would appear she's developed a resistance to it."

"Fantastic," Bauwerji muttered. "I'll be up as soon as I can. I want to talk with her again."

Merspeth stopped her from walking away. "Ma'am... what do you suggest we do?"

"Do?" She looked at the unconscious Sau. "We are currently hosting a prisoner from a race we know nothing about, and we just discovered she's a powerful telepath with the ability to take out a dozen people over a distance of half the station. We have no way of stopping her, and as of right now we have no way of knocking her out or rendering her helpless. You can think up ways out of this mess and tell me if you come up with anything."

"Yes, ma'am. Will do."

She sighed and pushed a hand through her hair as she walked

back to the lift. It was time to have another conversation with the Socigines. Her hand went to the bandaged wound on her side and hoped this talk led to less bloodshed.

CHAPTER TWENTY-TWO

CORDWAINER WAS in the lab, hands flat on the table and hir head bowed. The results of their examination on the Socigines was in front of hir. Ze had looked over them and also examined the schematics of the Roadblock technology to determine if it would be possible to do what Admiral Reshef proposed. Based on Captain Drayton's testimony, ze believed it could. The rock allegedly contained the genetic building blocks that had evolved into every known race. It was a pure sample. If someone got their hands on that, they could compare it to the sample of each race as they existed now. Separate out the differences and one would have a weapon that targeted only Balanquin, or only Humans, et cetera and so on. The rock would make it viable to use on a planetary scale.

Ze noticed hir hands were trembling, so ze curled them into fists and flexed hir forearms to stop the tremors. The door opened behind hir and Cordwainer turned to see Jocia standing in the doorway.

"Hello, Dway."

Cordwainer offered her a weak smile. "Jocy. I was expecting Officer Crow."

"Are you sharing yourself with her?"

"No. No one else." They embraced and ze kissed the side of Jocia's head. "I called her because our guest has awoken. She will be here soon. But I am very glad to see you, my love."

"You sound distraught." She leaned back and put her hand on the back of Cordwainer's head, below the line of hir charcoal-gray hair. "What do you need from me?"

"A promise." Ze looked at the reports again. "I don't know what to do, Jocia. The Socigines could create extinction-level events with this weapon. In a year Humans could be a bad memory. The Ladronis could only exist in history books. But if I do this, if I am instrumental in creating something so heinous, how could you ever be with me again?"

Jocia dropped her hand to Cordwainer's shoulder. "Darling, is that what you're concerned about?"

Ze faced hir lover but refused to meet her eyes. "Your people are pacifists. It's bad enough you fell in love with someone from another race, let alone one known for our aggressive tendencies. But I would be giving the Aphelion Project the means to cause genocide. How could you possibly still be with me after I'm a party to that sort of atrocity?"

"Because I adore you, Cordwainer." She moved her hands to Cordwainer's cheeks. "Ladronis abhor violence and causing injury to others, it's true, but it goes deeper than that. We're not automatons who see everything in black and white. If you were to strike me in the face, I would dodge or block your hand. If you persisted, I would perhaps shove you away from me while retreating. We believe in doing as little harm as possible. It's not always possible to do no harm. I believe you Human doctors take an oath to that effect."

Cordwainer said, "It's a little different."

"Regardless. Whatever you do, it's not coming from your heart or your soul. You're not lashing out and causing death from a place of anger."

"I'm just providing the means for it to be done."

Jocia thought for a moment. "Millions of years ago, ancestors on both our planets found a sharp rock and fashioned a grip for it. They sharpened the edge on other rocks until it could pierce skin with a single jab. They used it to hunt animals for their food. They killed to stay alive. You're doing this to keep us alive. And just like those first bipeds, you're not to blame for what is ultimately done with your creation. I have heard your part of the Great Chorus, and I know it is true and good." She kissed the corners of Cordwainer's mouth. "You don't have to worry about me, Cordwainer. Whatever happens, I will be with you when it is all over."

"Thank you, Jocia."

"Of course. I owe you my life." She grinned. "They brought me here after I lapsed into a coma on my trip here. I was so unprepared for the silence once we left our solar system. If you hadn't known to give me back my music..."

"Someone else would have thought of it eventually."

Jocia shook her head. "No one else on the station had studied our people closely enough to know how vital music was to us. You brought me back with a song. And I asked your name, and you said Cordwainer Littlefoot. It was more than beautiful... it was musical. I had never met a Human before, and the first one I encountered saved my life and had a name I could sing forever."

Cordwainer actually chuckled. "I remember the song you wrote for me. I was so touched." That night they kissed for the first time. Cordwainer remembered awkwardly explaining the fact ze was gender-neutral and what that meant for intercourse. Jocia had been so tender and understanding. She let Cordwainer take the lead just to ensure nothing went farther than ze was comfortable with. It ended up being the best sex ze had ever had.

Ze brought Jocia's hands to hir lips and kissed the knuckles. "You have successfully calmed my nerves. *Voquay.*"

"You're very welcome," Jocia said. "Come to me when this is all over. We can bathe together."

Cordwainer had initially been put off by how much time hir Ladronis lover spent underwater. They weren't amphibious, but they soaked whenever they could. Now it felt odd to lounge in a chair or on a couch when ze knew ze could be in a tub.

"With luck, this will all be resolved soon." Ze nodded toward the door, where Bauwerji had just arrived with a group of security officers. "The Socigines is in the same room as before."

Bauwerji nodded and continued deeper into the med center. "Stay out here."

Cordwainer watched as Bauwerji led the security officers away. "You don't have to stay with me for this."

Jocia gripped Cordwainer's hand. "There's nowhere I have to be. Believe it or not, the Aphelion Project doesn't want a pacifist hanging around their scheming sessions. Besides, I have a task to accomplish here. The mental well-being of the woman I love. If there's anything I can do for you to ease the stress, let me know."

Cordwainer squeezed her hand, wondering how ze had gotten so lucky in love, and looked down the corridor. Hopefully there was still a way to peacefully conclude their newest first contact, but at the moment the possibilities seemed to be dwindling.

The isolation room holding the Socigines was originally designed to quarantine crews of incoming ships. It was absolutely secure and completely cut off from the rest of the station to prevent accidental exposure to any viruses or virus-carrying vermin that might be brought in. Apparently the seals weren't tight enough to prevent the Socigines from reaching out with her mind. Bauwerji approached alone, signaling the security officers to remain near the door.

The Socigines was still in the carrier they'd used to remove her from the ship, but the top half of the shell was removed. It had been tilted so someone standing in front of the cell could see her, and vice versa. She was strapped down by both arms and across the chest. Another strap went around her skull to keep her head from lolling. She looked groggy, but she was definitely conscious. A smile slid across her face.

"Bauwerji Crow. I'm surprised. Many species wouldn't have recovered from a cut at all, let alone this quickly."

"I had a good doctor. And ze's the same one keeping an eye on you. If we get tired of having you around, ze can make it look accidental."

The Socigines laughed weakly. "I also have to admit I'm surprised you were able to keep me unconscious for so long. You had an opportunity to speak with my soldiers before I eliminated them. I hope they didn't give away too many of my secrets."

Bauwerji crossed her arms over her chest. "We need to talk about how to make you go away without any unnecessary bloodshed."

"There will be bloodshed no matter what the outcome," the Socigines said. "We don't aim to defeat you. Our purpose is your eradication. You occupy a small quadrant of the galaxy. You are a scourge. Your wars and your insignificant civilizations. You destroy your planets and then spread out into the universe to continue your reign of terror. We've seen this station before and the sea of detritus that orbits it. We've observed your planets become fuzzy with satellites and space trash. This endeavor is only our first gambit. If we fail, if we cannot acquire the stone to create our weapon, then we will take drastic measures. We will create enough supernovas to cleanse this entire area of space. Not a single Balanquin or Paisian or Ladronis will survive. It would leave your planets uninhabitable... but they're pretty much uninhabitable now."

Bauwerji said, "The universe is a big place. Why don't you just stay where you are, we stay here, and neither of us sees the other ever again?"

"The time will come when you're not content with your corner of the sea. Even the Humans have stretched out to the limits of their reach. You are dozens of light years from your home, are you not? One thing you all share is the urge to sprawl. To explore and colonize. The entire history of the Humans is built upon spreading out and obliterating the natives. It may take centuries, it might take millennia, but eventually they will wash upon our shores and try to take what is ours."

"So this is a preemptive strike," Bauwerji said.

"This is necessary. This is crushing a virus before it has time to become fatal. We are cutting out the cancer."

"You never answered my question. What will make you go away and leave us alone?"

"I didn't need to answer your question. There is nothing you can do to prevent this."

Bauwerji stepped closer to the field separating them. "We can destroy you and the other three bitches you brought with you."

The Socigines smiled wider. She seemed more alert now, and she clucked her tongue in disappointment. "Someone did speak. That is unfortunate. Well, it doesn't matter if you know they're coming. Now that I'm awake they hear me. They see me and feel my mind in theirs. They can see what I see, they know what I know, and they're going to be coming for you, Bauwerji Crow."

Bauwerji looked into the Socigines' eyes. "I hope so. I hope they can see this right now, because I'd like to say something to them. My name is Bauwerji Crow, and I'm the second in command of the Aphelion Project Station Quay. I was born on Pelorum. I was blown up at my graduation from the military academy, and I survived ten years living in the desert fighting an unwinnable war. I withstood countless violations from our 'saviors' before I finally drew first blood in that conflict as well. Our people turned the tide of the Cetidroi War. Coming after us only saves us the trouble of coming after you. You think we're a virus? That's fine. But this is our turf, and you don't get to take it with some kill-switch. If you want us gone, we're going to make you fight for it."

The Socigines laughed. "Strong words, Bowery."

Cordwainer appeared amid the soldiers. Bauwerji looked at hir, and ze gestured at the air above hir head, then pointed at the quarantine unit. Bauwerji nodded.

"Sweet dreams, Socigines. We'll see you when you wake up."

A new gas began filling the room. The Socigines breathed deep and closed her eyes. "Oh, my. Well, well."

Bauwerji watched until it was clear the alien woman was losing consciousness again. Once the Socigines' head had lolled forward against the strap holding it in place, Bauwerji walked to where Dr. Littlefoot was standing.

"I put together a new cocktail. It would likely kill any of us, but I diluted it enough that it should keep her unconscious for... well, a few hours. That's based on her reaction to the initial dosage and the original drug we used."

Bauwerji nodded distractedly. "She called me Bowery."

"I was under the impression that many call you that."

"Humans," Bauwerji said. "People who don't take the time to pronounce it correctly. But how would she know that? How would she know that specific mispronunciation?"

"I... I don't know."

Bauwerji said, "We know that she can reach out telepathically. We know that when she's awake the power is strong enough to knock out all of her men in one fell swoop. But what if it's still present when she's unconscious, just weaker? What if she wormed her way into the brains of whoever was at the docks when we brought her aboard?"

Cordwainer looked horrified at the thought. "You think she read our minds?"

"I don't know. I don't even know how to check. But right now, we need to keep a careful watch on anyone who was in close proximity to her."

"Even me?" Cordwainer asked.

"Even me," Bauwerji said. "We can't afford to have anyone compromised when her three friends show up. If anyone starts acting unusual, I want to know as soon as possible. Let me know if she wakes up again. And Doctor... the device we asked you to build..."

Cordwainer nodded. "Yes, I-I know. I'm working on it."

"Good. Once Cicero gets back with the stone, we're going to have to move quickly. There's no telling how much time we have before we need a working version of it."

Cordwainer said, "I'll do my best, but we won't have any way of testing it before we're in the heat of battle."

"Yes, we will," Bauwerji said. "You just knocked out the test subject."

CHAPTER TWENTY-THREE

CICERO TOOK the *Sastruga* along the curve of the Kuiper belt until the Quay was no longer on their sensors. When she was positive they wouldn't be spotted, she set them to drift and summoned the crew into the common area. By the time she arrived, everyone else had gathered around the table. She detoured to the kitchen and found a box of *ti so py*. They were small round candies, about the size of a thumbnail, and tasted like chocolate mixed with dirt and ash. Humans seemed to be the only species that hated the taste, so she kept the stuff around for the crew. She took her seat at the head of the table and put the box down in the center.

Irias reached into the box and took out a piece. "I assume you didn't summon us for a snack."

"No. We need to have an official vote about what we're going to do with the rock." She had lied about stashing it somewhere safe. It had been a calculated gamble in the event she needed to get her ship and crew away from the station without hurting anyone's feelings. The rock was actually stashed in one of the hollow support legs of the table they were currently sitting around. "We can turn right around and go back to the Quay, hand it over, and let whatever happens happen. Or I can suit up, go out, and chuck it into the Kuiper belt where no one will ever find it. You've all had a chance to think about this, but now we need a decision."

Aryana, who hadn't been present for the debate at the station, said, "I want to throw it out. I saw what it did to the Karezz man. Giving anyone the ability to do that to a whole species is just wrong."

Irias said, "I tend to agree. I don't like the idea of arming anyone."

"We've armed people before," Enatel said. "The difference is that now we know about it."

Sery said, "And we'll be directly affected by this. If the Wakerran aren't stopped, they'll wreak havoc on this sector. Who knows how many will die? What if we had something like this when the Cetidroi attacked? Thousands of lives could've been saved. The space around the Quay could be clear of debris. This is a chance to end the war before it can begin."

Zennes said, "So we combat them by creating the very weapon they want to build? Right now it's a hypothetical threat. If we take this rock back to the Quay, we bring it one step closer to reality."

"Presumably this isn't the only fragment out there," Cicero said. "The Wakerran might end up with the weapon anyway. This rock may be the Aphelion Project's only chance of leveling the playing field."

Kela had remained silent through the debate, but she finally spoke up. "We can't argue hypotheticals. We have absolutes. We have the stone. The Wakerran are coming. Admiral Reshef is counting on this plan. If we take it away, we leave the Quay defenseless until they come up with another defense. And if they're not able to think of anything to fight back..." She shrugged. "There are infinite possibilities about what may happen in the future. But the course we're on now, our options are handing over this stone or leaving the Quay to be destroyed."

The crew fell silent.

Cicero said, "I vote we take the stone back."

"Aye," Zennes said.

Irias nodded. "Aye."

Around the table, everyone marked their agreement. Cicero crouched and reached under the table to disconnect the hollow leg. It was heavy with the weight of the stone within. Relatively speaking, when it came to space debris, the thing was minuscule. She thought of the impossibility of its discovery on some forgotten world, buried in silt and topsoil. And then the procession of hands it had to pass through before it was delivered to her by a Karezz trader.

"The man who died," she said suddenly. "The man who brought

this to us. What was his name?"

Everyone looked at someone else, blank looks passing between everyone. Cicero remembered him mentioning it on the way back to the ship, but her mind had been on other things.

"Fine. To whoever he was, in his honor, we will take this back to the Quay and give them a fighting chance against our latest enemy."

Cicero dismissed the crew back to their stations. Kela followed Cicero to the bridge and took a seat at the sensor display.

"We are doing the right thing, aren't we?" Cicero asked as she entered the station's coordinates.

"I don't know if there is a right thing," Kela admitted. "In a kill or be kill situation, you only do what must be done and hope you can live with yourself afterward. Giving the stone to Admiral Reshef is a choice I think we can live with."

Cicero said, "I hope you're ri~"

Kela interrupted her. "Company." She swiveled her chair to face the sensors fully. "They're right on the cusp of our range."

Cicero said, "Identifiers?"

"It matches the Wakerran ship that attacked us earlier."

"Communications?"

"We're too close to the Kuiper belt. Too much interference to cut through. We could move out away from it, but it would make the trip back to the Quay even longer."

Cicero cursed under her breath. "We can't afford to waste the time. Don't bother coming about. Just turn the engines and push us backward. The second we're within radio range, send them a blast to know what's going on."

"Full reverse blow. Dangerous..." Kela said, but she was already complying with the order. "The entire trip back to the Quay?"

"If you can see an opportunity to whip around without losing speed, take it. But otherwise, yeah."

"Dampeners aren't going to like that."

Cicero turned on the intercom. "Everyone hold on tight. We're about to have a very rough ride." She looked at Kela. "Progress of the Wakerran ship?"

"They're moving slow. If we push, we'll be able to get back to the station in time to warn them."

"Go, then."

She was thrown forward as Kela accelerated, but she caught the arms of her chair before she fell to the floor. Something clattered in the body of the ship. Guilt was overwhelming her; she had wasted time Dr. Littlefoot could have been using on the weapon. If she'd skipped the debate and the vote... but then she wouldn't be certain she had her crew's support. And on the positive side, by being so far outside the Quay's sensor range meant that they'd seen the incoming Wakerran ship long before anyone at the Quay would have.

She just had to pray the warning was delivered in time to make a difference.

Bauwerji was in the pilothouse, pacing up and down the center aisle between the wells for want of anything better to do. She felt in her heart that she hadn't seen the last of Cicerone Drayton, but she couldn't shake the fear. On Pelorum there were ceremonies, rituals that bonded one soul to another. She didn't know if Cicero would be amenable to partaking in one, but she regretted that she'd never asked. Cicero, the thief. Cicero, the Human. Cicero, the conniving and dishonest smuggler. A woman who looked at Bauwerji, the soldier, the terrorist, the fugitive, and saw a kindred spirit. They were more than the crimes they had committed. She doubted she would ever meet anyone she loved more or who could understand her better.

A yeoman said, "Officer Crow, incoming message on the emergency bandwidth. It has the *Sastruga*'s call sign."

Bauwerji ignored the fact her heart had just leapt into her throat and feigned calm. "That was quick. What's their ETA?"

"She didn't specify, but... *stalif*, they're coming in quick. And... backwards."

"What?" Bauwerji said. "Open the channel." She heard the chime. "Cicero, what the *stalif* are you doing?"

"Wakerran ships, Bauwerji. I'm sending you their coordinates and bearings right now. They're coming slow, but they'll get there right behind us. Throw up your defenses *now*, Bauwerji, right now."

"Do as she says," Bauwerji ordered as she opened her communicator. "Admiral Reshef, high alert. We have a report that a Wakerran ship is incoming."

Moments before the alarms began sounding, the lift delivered Selina Rogers to the pilothouse. Bauwerji grunted quietly when she saw the doors closing behind the Acapsian ambassador; the lockdown would prevent her from leaving.

"Miss Rogers, I'm afraid you have to find a place to sit down and be quiet until this crisis is over. We could secure you in one of the empty offices—"

Selina snapped, "Shut up, Bauwerji!"

Bauwerji's attention was momentarily diverted. Selina, like almost every other Acapsian she'd met, was the epitome of calm, unflustered reserve. But now Bauwerji could see that Selina's hair was unkempt. Her face was beet red, and her eyes were wide enough that Bauwerji could see the blues around her irises. She was trembling, her hands curled into fists at her sides. Admiral Reshef had come out of her office and was watching the standoff with concern.

"We don't have time for this," Bauwerji said. "Whatever is wrong with you, we can discuss it when things are a bit less hectic."

"No, I don't think we can." She brought her hand up, and Bauwerji could see blood dripping from her palm onto the cuff of her sleeve. "I'm supposed to kill you. This voice in my head keeps telling me to kill you. And I... I've been able to stop myself so far. But I don't know how much longer I can hold back. The longer I wait, the stronger the urges g-get. I tried to stop myself. I did."

By now, a handful of yeomen had abandoned their stations to surround Selina. Bauwerji could hear another directing Cicero through the fleet of debris. Any minute now, they would have a Wakerran ship on their doorstep.

"I don't know if I'll hurt anyone else if they try to stop me," Selina said, "but I think... I think they should try. I think they should try very soon..."

She was tackled from behind, and then the soldiers piled on. Bauwerji moved forward and wrestled her weapon out of the confines of her jacket pocket. "Move," she said to a yeoman blocking Selina's neck. She pressed the barrel against the ambassador's neck and pulled the trigger. It was set to disable, and hopefully it would be strong enough to keep her unconscious until the threat passed.

Indira said, "What the hell was that all about?"

"Sorry, ma'am. I hadn't gotten a chance to debrief you fully." That was a lie. She'd been so distracted about Cicero's departure that she'd forgotten to tell the Admiral about what she'd discovered. "The Wakerran has telepathic abilities. Dr. Littlefoot and I speculated that she might have gotten her hooks in someone. Mentally. Took control. I guess we know who she picked. *Chau* knows why her, but... I guess... someone I wouldn't suspect? Someone I would let get close enough to hurt me." She shrugged and gestured for a yeoman to take her away.

"Officer Crow," another officer said. "The *Sastruga* is coming too fast. She's too close to slow down and she doesn't have the maneuverability to hit the docks flush. She's going to crash."

Indira called a warning to the docks to brace for the impact. Bauwerji stood up and watched on the screens as the *Sastruga* came at them like a bullet.

Bauwerji stood up slowly and tensed.

Indira said, "You know... it would be quite ironic if the station is destroyed by an accident moments before the Wakerran get here. They'd never find the stone in the wreckage. It would technically be a win."

Bauwerji couldn't help but laugh. "How Human of you, Admiral."

Whatever response Indira might have made was drowned out as Cicero's ship collided with the docks, sending a wave of tremors through the entire station. Bauwerji and Indira were knocked off their feet. The screens flickered blank seconds before the lights went out.

CHAPTER TWENTY-FOUR

THE SUN shone brightly overhead. She stood shoulder-to-shoulder with her fellow graduates; the four-hundred-and-eighty-second class to graduate from the Balanquin Military Institute. Her hair was braided to honor the four generations of women in her family who came before her, hands clasped behind her back and chin held high as the *opvoedor* read out the name of each student. In a matter of minutes, they would be released as full-rank ensigns in the protector elite.

Even in her dreams, she never saw the attack coming. It announced itself with a roar and a wave of heat against her back. In thirty seconds, half her graduating class was eradicated. The *opvoedors* on the stage was incinerated in the initial blast. The initial address echoed in Bauwerji's ears as she ran for cover: "Family. Friends. Prestigious Alumni. We are all gathered here today." Another blast destroyed the risers. Bauwerji saw bodies falling, clothes and skin burning as they hit the ground.

For the first time in two centuries, the Balanquin were at war. The opening salvo had left them defenseless. In the coming weeks, their shipyards would be targeted and destroyed. The Catarrh had spent years plotting and planning the best way to cripple their enemies before a single shot could be fired. Their patience had paid off.

A screaming alarm cut through the memories, waking her up

from where she had fallen. She was in the pilothouse, which was lit green by emergency lighting. She tasted blood in her mouth and turned her head to spit it out as she got back to her feet. The yeomen were either slumped in their seats or frantically speaking into headsets as the screens in front of them flickered. Bauwerji squeezed her eyes shut and then opened them wide so she could focus. Admiral Reshef's voice cut through the din.

"–defenses and life support are the priorities. Repair them first and we'll get to the other shit when we can."

Nerea Paisian nodded before the nanoids making up his body began breaking off into swarms to tackle the repairs. Bauwerji approached Indira from behind.

"What are your orders for me, ma'am?"

Indira looked at her. "Lords. Are you okay?"

"Fine." She touched her face and felt sticky blood on her cheek. "I don't exactly have time to stop by the infirmary and get patched up. Give me something to do."

Indira sighed, giving up the futile argument she had planned. "We lost all sensors and communication in the docks. If your friend survived that reckless stunt, go down there and escort the stone to the med center. I want Cordwainer to have it as soon as possible."

Bauwerji nodded and headed off. She took the time in the lift to wipe the blood from her face. She'd fought with worse injuries and had the scars to prove it. She'd gone up against a Catarrh squadron with two broken fingers and a cracked patella, and that was in the desert. Despite the current situation, the Quay was still temperature controlled. It would be easy.

Her destination was the pavilion. As soon as the alert sounded, all non-essential personnel should have remained where they were or found a safe haven. She exited the lift and looked down at the row of shops and delicatessens, glad to see they'd all complied. She began jogging toward the docks when she caught movement from the corner of her eye. She glanced to the side and saw Constable Heely running to intercept her.

"Constable," she said. "Have you been briefed on what's happening?"

Heely kept her hand flat as she swung her arm around, cutting the back of her hand against Bauwerji's throat. Bauwerji's forward momentum helped give the blow more strength. Her air was cut off as she fell flat on her back, coughing violently as she gripped her throat. Heely stepped over Bauwerji to straddle her body and bent down, wrapping her hands in her tunic to haul her up. Bauwerji threw a punch into Heely's stomach. The angle was wrong and the blow didn't deliver much pain.

"I've always regretted that I was never assigned to Pelorum. The fun I could've had with you." She twisted at the waist and hurled Bauwerji against the wall. Her shoulder hit hard enough to dent the metal, but she didn't have a chance to crumple to the ground. Heely was on her again, hoisting her up and slamming her back against the wall. Bauwerji's feet weren't touching the floor.

"You know I've never tasted a Balanquin? I'd prefer male, but I hear the ladies have parts that are serviceable. Is that true? You got a dick for me, Bowery?"

Bauwerji spit in the Karezz woman's face. Heely stepped back, let go of Bauwerji, and waited for her to fall forward before kneeing her in the stomach. Bauwerji gasped for air again as Heely grabbed a handful of her hair and hauled her through a doorway. As she tumbled, Bauwerji saw that it was an abandoned Human diner. Plates and glasses had fallen from the tables, and food was smeared over the tile by patrons attempting to flee to safer locales. Bauwerji hit the floor hard and looked back to see Heely looming over her in the darkness.

"This isn't you, Constable."

"Oh, it's me. I've been fighting the urge to do this for so long. In a few days, I won't have the chance. You're an endangered species, Bauwerji. As soon as the Wakerran get here, I'm going to hand over the stone. And they'll hand over Pelorum."

Bauwerji grunted and started to get up. "She got to you, too. The Socigines. She's in your head, Mara."

"I'm fully aware of that." She kicked Bauwerji down again. "I was so curious about her. When I looked into the pod, I could hear her offering me answers to all of my questions. The Aphelion Project neuters the Karezza. It treats us like their guard dogs. Cowed. Trained. Fenced in." She grabbed Bauwerji's hair again and forced her to stand up. She slammed Bauwerji against the counter. "But you know better than that, don't you? Balanquin know what the Karezza are capable of." She closed her fist around Bauwerji's throat and squeezed. "You know exactly what I'm going to do to you, isn't that right, little Balanquin?"

Bauwerji managed to nod. "I do. That's why I won't regret this."

She'd been gripping the shard tightly enough that blood was dripping down her hand. She had picked it up when she hit the ground, afraid she wouldn't have a chance to use it. For a moment she was afraid it would make her hand slip, but she managed to shove it into the soft meat of Heely's gut with no problem. Heely backed up, startled by the counterattack, and Bauwerji swung her other hand up. The serrated knife sank into Heely's shoulder and seated itself with a satisfying and sickening thump.

Heely rocked back on her heels. Bauwerji clenched her teeth and braced herself against the counter. She brought her foot up and kicked the plate shard, sinking it even deeper into Heely's body. Blood poured out of the other woman's mouth as Bauwerji used her fist to hammer the knife down to its hilt in Heely's shoulder. Heely took another step backward and slipped on some spilled food. She went down, and Bauwerji kicked a chair out of the way so Heely would land flat on the floor.

"I would've had to pull my punches if I thought the Socigines *jika* was in charge of you. Thanks for taking away my moral quandary."

Heely gasped for air, but Bauwerji wasn't interested in witnessing her death throes. She walked out of the deli and stepped back out onto the concourse. The first thing she saw was someone else running toward her, and she braced herself for a fight she knew she wouldn't win. She relaxed when she saw that it was Cicero. She was also bloody, her uniform blouse torn to reveal the blue-gray undershirt. She was cradling a wrapped bundle the size of a large baby against her stomach as she ran.

She slowed when she saw Bauwerji. "What the hell...?"

Bauwerji waved her to go on. "Threat neutralized. Go. Get the stone to Dr. Littlefoot."

Cicero picked up speed again. "Be safe."

"You too," Bauwerji said.

She watched Cicero disappear around a bend. She took a moment to consider her next course of action. Her orders were to escort the stone, but following that order would only slow Cicero down. The next best choice would be to confirm the docks were still salvageable. She used the rail to keep herself upright until she trusted her legs to support her on their own. Her feet shuffled a bit, and she gripped the rail tightly enough that she was afraid of denting the metal, but she continued onward.

"Bauwerji."

The voice came from her earpiece, mired in static and half-lost. But it was undeniably Cicero. "I'm here. You're fading, but I can hear you."

"Don't die. I've finally decided how much I'm willing to give up to be with you. So if you die now, it would be a really shitty thing to do."

Bauwerji smiled weakly. "I don't want you to give up anything. I just want you to be with me as you are, Cicerone."

"Whatever," Cicero said. "The point stands. Don't die, darling."

"I'll do my best. Some reckless asshole crashed her ship into the station."

"Yeah. I probably could've thought that through better, huh?"

Bauwerji grunted. "I will stay alive for you, Cicero."

"Then I'll do the same for you."

"You're breaking up. We'll speak later."

Cicero's farewell was lost in the next burst of static. Bauwerji ended the communication and descended carefully into the docks. The *Sastruga* had left some very obvious damage in its arrival; the four docking clamps on either side of the slip were twisted and bent in horrible angles. One had lost its diamond-shaped head completely. Dockworkers were frantically hurrying about to minimize the threat level. Bauwerji could see the shimmering wall of light that marked the end of atmosphere and the beginning of deadly space. They could survive a brief failure, but anything more than a few seconds would be catastrophic. She looked for someone to request a status update and decided everyone was too busy to waste time filling her in.

The *Sastruga* itself was heartbreaking to see. It rested at a horribly unnatural angle in its slip, tethered but only barely by the few cranes that were still intact. It was steaming, and the exterior plating was missing in several vital areas. Cicero's crew was out of the ship, some nursing injuries while others seemed more concerned about fixing their ship's damage.

Bauwerji decided there was nothing she could do but get in the way, but there was another option available to her. She ran through the sea of people, ducking one way to avoid a person and turning sideways so she could get around a machine, her eye always on her destination. A small private slip at the absolute end of the docks, a private berth where she was allowed to keep her personal ship, the *Biju Sprinter*. It was a Balanquin *bracijera*, the 'little ship that won the big war,' as Indira often called it. The ships were so small that Cetidroi weapons couldn't lock onto them. They were maneuverable enough to get up close and take out the weapon emitters. She could only hope the Wakerran had the same weakness.

It was also the ship that had, against all odds, carried her twenty-one hundred light years to safety after she fled her home planet. The Sprinter meant hope in the face of impossible odds, survival where everyone else could only see death and loss. It was a sleek needle, black with orange accents, a flared tail section. She activated the code that would wake up its systems and climbed inside.

Piloting a *bracijera* ship required lying on her stomach, legs clenched around the center saddle, hands extended out past her head. It felt as if she was wearing the ship when she flew, her hands manipulating the out-of-view controls as the movement of her body dictated the minute changes in trajectory.

Once the engines were warm, she opened a channel. "Officer Crow to Admiral Reshef."

"I'm here, Bowery. Give me good news."

She flexed her hands on the grips that would guide the ship. It was like slipping on an old glove. "You assigned a great crew to the docks. I couldn't get a sit-rep because everyone was moving too damn fast to get things up and running again."

"That's good, I suppose."

"And..." She hesitated to mention this, but Indira needed to know a crew member was gone. "I killed Constable Heely."

Silence from the other end. "You what?"

"Indira. She attacked me. She was being manipulated by the Wakerran, but she was in control of her actions. She tried to~"

"I can guess what she tried to do," Indira said softly. "Are you okay?"

"I'm... I'll be fine. I just wanted to tell you she wasn't going to be available."

"Right. Bauwerji, I'm sorry."

"Don't be. Don't think about it right now." She fired the engines.

Indira said, "What was that? Where are you?"

"I'm in the *Biju Sprinter*. I'm going to see what damage I can do to that Wakerran ship."

"Bauwerji~"

"Listen, Indira. If the worst happens... find Cicero. Tell her... tell her that... I'm... sorry I lied."

Indira said, "I will, Bauwerji. Godspeed."

"Thank you." She took a deep breath, closed her eyes to whisper a prayer, and disengaged from the slip. She was propelled backward through the force field and, once she was clear, swung her ship around to face the scattered field of broken ships. Beyond it, looming large but still hundreds of thousands of miles away, the Wakerran ship slid forward like an *ayyijatopac* in the reeds. Bauwerji locked eyes with the ship as if she could see its pilot through the bulkhead. Then she lowered her chin and set off for the first engagement in what she hoped and prayed would be the last war she ever fought.

CHAPTER TWENTY-FIVE

THE MED Center had been locked down since the impact, operating on emergency power that cast everything in a pale green glow. Cordwainer was running tests on the Roadblock tech to make sure there weren't any bugs to work out. Down the hall, near the Wakerran woman's cell, at least a dozen soldiers were standing guard in the event of a power failure. Cordwainer doubted the woman would be able to move under her own power even if the force field did collapse, but she appreciated the extra protection.

Jocia was pacing nervously. Every few minutes she would move to the screen and try to contact someone for an update, but it never responded to her tapping. When she walked over to it again, Cordwainer bit off a sigh.

"It's obviously broken."

"I know that, Dway."

"Then why do you keep trying?"

"Maybe they fixed it."

Cordwainer couldn't hold back hir sigh. "I believe they have more pressing concerns to deal with first, darling."

"What does it hurt to try?"

"Because you are making me anxious."

Jocia said, "At least you have a project to keep you occupied."

"Yes, I am very grateful for this doomsday weapon to keep my mind busy."

Jocia went to the sink and ran the water. She cupped her hands under the flow and closed her eyes. After a moment she brought her wet fingers up and touched the tips to her face. Small droplets rolled over her features before dripping off her chin. Other tributaries ran down her palm, under the cuffs of her gown. She lowered her hands and breathed in the scent of the water. It was different here than it was on Ladrona. Filtered and purified. She licked her lips.

"I'm sorry, Cordwainer."

"Don't be," ze said. "The stress... the not knowing. It's getting to me, too."

Jocia moved closer and began to reply, but she was startled by the door being flung open. She didn't think before she acted, lunging to stand between Cordwainer and the running Human who had just appeared. Jocia, who had spent her entire life dedicated to non-violence, threw out her arms in anticipation of stopping the attacker by any means possible, her heart thudding against her chest as she envisioned all the ways someone could hurt Cordwainer.

It was only a moment before she recognized Captain Drayton. The Human recoiled at the sight of an attacking Ladronis, pulling the bundle she carried tighter against her chest as her eyes widened in surprise more than fear. Cordwainer put a hand on Jocia's shoulder and gently urged her to one side.

"It's all right, Jocy. Thank you."

"I... was only afraid for you."

Cordwainer smiled. "I know, darling. I know."

Cicero held out the bundle to Cordwainer.

Jocia's breath caught in her chest as she realized what it was. "That's the stone? The... the piece from the beginning of the universe?"

"Not exactly," Cordwainer said as ze took it. "It's one of the fragments that seeded life in this corner of the galaxy. Hopefully there's enough genetic material left on it to use as a deterrent for the Wakerran." Ze looked at Cicero. "Admiral Reshef warned us that time is short. How close are they?"

Cicero said, "They're extremely close."

Cordwainer turned back to hir work. "Then I should get to work."

"You don't need me here for that, do you?" Cicero asked.

"No. Why? Where are you going?"

"There are two other Wakerran ships out there somewhere."

Jocia said, "You won't be able to leave. Admiral Reshef will never clear it."

"Then maybe I just won't ask Admiral Reshef. I'm not in her chain of command. You need the Karezza and Paisian fleets here to protect the Quay. You also need a pair of eyes out there making sure you don't get piled on." She went to the door but stopped just before she passed through into the corridor. "Look... it goes without saying that I don't want you saying anything to anybody about this. But... Bauwerji in particular. If Bauwerji comes looking for me, just say you don't know where I am. I made her a promise about something I'm not sure I can keep. But tell her I love her."

"She knows," Jocia said.

Cordwainer said, "But we'll tell her anyway."

"Thank you, Dr. Littlefoot. Ephor Wison. Good luck to you both." She tapped her knuckles against the door and then was gone in a flash.

"Reckless and foolhardy," Jocia said softly.

Cordwainer said, "Yes. They deserve each other."

Jocia grinned and touched Cordwainer's shoulder. Cordwainer had carefully unwrapped the stone to examine its craggy surface. To think of the potential horrors this simple rock could unleash made her shudder, and she squeezed her lover's shoulder in a show of support.

"Is there anything I can do?"

"Pray."

"As hard as I possibly can, darling."

Cordwainer took a deep breath, let it out slowly, and then ze got to work.

The docks were still hectic enough that Cicero knew she'd have no trouble launching without being noticed. Her crew was still standing around the ship like evacuees waiting to see the building they'd just fled collapse before their eyes. Kela saw Cicero coming and moved to meet her halfway. "Rough," she said in response to Cicero's unasked question. "Extremely rough. It would be the worst ride we'd ever taken. But it'll hold together."

Aryana joined them. "We'd vent atmosphere in a lot of places. But I can minimize the effect it would have on us by shunting it through unused portions of the ship. We'd have to be very careful about where we went and what doors we didn't open, but we could make it."

"Sensors?"

Enatel said, "Uh... how sensitive would you need them?"

"I want to follow the Wakerran energy signature back to where they came from."

He rubbed his chin and bared his teeth as he considered her request. "Yeah. That's a definite. We might have to be a bit tunnel vision about it. Staring straight ahead while ignoring behind us and to the sides."

Cicero said, "What would our top speed be?"

"Snail's pace," Aryana said. "The engines really didn't like being pushed backward like that. It's going to take everything I have to nudge them back up to a bare minimum."

"Do what you can. I have faith in you, Yana." She walked over to the crew with Kela and Aryana trailing her. "I don't necessarily need the entire crew for this job. I just need eyes and a few hands at the controls. So if anyone wants to stay behind, play it safe, there wouldn't be any judgment. Your place on the crew would still be there when we came back."

"If you come back," Zennes said.

"Right."

Enatel said, "All due respect, ma'am, but where exactly could we stay behind and play it safe? Here at the Quay, with a Wakerran ship bearing down on us? If I'm going to face death, it's going to be aboard the *Sastruga*, just like my wife always warned me."

Cicero smiled as the rest of the crew agreed with him. "Then okay. Climb aboard and buckle up. As an ancient Human once said, fasten your seatbelts. It's going to be a bumpy night."

The overhead lights came back on first, followed quickly by the yeomen getting back full control of their stations. Indira tried to find some relief in those facts, but she could only think about Bauwerji's confession. Heely was dead, murdered while attempting to assault the station's second-in-command. Who knew how many other people were under the Wakerran's control? Were there dozens of time bombs all around her just waiting to go off?

She looked at the screens. Three Paisian ships were hovering just beyond the debris field. Seven Karezza warships had also arrived and were lined up with three to port and four to starboard. The Wakerran vessel was now visible, but it was remaining at a discreet distance. She didn't know if they were waiting for the other two ships, or if the Socigines they had in custody was supposed to send a signal. Either way, every screen was filled with the promise of doom and another war.

"Ma'am," one of the yeomen said, "we have an energy signature near the docks. Someone is taking off without clearance."

"Could it be left over from Bauwerji's departure?" She crouched behind the man, remembering his name was Sior.

"No, ma'am. This is much larger. They're trying to hide themselves." His fingers danced across the control panel. "It's the *Sastruga.*"

"What the hell?" Indira muttered. "Can you open a channel?"

Sior began to shake his head. "Wait... yes. Possibly." He typed again. "They're trying to block any communications, but I can use the emergency channel override to punch a hole through."

Indira said, "Quick thinking, Yeoman. Remind me to put you up for a promotion when this is all over."

"Please don't, ma'am. I like my job too much."

She smiled. "A commendation, then."

"Thank you. Channel is open."

Indira said, "This is Admiral Reshef calling Captain Drayton. Can you please tell me what in the hells you think you're doing?"

"Trying to make up for breaking your station, Admiral. Leave this channel open for us and we'll tell you where the other Wakerran ships are and when you can expect them."

"Damn it, Cicerone..."

Cicero said, "We've all got to do our part, ma'am."

Indira rubbed one knuckle against her lip. There was no point in arguing or trying to make her turn back. They could have sent some towships to bring her back by force, but it wasn't as if they had soldiers to spare. "The Aphelion Project thanks you for your assistance, Captain Drayton. Consider any punitive measures for what you did to the Quay cleansed from your record."

"Thank you, Admiral."

"*Sahrah nahsiba*, Cicero."

"You need the luck more than I do."

"There's enough to go around. Besides, the Wakerran are nothing compared to what Bauwerji would do if she found out I let you leave."

Cicero laughed. "You may have a point there. Going mute, but I'll still be here if we find anything. *Sastruga* signing off for now."

Indira put a hand on Sior's shoulder. "Guide her through the wreckage, alert the Paisian and Karezza ships to let her through.

Monitor that channel and let me know if she provides any updates."

"Yes, ma'am."

She straightened and walked back down the aisle. She wanted to know how Cordwainer was doing with hir dreadful project, but she also knew giving constant updates would only delay it. She didn't know what the Wakerran were waiting for, but she was positive that their patience would run out sooner rather than later.

"We're clear of the debris field," Kela reported.

Cicero nodded to her and faced forward. "The other ships?"

"They're not reacting to us. Maybe because they think we're one of the wreckages that broke loose."

"A possibility," Cicero said.

"There's another ship out~ Captain, it's Bauwerji's Sprinter."

Cicero stood up and moved closer to the screen. "What? What the hell is she doing out there?"

"It looks like she's heading directly toward the Wakerran ship."

"Bauwerji, you stupid stubborn *faihjoh*..." She put her hand on the corner of the screen where a small yellow dot indicated the ship of the woman she loved.

Bauwerji looked at the screen as another ship broke away from the debris field and set a course away from the blockade. She almost ignored it, focusing entirely on the Wakerran ship ahead of her, but something clicked in her mind and made her recognize it for what it was. The size and shape matched. The trail of heat and energy in its wake indicated near-critical levels of damage... without a doubt, it was the *Sastruga*.

"Cicerone, you stupid stubborn *bijesan*..."

She turned off her communicator in case Cicero was trying to talk her into going back, but the *Sastruga* took a different bearing. Bauwerji couldn't waste the brainpower trying to think of what she was doing. She focused on her mission, which began and ended at getting herself to the Wakerran vessel. It had looked huge from the docks, but each passing second proved just how massive it truly was. She scanned its hull for any weaknesses she could exploit, specifically weapons ports she could disable. That was how they'd finally defeated the Cetidroi.

Unfortunately, it seemed as if the Wakerran weren't going to be quite as accommodating. She pulled up under its curved belly and let her sensors pass across the expanse. Nothing. She picked up a few hatches which she assumed would open in the event of a firefight, but there was nothing she could exploit with the Sprinter's weapons. She pushed her right foot back, picking up speed as she neared the stern of the enemy vessel. The engines were exposed. But there was no weapon on her ship that could do any damage to them.

No weapons on the ship... but the ship itself?

She tightened her grip on the controls. "One last hurrah," she said. "We said this would be our last war, Biju. Might as well make it count. Add a Wakerran vessel to the remnant fleet." She wet her lips and plotted a course that would bring her around to fly directly into the engines. She didn't know what it would do, necessarily, but there was no technology that could survive a kamikaze run like that. She had her finger poised to enact her flight plan when all of her systems died. Sensors went dark, the running lights flickered and left her in the dark, and she could feel the air grow still.

Her ship was dead, but it was still moving. Backward. She lifted her head and looked through the canopy to see the Wakerran ship growing large again.

"Shit. They hooked me."

She jabbed at her communicator and, in a last ditch effort, grabbed for her ejector. She would have preferred dying in the vacuum to whatever the Socigines had in mind, but it was no use. It seemed that she was going to be getting a front-row seat to the first battle of their new war.

CHAPTER TWENTY-SIX

THE BIJU *Sprinter* was towed into the hangar bay of the Wakerran ship, where Bauwerji could see a squadron of small fighter ships waiting to be sent out. Sautoriau mercenaries were also waiting for her in three rows of three. It was quite a response; she wondered if she should feel honored that the Wakerran considered her such a threat that she sent so many guards to escort her.

The ship landed with a quiet thump, and the Sau surrounded it with their weapons drawn. She was ordered to surrender herself without delay or belligerence. The canopy slid back and she pushed herself up into a crouching position on the saddle. One of the Sau climbed up to secure her wrists before hauling her out of the cockpit.

"If you do anything to my ship, wait until I'm dead. Otherwise, I'm coming after you."

The Sau looked over her bloody, bruised form and hissed through his teeth. "I doubt we'll have to wait long."

She was limping when they led her out of the hangar. She was covered in sweat, and something was dripping down her face. Whether it was blood or sweat, she couldn't tell. The Sau enclosed her in a circle, all of them at least a head taller than her, all of them armed to the teeth. Whenever she was too slow, they nudged her forward with a clawed hand or the butt of their gun. She shuffled her feet, the right one dragging because it wouldn't step properly.

That could be a problem in the future. If she had a future.

The corridors were identical to the last Wakerran ship she'd been on. She had memorized the layout the first time, so she didn't have to expend her attention to remember the way back to the hangar. Instead she tried to think of a way to still be alive in ten minutes, to need the escape route. Currently the only thing she could fathom was if Indira activated the weapon and wiped out every Sau aboard. She could take care of the Socigines herself, if necessary. Almost as if to mock that idea, she felt a flash of pain from the cut on her side from her first encounter with the Wakerran people.

They arrived at the bridge, where she saw the first difference from the first ship: this Socigines had a vast control center built up around what looked to be a throne. She was svelte and gorgeous, her legs folded up underneath her. She smiled when Bauwerji was brought into the room but kept her dark-eyed gaze locked on the screen in front of her.

"I could have just destroyed your ship and moved on."

"Thanks for choosing the personal touch," Bauwerji said.

The Socigines grinned wider. "I know I look different from you, but we have met before. Twice now. I almost feel as if I'm about to wage war against you, Bauwerji Crow."

She started to respond, but a thought occurred to her. "Telepathy, right? That's how you're connected to the other Socigines?"

"No," she said, "but it's close enough for you to comprehend, so if you wish to call it that..."

"And you can only invade someone's mind if they let you in?"

The Socigines said, "As you can tell by the fact I'm not making you kill yourself right now."

Bauwerji stepped away from her Sau escorts. "I want you to think about something. Your twin, or double, or however you think of yourselves, is our prisoner right now. She's locked in a cell with at least a dozen weapons aimed at her. Will you feel it when she dies? Never mind. I don't care. It doesn't matter. What does matter is that she managed to take control of two people on our station. One is dead and the other is in custody."

"Foot soldiers. What do I care?"

"You care because of what that represents. You think you can wipe us out with some superweapon? Good luck. You might take out a species. You might defeat a planet. A few billion lives lost. It would be a tragedy. But you know what else it would be? A call to arms. Every species in this quadrant would rain down hellfire on your heads."

The Socigines smirked. "Well... except the Ladronis."

"Wanna bet?" Bauwerji stepped closer to the throne. The Sau brought up their weapons, but Bauwerji ignored them. "I'm giving you permission to look inside my head, because I want you to fully appreciate what I'm about to say. Go on. Go way back. Know who is speaking to you. My name is Bauwerji Cro~"

"Daughter of Omjia Crow, Kellen Crow, and Jania Crow. Granddaughter of We'quean Crow. Great-granddaughter of~"

She blinked away the memory. For a moment she had been back there, standing in the clay dome of the *opvoedor's* study. She looked at the Socigines and focused on another memory from about a year later, on a warm mid-year night, when the heat lingered long after the sun had set. In the middle of the wildflowers, when she

crouched and used her blackened fingernails to pluck a wild-haired flower from its stem. Bochelm, the girl who had been racing ahead in the moonlight, came jogging back. Her skirts swayed around her hips like part of the night that had broken free to clutch at her body. She crouched and pushed her hair out of her eyes. Bauwerji held up the flower and touched Bochelm's nose with it. Bochelm waved her hands, ducked her chin against her chest, and sneezed.

"You sound like an ardilja."

"I do not." She rubbed her nose vigorously with the back of her hand.

Bauwerji snickered and twisted the stem of the flower between her finger and thumb. "It's okay. I think they are very cute."

Bochelm pulled her lips back to reveal her upper teeth, wrinkling her nose and crossing her eyes in a mockery of an ardilja. She curled her fingers and made chittering noises. "Am I? Maybe I am! I am a nasty little pest hiding in your trees!"

"You are more of a pest than a whole clot of ardilja!" She threw the flower at Bochelm and stood, turning to flee. Bochelm pursued, but her skirt hindered her ability to sprint. The space between them grew until finally Bochelm stopped and put her hands on her knees.

"Bauwerji! Please, don't leave me behind!"

Bauwerji stopped and turned. She looked at her friend, the desperation in her eyes, and jogged back to her. "I was only playing."

"I know." She touched Bauwerji's cheeks. "Don't leave me."

"I won't. Not ever." She tilted her head and touched her lips to her friend's. Bochelm collapsed against her, and Bauwerji opened her mouth.

She felt herself growing against her uniform trousers, aroused in a way she never had been with her male partners. Bochelm felt it against her hip and moaned into Bauwerji's mouth.

They made love there, standing, their clothing pushed aside rather than removed. Bauwerji wept when she came, and tears rolled down her cheeks when her best friend knelt in the mud and took her erect clitoris into her mouth. It was glorious, more than she had ever hoped for. She opened her eyes and looked up at the stars as she climaxed against Bochelm's tongue, knowing that her destiny was in the stars and in the love of a beautiful woman.

She flinched away from the memory, the unexpected pain at remembering her lost love. Bochelm had survived the initial Catarrh attack, but they lost track of each other soon afterward. Bauwerji assumed she was dead, but she had no way of knowing for certain. Her heart ached but she focused on the Socigines that had just experienced the same moment.

"A little girl, barely in her twos, picking flowers in the moonlight. So simple. We thought we had known hardship. We didn't know a goddamn thing. We didn't know what fear was. We didn't know how far we could be pushed and still survive." She took another step closer. "Look again. Look ahead five years and see what that girl was doi–"

Don't see him as a person, she told herself. If you see them as people, you're done. You can't do what needs to be done and your people die. Your people fucking die, so stop crying and do what needs to be done. She was speaking out loud, she realized, and she pinched her lips shut so she wouldn't get blood in her mouth. The Catarrh lay underneath her, the bone of his skull-plate shattered. His teeth were around him on the ground. Bauwerji realized she was crying.

She pulled upward on the knife and peeled away another strip of muscle. Her hands were trembling when she dumped it in the upturned helmet. Meat was meat. Catarrh meat was stringy and tasted odd, but it was protein and she needed protein. All her people needed a proper meal. She swallowed her bile and cut into the soldier's body again, fresh tears washing the dirt from her face.

Don't see him as a person, she told herself.

"That was my first war," Bauwerji said. "What do you want to see next? My Karezz supervisor telling me to take my jumpsuit off so he could fuck me from behind while I worked on the Sprinter? How about when my ship was skimming close enough to the Cetidroi warships that I could see the rivets holding it together? I could feel the heat coming off of it. How about the smell of burning flesh because I stood by and watched as a Catarrh transport burned? I'd jammed the doors. I lit the incendiary. And I burned seven men alive. Or how about this one?"

Bochelm and Bauwerji lay together on a high platform, nestled against the ceiling of their room. They had just finished making love. Bauwerji was still sore, her thighs still wet. Her hair was loose, the braids meant to honor her family not yet tied. Bochelm asked, "Where would you like to be stationed?"

"With you."

Bochelm kissed Bauwerji's nipple. "No. Seriously. Where?"

"Somewhere quiet. I would like to be stationed in a tall tree somewhere. Taller than all the others around it so I have a carpet of green under my feet. And at night, I can see the moons and the stars and I can smell wildfires in the distance."

"Sounds peaceful."

"Mm. Somewhere peaceful. A quiet place." She nuzzled Bochelm's hair. "That would be paradise. Especially if you are there with me."

"I never got my quiet place," Bauwerji said gravely. "Look at me. My side is barely stitched shut. I'm covered with blood. I think I might've broken my leg, and I don't even know where. My hand... I cut open my hand on a broken dish I used as a shiv. I have killed. I've slaughtered people. The girl who dreamed about spending her entire life in a tree killed someone less than an hour ago because she was in my way."

The Socigines was no longer smiling. "What does any of this have to do with our current stalemate?"

"Because I want you to know exactly what you're doing. You're a scout, right? You're supposed to report back to the Wakerran what they can expect if they invade us?" She held her arms out to either side and stepped back. "This. They can expect me, and entire planets of people like me. You tell us it's a hopeless fight? You threaten us with destruction? Then you'd better kill every *prolekta* one of us in the same instant or the survivors will come after you. We will sacrifice everything. The things that make us who we are? We'll toss it aside so we can survive. If you go to war with us, we will fight. We may not win. But we'll take as many of you with us as possible."

The Socigines said, "The Wakerran are prepared to do whatever is necessary..."

"For what? Why? Just to say it was done? If you get that stone, you waltz in here... say you take out the Karezza first. Please do. You'd be doing everyone a favor. But the Paisian won't stand idly by. I think your ships won't stand up against one of theirs for long. That's why you're just sitting here. You're waiting for your pals to show up and lend a hand. But if you declare war on us, we're not going to play fair. We're not going to wait for your reinforcements."

"Your fellow species are... not... capable of..."

"War. The great innovator. Some of the greatest and most terrible things have been invented to wage war. Can't wait to see what the Occamian come up with. Or the Irikoan. Or if the Sau wise up and realize you're just saving them for last." She looked at the mercenaries. "You consider that at all? If your little goons decide to have an uprising before you destroy their planet?"

The Socigines looked distinctly uncomfortable.

"How much is it worth to you, Socigines? How many Wakerran are ready to die just to clean out this sector? This cluster of races they've never even met? How many are willing to lay down their lives for this cause? Can you even estimate how many it would take? You have a chance to find out. Roll on, open fire, and start this war for your people. Go to war against every Balanquin, Karezza, Occamian, Irikoan, Paisian, and Karezz in this system. You might wipe some of us out. You might exterminate all of us eventually. But the Wakerran are going to suffer heavy losses before they achieve that victory. Earth made a bomb and destroyed an entire city full of people. Mars made a bomb that rendered an entire quadrant inhabitable. So I'm going to ask you one more time."

She stepped up to the base of the throne and looked into the Wakerran woman's dark eyes.

"Is it worth it? Is this a war you really want to wage?"

Silence from the Wakerran. Bauwerji could hear the Sau mercenaries breathing from across the room. She was trembling, from fear or blood loss or shock, she didn't know or care. She refused to look away from her opponent.

"My sister is unharmed?"

"Nothing that can't heal."

"You will release her at once."

"If you want her, you're more than welcome to have her."

The Socigines curled her hands into fists. "We will come into conflict one day, Bauwerji Crow. Perhaps not in your lifetime, but it is inevitable."

"Maybe so. We'll be waiting for you."

"Take her back to her ship." One of the Sau made a shocked noise. The Socigines ignored it. "I will expect my sister to be delivered at once."

Bauwerji said, "The sooner she's off the station, the happier we'll all be."

She turned and walked away. The adrenaline was fading, and now she could feel pain coming in from all corners. She was almost to the door when the Socigines spoke again.

"Balanquin." Bauwerji turned. The Socigines was again facing forward. "You're a formidable opponent. I would not be eager to go against you in a fight. And you don't have to worry. I have released my hold on your mind."

"Good," Bauwerji said, since she couldn't think of any other response.

"I hope we meet again."

"All due respect, I don't. Once you have your sister, you're gone. You stay on your side of the universe, we stay on ours."

The Socigines nodded slowly.

Bauwerji turned and limped back into the corridor. The Sau followed her, confusion radiating off them like heat or a bad smell. They trailed her all the way to the hangar and stood silently as she mounted her ship, settled on the saddle, and sank forward. She caressed the controls, exhaustion settling over her like a cloak as she fired up the engines. She was still trembling as she activated the reverse thrusters out of the hangar and back into the gentle currents of space.

Once she was clear of the ship, she opened a channel to the Quay. "Officer Bauwerji Crow to Admiral Reshef."

"Bauwerji? Please tell me you're in one piece. You fell off sensors a while ago."

"Mm. Yeah. Sorry. Got... snapped up. Listen, 'Dira. You have to release the Socigines. Let her go back to her ship."

Indira said, "You negotiated a prisoner exchange?"

"Mm-hmm."

"Not to sound ungrateful, but what do we get in return?"

Bauwerji sighed. "Peace, Indira. We get peace."

Silence. And then, "We're preparing her for transport now."

"Good. I m-might need some help at the docks. I think I can get the Sprinter home, but I'm feeling really weak, Admiral. Feeling tired."

Indira's voice was soft. "I'll be there for you, Bauwerji. I promise."

Bauwerji nodded. "Good. I'll see you... I'll see you then."

"We'll light the way for you."

Bauwerji opened her eyes and looked out ahead. Past the Karezza and Paisian blockade, through the sea of broken ships, the Quay shone like a beacon. It was fully powered, it would seem. All systems go. It looked like Heaven. Bauwerji smiled at the sight of it and tightened her grip on the Sprinter's controls. It wasn't as far away as it looked, she decided, and she pushed her foot down to speed her return home.

CHAPTER TWENTY-SEVEN

INDIRA LED the guards into the Med Center quarantine area to personally oversee the Socigines' release. The woman already had her hands lifted in surrender when they arrived at her cell. Indira stopped in front of the force field and crossed her arms over her chest. She watched the Wakerran for any signs of betrayal or subterfuge, but she seemed... perturbed more than scheming. Dark eyes met Indira's and her lip curled into a sneer.

"I was outvoted," the Socigines said.

"I don't know what that means. But I assume you're aware of what happened aboard the other ship?"

"Surrender in exchange for my life."

Indira tried not to look happy, despite feeling overwhelmed with pride at what Bauwerji had accomplished. "What did she say to you? To... the other you?"

The Socigines thought for a moment. "If this force field dropped and I attacked you, what would your response be?"

"We'd fight to the last man," Indira said. "You might kill me and all the men standing behind me, but you'd never get off this station alive."

The soldiers around her didn't flinch or waver in their attention on the prisoner. The Socigines scoffed and shook her head.

"Suicidal. But I suppose it supports the theory."

"What theory?"

The Socigines ignored the question. "Release me back to my vessel. I and the others will return from whence we came."

Indira nodded to the guard. He stepped forward and dropped the field. Other soldiers moved in to manipulate the hoverpod to carry the Socigines back to her ship. Indira stepped out of the way and followed as the prisoner and her escorts made slow progress through the med center, careful not to bump its edges against anything.

The lab was just off the main entrance to the Med Center, and Indira changed course so she could step inside. Jocia and Cordwainer were sitting together on a recessed bench, holding hands and comforting one another. They both looked up as Indira entered.

"The Socigines is being taken back to her ship, and it seems as if the Wakerran are truly surrendering. Dr. Littlefoot, the weapon you were working on. I want it destroyed. Along with any notes you might have taken on it."

Cordwainer tensed. "If this is just a ruse on the part of the Wakerran..."

"I don't care."

"The Aphelion Project will surely want the research," Jocia said, "regardless of whether it will be immediately useful."

"I don't care. I ordered the creation of a weapon that could cause genocide. I don't want the blueprints just lying around for someone to find and take advantage of. The Aphelion Project can remove me from this position if they don't like it. I want every scrap of that thing destroyed. Understood?"

Cordwainer breathed a sigh of relief and closed hir eyes. "Yes, ma'am. Right away."

"I'm sorry, Cordwainer."

"You were only trying to protect us all," Cordwainer said. "That's a heavy burden for anyone. The important thing is what you're doing now."

Indira said, "I hope so. But it's going to have to wait. You just got a new patient."

Cordwainer kissed Jocia's hand before ze stood up. "Who?"

"Bauwerji. I get the feeling she's going to need your help."

They left together and headed for the docks. Indira wanted to actually watch the Wakerran woman board her ship and depart the station, but she also needed to be at the docks when Bauwerji arrived. She'd been there when Bauwerji arrived the first time. She was a refugee, unconscious and clinging to life, desperate for a safe harbor. Indira had made a choice to stand with one lone Balanquin against the entire Karezza fleet, risking the alliance the two races enjoyed. Bauwerji had repaid that trust dozens of times in the intervening years, but now she had literally saved them all from destruction.

The absolute least she deserved was a proper homecoming.

Bauwerji didn't know how she docked the Sprinter, or how she was transferred to the Med Center. That was where she woke up, in one of the most comfortable beds she'd ever been in. Her entire body was numb. She could feel poking and prodding, but there was no sensation associated with the touch. She opened her eyes and looked down to see Cordwainer rolling a sheet of restorative gel across her bare abdomen. The doctor sensed ze was being watched and looked up. Ze smiled when ze saw Bauwerji was awake.

"You should still be resting."

"Tell that to the doctor."

"I am the doctor."

Bauwerji squinted skeptically at her, then dropped her head back onto the pillow. "What's the damage, Dr. Littlefoot?"

"You broke your leg in one place; a fracture. You sliced your hand open. Bruised larynx. Various cuts and abrasions. Massive blood loss. Dehydrated. Stubborn and mule-headed and reckless."

"Those aren't medical."

"No, but they're certainly chronic." Ze squeezed Bauwerji's hand, then nodded at the next bed. "You should know... she's going to be all right."

Bauwerji thought ze was talking about Mara Heely and turned her head in disbelief and horror. Instead she saw Cicero lying in the next bed. Her face was covered by an oxygen mask, her eyes closed. She looked peaceful.

"What happened to her?"

"The *Sastruga* was in horrible shape, but she insisted on going out to find the other two Wakerran ships. Life support was failing, the whole ship was about to break apart. She told her crew to take the life pods to Taplinid. She was going to stay behind. Keep looking. Kela got in contact with a cargo ship captain and they salvaged the *Sastruga*. Brought Cicero back here. She was clinging to life, but we brought her back."

"Thank you," Bauwerji said.

Cordwainer squeezed Bauwerji's hand. "Thank you. Admiral Reshef told me what you did. You saved my soul from a darkness I would never have been able to erase. For that, I am in your debt."

Bauwerji said, "You saved Cicero. We're even."

"We'll see about that. For now, I was serious. You need your rest." Ze finished dressing Bauwerji's wound and pulled the shirt down over the bandages. "I'll be in to check on you in a while."

"Thanks," Bauwerji said again.

Cordwainer turned off the overhead lights before ze left, but the ambient lighting from the desk and behind the beds was enough to see by. Bauwerji pushed down her blankets, checked to make sure she wasn't strapped to or pierced by anything, and checked the brace on her right leg. She moved carefully, putting all her weight on her left leg and bracing her arm against the wall to hop the short distance to Cicero's bed. She sat down on the mattress and lay back before rolling onto her side. She draped her arm across Cicero's midsection, her head on the Human's chest, and almost immediately fell back into a deep and restful sleep.

"Standing here today..." Lalan Paget bit her bottom lip and squinted at the screen. Her thumb rested on the record button of her device, but she moved it to the delete key. She was standing on the concourse above the pavilion. She could smell the blended aroma of several worlds' cuisines rising up to create melange of odor that she had grown to find appetizing in her short time aboard the station. Admiral Reshef had been true to her word about providing access once the threat was over, but having all the information put Lalan in a difficult position. Earth deserved to know what was happening on its furthest-flung outpost. But did they need to know how close to destruction they had come? What did it benefit them to know their lives had been so close to ending? If not for the words and deeds of one Balanquin, the universe could have been mired in another war.

Did they need to know? What purpose would it serve to tell them once the crisis was averted? She walked from the screen to the railing that overlooked the pavilion. She saw Bauwerji Crow and Cicerone Drayton seated together outside the Balanquin eatery. They both wore Med Center shawls, and Bauwerji's face was purple and black in spots from bruising. Across the pavilion, Ephor Wison carried a tray with two Ladronis meals on it. Dr. Littlefoot, either on a date or choosing to have a meal while keeping an eye on hir patients, sat nearby. Ze stood up and helped hir partner set their table.

On the far other side of the pavilion, facing away from the crowd, Selina Rogers was hunched over a bowl of something Lalan couldn't identify. It was peculiar to see an Acapsian purposefully avoiding the sight of others dining, she had learned, so her attention was drawn. It wasn't surprising, she supposed, giving what she had heard about the ambassador's ordeal. Dr. Littlefoot had confirmed the Wakerran no longer had a hold on her mind, but it was certainly bound to leave an imprint. So many dark thoughts, which she had fought for so long. Lalan hoped she would be able to overcome the assault.

Lalan pressed record again. "The people serving aboard the Quay were again reminded this month of just how dangerous the universe can be. But in turn, they proved to be the best of the best. They pushed themselves to the edge in mind, body, and soul to ensure survival for the rest of us. In the end, they achieved victory without a single battle being fought. Lives were lost and blood was shed, but the peace remains intact. The heroes of the Quay would balk at being called that, but it is exactly what they are. This is Lalan Paget for the Home Press, signing off."

She slipped the recorder into her pocket. She would transcribe it later, polish it up a little, then record it properly and send it off to the Home Press offices. She had no idea what the publishers would think about her angle. She didn't know if they wanted the Quay officers presented as heroes or scapegoats for wasteful spending. She didn't much care about their opinion. She would report what she saw and, if the bosses didn't like it, they could replace her.

She pushed away from the railing and decided to go see what culture's food would pique her appetite that day.

EPILOGUE

THE COUNCIL gathered in the pilothouse at the chosen time. Bauwerji and Indira were already on-duty, and Cordwainer left the Med Center in the capable hands of hir nurses to attend. Jocia arrived not long after her partner. Lalan Paget was there to record the moment for posterity in case it ever became common knowledge. She was under strict orders to only film the people, not what was on the screen. Indira didn't want future people to know even the vaguest description of what the stone looked like for fear they might try to find it themselves. Selina Rogers had initially declined her invitation, but a plea from Bauwerji convinced her to be there as a representative of her people. She stood well away from Bauwerji, just in case there were any lingering directives from the Socigines. Cicero was also present, since her crew had been instrumental in recent events and because what they were about to do was her idea. The *Sastruga* was grounded until a multitude of repairs could be done, but Cicero didn't mind the extended layover. Admiral Reshef was donating much of the work and parts on behalf of the Aphelion Project out of gratitude for everything Cicero had done to help fight their latest threat.

Their officers stationed at the far reaches of occupied space reported that the Wakerran ships had indeed returned to the unknown from whence they came. The observers were sheepish about letting the four ships get past them in the first place, but

Indira was certain they had been craftier coming in than they were going out. They weren't attempting to hide when they left, so they didn't bother making themselves inconspicuous. Either way, it seemed as if the Wakerran were truly living up to their end of the bargain. That meant it was time for the Aphelion Project to officially get rid of its ace in the hole.

The group stood in a small cluster at the back of the pilothouse, waiting for word from a yeoman that the payload was ready. When she received the nod, Indira stepped forward to address the group.

"Thanks to the actions of Officer Bauwerji Crow, and everyone standing here today, we were able to sidestep a major disaster. The war with the Wakerran would have been devastating. But that is not what I'm talking about. In the face of the Wakerran threat, I asked Dr. Littlefoot to create a weapon that would have made us monsters. To use something so heinous would have been irredeemable. Dr. Littlefoot's research into the weapon has been destroyed, but there's still the possibility someone could still make the weapon if they had the stone."

She nodded to the yeoman, who spoke to someone in the weapons bay.

"That is why, on a suggestion from Captain Drayton, we're shooting the stone into the Kuiper belt. There it will orbit, get caught up in some planetoid's gravity, impact on some barren moon... who knows. It will be lost. And while there is still the possibility that someone will one day find it, or that one of the other shards will be discovered and this whole thing will start up again, the threat will be gone. The temptation to create a sword to hold over the head of our enemies will be gone. I thank you for joining me on this auspicious moment, when we say good riddance."

She turned to face the screen and lifted her hand. When she dropped it, the yeoman fired. The group watched as a streak appeared on the central screen, only to be swallowed by the stony sea beyond the station.

"And that is that," Indira said.

"Good riddance," Bauwerji said.

Indira turned to the group. "Thank you all for being here. And thank you for the parts you played in preventing disaster."

Once the others departed, Indira moved to stand beside Bauwerji. "I've heard that a new security officer is being assigned later this week. Promotion from within the ranks, from what I gather. Whoever it is, it won't be a Karezz. I assure you of that."

"Thank you, 'Dira."

Indira nodded and faced forward. "Things are practically back to normal. For now. There are a million billion asteroids out there, but I still fear someone will find the one that could end so many lives."

"Or one of the others," Bauwerji said. "There are bound to be more, covered with the same genetic information that made this stone so dangerous. We don't even know how the Wakerran found out it existed, where it was found, who dug it up…"

"Please," Indira said. "I'm going to have nightmares as it is. I don't need more facts." She sighed. "And then there are the others. First the Cetidroi, now the Wakerran? Who knows what other races are out there beyond our scope? Just waiting to come sniffing around their neighbors."

Bauwerji said, "We forced two of them to run back where they came from. If anyone else shows up, we'll do the same thing."

"Good attitude." She checked the time. "I should go back to my desk. Let's grab a meal after duty, ai?"

"Sounds good."

Indira smiled and went to her office. Bauwerji walked purposefully down the central aisle, hands clasped behind her back as she scanned the workstation of each yeoman she passed. Her leg was in the odd middle-ground where it was nearly healed and she was almost so accustomed to the brace that she barely noticed it anymore. She could stand and walk without any apparent difficulty. The bruises and cuts would take longer to fade away, but soon they would be gone as well. The officers in the wells to either side of her were mostly Human, although there were a handful of Occamian, Acapsian, and Ladronis as well. Everyone on the Quay was far from where they were born, she realized, but none of them were far from home.

Her earpiece chirped with an incoming signal. She tapped to answer it. "Executive Officer Bauwerji Crow of the Aphelion Station Quay. How may we assist you?"

"This is Captain Cyriaca of the Irikoan freighter *Jetlucani* requesting permission to dock at your fine station."

She smiled; Cyriaca was an agreeable old flirt. "We read you fine and clear," Bauwerji said as she crouched to look at one yeoman's screen. "You have been cleared to approach on trajectory nine-nine-one-four-one-two. Yeoman Pahleis will guide you safely in. Try to be kind to him, he hasn't been assigned here very long."

"No promises, Bauwerji."

Bauwerji smiled and stood, clasping her hands behind her back. "You're in safe hands with him, gentlemen. Allow me to be the first to welcome you back to the Quay. We hope you enjoy your stay."